It's been so long since I last saw the Sun; I've forgotten what it feels like.

I see it now, yet not with my waking eyes.

Though everything is grey...

A tale of unprecedented woe

OVERMORROW

Penned by the well-worn quill of

Lordt

Published by New Generation Publishing in 2021

First Edition

ISBN

Paperback	978-1-80031-031-5
Ebook	978-1-80031-030-8

www.newgeneration-publishing.com

 New Generation Publishing

The Blacke Estate

The Reaching Peaks

Slyce

Richter

Swagger Inne

Somhremyre

Slaughter

Champ

Thee Endless Meadowe

The Laste Inne

The Gre

The Bleak Realme of

Winter Gloaming

By unknown survey,
The lay of the land concerning
A place so wrong
As to become Obsession

Mneme

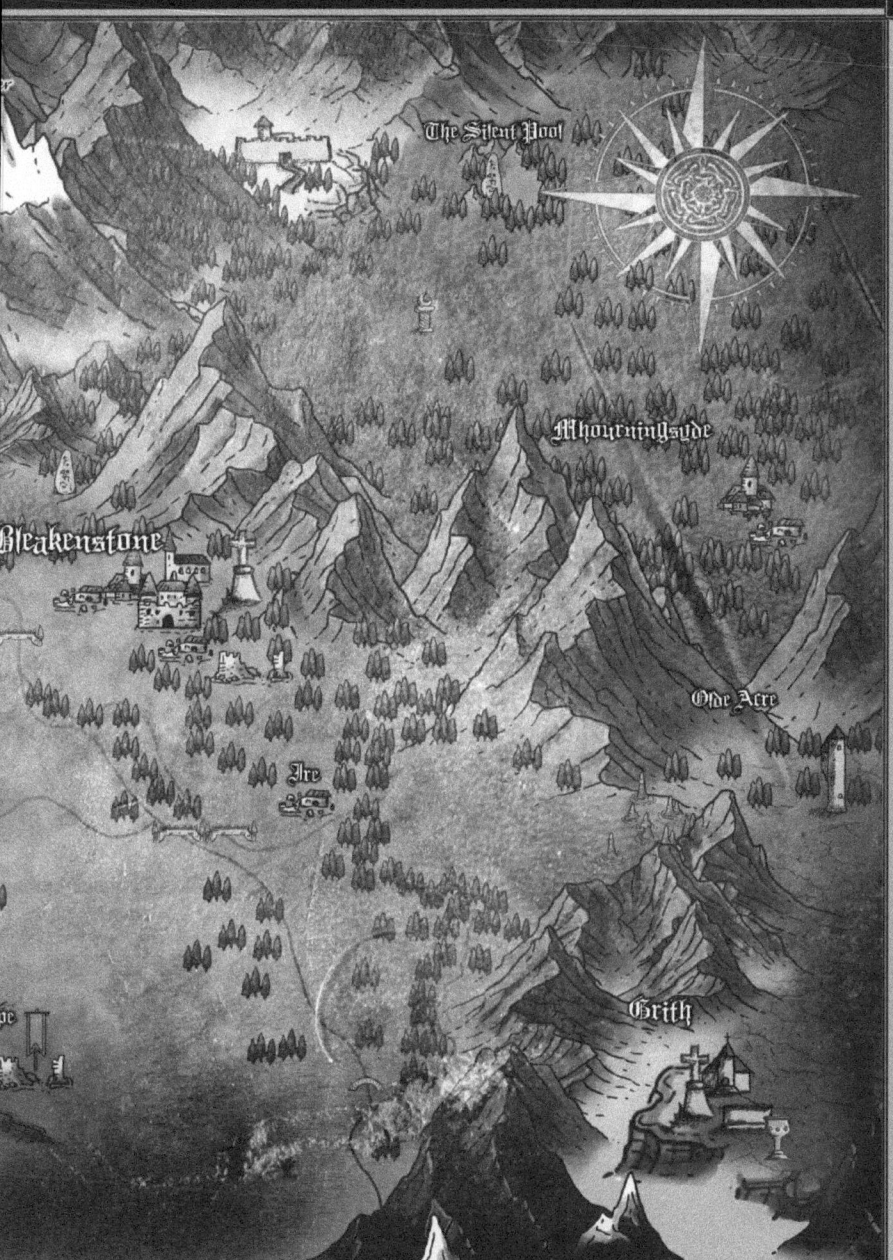

Part I

Prologue
A typical Scene

The plain was still, save for the mist upon it.

The Moon held control of the sky, but not for too long.

The hour was late, or early, but subtly in-between that dark fabric and the shimmer on the horizon.

The ground was hard and raw, the air about it cold and damp; like a tomb without.

The plain was still, save for the breeze that would lift the mist but for a moment, and so reveal the dead who lay prostrate upon the land like so many spent matches; discarded and forgotten.

From the depths, a few insignificant clouds hung overhead, threatening, but nothing more.

The plain was still, with the right light in the wrong place; repetitions of grey, lost within an endless flourish.

Limited moments seen through layers like solitude; pale hues of suffocating wonder.

Winter gloaming long burned down against a vast, empty fireplace, breath clinging to the air for longer than seemed possible. When had it gotten so dark...

A strange place then, to look long enough to see beyond the resplendent veil and into the saturne...

And still was the plain.

~

Yet, in a place of discordant nightmare, the hunched silhouette of a man could be seen within the corner of a damp, stone room; a cell, if you will.

The door.

Dishevelled and broken, a once handsome figure with a knot of dark, matted hair, rank with lice, cast eyes up for the first time in well over far too long.

Clad in torn leather and sporting an unkempt beard of moss and ashes, he remained in the filth that adorned his home of late, but granted himself a look at what was to come.

Gaping pupils withdrew to pinpricks as light from the hallway streamed in like so much fallout, revealing rents upon the walls. Trapped between worlds, each mark an heirloom; each moment a maddening charade.

Footsteps made their way towards him, harsh as tin pans after a hard night of debauchery and gross consumption of ale.

Those were the days.

Rudely awakened from his reverie by the reluctant sound of iron against iron, it could only mean one thing.

He lowered his gaze.

Torchlight ebbed and flowed like a sorry dance, and the voice that accompanied the spectacle was not expected, yet not unknown.

"Edgar, how do you fare?"

There was a sad quality to those words; the rumpled, parched tongue of autumnal herald.

"Same olde day, same olde night", he replied.

It had been some time since he had last spoken and the words caught in his throat like crushed leaves generously dipped in thick honey.

"Look at me, Edgar"

Obliging, his eyes adjusted just enough to make out a shapeless form made of mindless structure... There was familiarity there. There was understanding.

But that moment went by, moving swiftly, as of smoke over running water; a decaying thought within a monochrome realm.

The visitor regarded the surroundings with open disdain.

"Things have not gone as planned, I see"

They held the light up a little further, checking for signs of injury or pallor on the other, though the results held little encouragement.

Edgar lowered his head once again.

"Look at me", the visitor whispered, more harshly this time, holding the torch at bay. "I can dowse this torch if you cannot bear it, though I dare say times are dark enough"

A pale gaze complied with the request, accompanied by a morose comment devoid of hope.

"To heal these eyes is tomorrows cause, for today is all so black"

A pause filled the silence as the prisoner swallowed to moisten his parched lips before continuing.

"And another thing I think you should know..." He looked around, mole-eyed, as if seeking something. "I won't be coming back".

The visitor held forth out a canteen, half full as it was, and Edgar drank deeply.

At length, he handed the vessel back, empty.

"As I await my judgement, I stand alone, slave to a distant power. My wish that I could taste life is all that remains" He held out his arms pitifully, knowing the result before it even came to bear. "Unleash these chains"

The figure stood silent.

As though bargaining with some unknown force in the aether, Edgar looked around once again. "I sent my soul to you in pieces. Will you hold them for me?"

Then the visitor moved up against the bars of the cell and gently crouched so that they could meet face to face and at a level gaze. "Edgar, with whom do you speak?"

At that, Edgar sighed.

There was a noise in the distance that faded away after a moment's frail tension.

Driven by fear, expecting something, the familiar stranger looked around, thinking that perhaps Edgar had been turned mad within his forsaken confines. Anger took hold then.

"Madness, Edgar, can't you hear yourself!? Madness!" The words echoed violently down the hall off every brick and every flagstone, effectively all but ending their time together.

"Call it what you will", Edgar responded meekly.

Then, just as quickly, that same anger melted into the slow tears of resignation.

Footsteps in the distance.

"Weep not for me. Die not for me. Save yourself, my friend. But don't look back...."

The visitor shook a lowered head. "Steeped in pain, your history, when will they forgive you?"

Once again, Edgar's head hung as though his neck could no longer be willed to support it. His lips barely parted as he spoke through his ragged, brittle beard.

"There's no luck left in the world anymore. Riven from my deity, you never showed me how to believe"

"Edgar, you have it wrong. There is no..."

Voices.

The torch guttered and waned as a draft crept through. Scant moments were left; all too little, all too late.

"Meet me where the parts divide and existence becomes a fragile thing... Cry not into the night, and hide not from the Rain..."

And as the stranger looked back one last time, the failing light limned what was left of the prisoner. There Edgar sat hunched, seeking something, yet finding nothing.

And then the book fell from his hands, its worn leather promising much as the visitor carefully reached out to take up the loosely bound pages. But leafing through did nothing to lift his spirits.

"Barely sane, your memories... Will they still know you?"

The door.

The stranger looked over their shoulder, clutching the tome to their chest like a long-lost lover.

"Edgar, what did you do...?"

Chapter I
Pleasantries

Inside the keep, two men exchanged pleasantries.

Somewhere a flint struck true; an exploratory foray amidst the glint and the gloom... most fortunate, given the circumstances, but why not? The sparks offered a brief glimpse of a bare, draughty dining hall. The gathering light stole what was left of the shadows, compelling an eidolon aspect against warded eyes, before it died back down.

A withered hand gripped the remnants of a well-worn stone. There was a chill tonight and supper had been forgotten.

"You do know what they do to people like you, don't you?"

A grim spectre of a man in all the world's finery scowled at Edgar from across an oaken table. Faded bracelets and jewels of all kinds adorned his every knuckle and wrists besides, shimmering but for a moment as though his hands had been bathed in nectar and frozen in time.

Silence.

"Introspection leaves no room for the living, Edgar"

Another spark.

Edgar sighed. "Feel free to put a hand in your purse and withdraw the coin with which to purchase some matches. You are frugal to the point of exhaustion, and I'm not just talking about that beeswax codpiece hanging at the rear of your vintage armoire".

Another spark, still no flame...

"Damn you!" raged the owner of the hand, casting aside the flint and sending the candelabra spinning to the stone floor where it rang out like a chime. "It's a quality armoire!"

Edgar grinned. "Damn yourself. That was some of our best silver".

The man glared daggers, though it would have been hard to see in the deepening dark.

"You have the whimsical smile of a Vampyre bathed in sunlight. Perhaps you have forgotten it is I who brought you here?"

Edgar gestured to the empty table. "And a fine spread you have laid on for us tonight, as usual. I must say the fact that I have had to ream a new hole in my belt is of only minor concern compared to that of saving bad coin on good matches"

"You make me sound like a miser", he replied with hot spittle.

More silence.

Edgar sighed. What lacked in light was made up for in hunger.

A grande clock struck eight and three, its misshapen hands moving into approximate positions with effort and under no small duress.

With that, the dining hall door creaked open like a sinking ship.

A sweat-stained, pustule of a man lurched in without so much as a by-your-leave and clattered a brass serving dish, laden with assorted roots, onto the table. Some of the platter may have even been meat, though it was hard to tell.

Edgar looked at the offerings, then to the man before him. Calmly, he pushed his chair back before long strides saw him lope from the room without afterthought.

The well-oiled gentleman remained to smack his lips and tuck a threadbare silken napkin into the neck of his shirt before perusing the victuals before him.

"Ah, Excellent".

~

That evening Edgar sat and brooded upon a decrepit stool by the window of his chamber. It was a place of abhorrent resplendence in memoriam of daylight, and dust motes spread over the room like a creeping veil.

Sparsely furnished though it was, his room had a bleak feel to it that few would appreciate; the dark timber flooring, the moth-eaten rugs, the skull codpiece draped from the end of the bed.

He was among those few.

The bed for that matter was always a source of misery for Edgar. He had often dreamt of four posts, yet had to settle for what could be considered little more than a child's cot, barely able to accommodate his tall, long-limbed frame. Oftentimes he could be seen splayed out in the centre, legs and arms crookedly finding their way out of the confines like a dead spider, unceremoniously stuffed into a matchbox.

Unperturbed by his presence, rain continued to pour relentlessly as it had done for some time, filling every nook and cranny like…pieces of the sky.

Edgar gazed upon the vista beyond, trying to decide if he preferred it augmented by the weather, or if it would look more appealing via thick, gossamer blindfold. Concluding that the only way that the scene could be improved is if it were cleverly inscribed upon expensive parchment with cheap charcoals, he slowly got up and moved toward his drinks cabinet. It was about the only piece of furniture free from dust, though it too was destined for a period of disuse, the empty bottles within offering up false hope and a prolonged thirst. Edgar let his fingers slide from the door, not bothering to close it.

Resignedly, Edgar manoeuvred to sit at the end of his bed, idly fingering a brass knob stick he had found discarded by an overflowing latrine some months ago.

He took a moment to adjust himself.

There was a sigh.

"Sit still for once, would you?"

A head appeared from behind a damp canvas, held aloft by a crude easel. Long sleeves, matted with coloured oils, gestured with annoyance.

The voice continued. "It's bad enough I have to paint your smug face as it is, let alone try and imagine what it might look like actually facing in the proper direction"

Edgar dismissed the comments.

"You know…I was saving this for a special occasion" he said quietly, carefully unscrewing the top of the walking implement. "But…"

He paused to extract a thin vial of unbroken, green liquid.

Shrugging, he uncorked the vessel and necked the lot, forthwith and without preamble.

The sensation was crisp, but warm, as the liquid made its way down his throat and into his stomach. There it sat pleasantly, leaking myriad reagents into an already fragile mind.

By this point, the man painting the portrait had given up entirely; tearing his shirt off and relaxing upon the nearby bed, leaving his tools cast aside like yesterday's chip papers.

Edgar regarded the scene.

"I've got nearly as much lichen for company as hair on my chin. I've twice as many books as I do shelves to arrange them on. And I own half-a-dozen ornate canes well before I am olde and frail. Yet, and what I don't, or perhaps even want to understand is, why I have a half-naked, third-rate artiste lounging around on my bed like it's some sort of public holiday?"

He paused, arching an eyebrow and piercing the figure with a sharp stare.

When no response was forthcoming, he resorted to more direct methods of communication.

"Herbynlocke, what do you want?"

The man said nothing, choosing instead to admire his work from the new perspective.

He sighed once more. "I am no painter, Edgar"

He paused, before sighing again.

"There was a time when everything seemed unreal. But that's gone now... They say omens are but figments of a deranged mind, but I know them to be truth..."

Edgar looked at him.

"You're no poet either. So stop sighing like you fell in love with the Moon but married the Earth"

There was a moment's silence.

"Look", Edgar added. "If it helps, I'll try and sit still"

He returned to his perch and resumed gazing out of the window, hand on chin.

Below he observed the sound of armoured boots upon rotten planks as a small group of bungling men-at-arms disappeared behind the decaying grandeur of an ill-tended gatehouse left to ruin.

He blinked only once and the mirage was gone. And he was left feeling jaded.

And then the empty vial fell from his fingers, shattering on the floorboards beside him like a carelessly placed festive ornament.

As the men below withdrew, the rain clattered about their metal skin, silence enveloped the night, and darkness overcame all.

Chapter II
Under The Willow

The temperature had dropped somewhat in the last hour, not that it really made a difference. The castle was frozen long ago.

Beyond, great mountains of snow and ice now reached up as though they strived to touch the very stars which glittered above them. Petrified and sacrificed to the wind, what trees remained stuck out like the teeth of an olde beggar; crooked and bygone, lost amidst a thousand facets of uncut radiance.

Edgar opened his eyes to a plume of breath, shivering as he sat up and reached for his cloak, draped over a broken chair.

Curious...

Squinting as shards of light reflected off the ice about him, he began to move, but the floor beneath him protested.

"Please... don't"

The voice came from behind.

Edgar nearly soiled himself right then and there, unashamedly and with full vigour.

"You're still here", he said, choking on the words as he spun to regard Herbynlocke, still shirtless, hunched by his easel and poised to paint, though the oil flaked openly from his brush.

Without thinking, Edgar tossed over his cloak, but it was next to useless in its current, brittle state.

He held out the cloak gingerly and regarded Edgar with knowing, before casting it aside.

"Unkempt, unshaved...If it wasn't for the quality of your attire I would assume you were a drifter".

Edgar stood there motionless, wondering what he had done to deserve such verbal abuse, and in his own chamber, no less.

Herbynlocke curled a lip and gestured to the window. "I will leave soon"

Edgar followed the gesture.

"Why are you…Still here?"

Herbynlocke smiled and drew a deep breath before slowly standing and carefully moving over to the window. Looking out he seemed distant.

"I came here to watch and to look and to be..."

He drifted off, leaving the howl of the wind to fill the silence.

On recognising Edgar's confusion, he continued.

"Every new day my heart breaks at the beauty of the world and the thought that one day I will not wake to see it", he gestured again, "And so I look..."

Edgar turned once more and moved to peer out from the window for himself. Paint broke away from where he had laid his hand on the sill and his breath momentarily clouded the vista before him. He took a moment before responding.

"I see only ice, snow, and what were once trees. I see a bitter death in a cold place and a pack of hungry wolves on the horizon"

But Herbynlocke was gone.

Edgar fingered his beard in thought, and then slowly he rose and moved over to the canvas.

It was blank. A forgotten page made of memories, of which there were none.

And then the floor gave way beneath him.

~

Bent double over a writing desk in the ground floor study, Edgar hesitantly looked up and he could see the roof of his chamber, wondering if it couldn't use a lick of paint.

His cloak, heavy with damp, fell about him like a spent sack, but he had no time to consider the cold, for he heard once again the baying of the wolves.

Groaning, Edgar managed to extract himself from the detritus. On the floor beside him was a note, penned in ink and sealed with tears, gone hard in the climate. Edgar stooped to collect it. Brushing his hair back and squinting in the gloom he could make out few of the words, but few enough were legible.

He turned to look out from the study window, before letting the note fall where it may.

After some time in contemplation, a thought occurred and Edgar reached into the drawer of the ruined writing desk to reveal a good half bottle of burgundy of no particular vintage or calibre.

He claimed the bottle forthwith before picking his way over the rubble towards an olde door.

Taking a generous swig from the bottle, Edgar leaned against the ruined frame. His mind reeled.

The castle groaned once more as various segments of masonry made half-hearted bids for freedom.

Tired eyes fell upon an oil painting depicting a skull and raven above an empty fireplace. Cold fibres show form and sorrow.

How he had loved that painting.

And now, as gaunt fingers ran over the peaks and troughs of the delicately painted oils, he dismayed as the work fell apart at his touch.

He took another step to find himself in the famously draughty hallway of his childhood home, remembering the countless occasions that he had been chastised for not keeping the rug free of leaves in autumn or dust in summer; a fruitless venture if ever there was one, as any acolyte knew, but still the scolding's rained as a fever through branch and bough; molten firelight and chilling night.

For that matter, he had not managed to keep the sconces lit either; a fact that was now undoubtedly moot.

The large, oaken entry door now gaped, crystalline, and twisted before him, offering a view of beyond.

Beyond?

Edgar had always dreamt of that. But he had never left the estate, not even once; as of a geas upon his body and soul. Yet he had lingered too long. And all too soon his world had dropped like summer ice cream upon the carpet of the past.

He edged closer to the portal before carefully passing through, squinting as the light shifted and changed.

Across the drawbridge, he turned to look out into the wilderness and the trees without. Not a leaf remained on branch nor ground. And the clouds overhead proposed further sombre acceptance.

Crumpling his cloak about him like cardboard Edgar retreated and backed into the hallway like a spider.

A fallen chandelier and several ceremonial swords were arrayed about the floor, causing him to choose each step with caution lest he tread upon an heirloom and hinder his path.

He proceeded to the kitchens in search of fodder and, after discovering several piles of mouldering slop, the finest thing he managed to lay his hands on was a butcher's apron that could be described grim at best and at worst, well… It was all there was. Suffice to say it did little to curb his appetite or clean his boots.

Beyond the kitchens was the cloister, accented with a beautiful willow, still standing, yet quivering like an olde man's mouth, unbroken banter upon limbs of which subtle labours drew down.

In recent months Edgar had spent many an afternoon under this particular tree, when he should have been attending to his duties, either lounging around or simply sat with a fist comfortably tucked under his chin.

Against the tree rested a rusty-looking rapier, once of fine quality. Edgar had never cared for it very well but didn't remember leaving it there. Now, finding himself alone he found its cold steel strangely comforting, though he doubted his skill to use it. Time had been a fleeting master, and what little finesse he once possessed had long since made way for other pursuits.

Slouching upon the ancient roots he took a swig from the burgundy and after a few minutes began to nod, the soothing warmth of the vintage promising cordial dreams.

He sighed then as memories assaulted him, his breath clinging to the cold air for longer than seemed possible.

And lower and lower he descended into the gloom.

Chapter III
Fireside

Edgar's eyes cracked open some while later, but it was still daylight and outside the wind was fierce. Drifts of snow spiralled endlessly around the top of ruined eaves.

It was only then that he realised how hungry he was. And what he wouldn't give for some salted pork…

The inexorable slopes surrounding the estate only served to increase how alone he felt, save for the wolves, which only crept closer, and the snowflakes that drifted down, only to disappear as he tried to befriend them.

Looking up he considered the approaching storm. He was only one bad night away from an untimely end; one in which no one would know that he had ever even existed, he mused.

Even if he could feel his fingers in order to record his demise they would be pitiful words, penned with a broken quill dipped in second-rate ink. And what parchment he might find would likely only now serve as bedding for the rats.

He had to get out of here, even if it meant baring his arse to the storm which, whilst both invigorating and mildly exfoliating, was something he could live without.

Retreating to the study, he took the sword with him and decided to wait out the weather for a while longer, under the guise of a man searching for rations or tools that might aid him in the coming days. Or so he told himself.

Deep down he knew a certain reluctance to leave was permeating his decisions, but he forced that aside.

Picking his way through odds and ends he found an olde leathern sack. Idly, he regarded the item, though he didn't bother checking the contents, it was empty, and he slung it over his shoulder like a fresh kill.

Nearby, a box of matches presented itself; a rarity, to say the least, having apparently remained unmolested by neither time nor tide. He struck one and lit a nearby lantern that lay cracked but still functional, a pale lavender oil clinging to the glass like a fine wine. It burned brightly with a comforting smell, and all of a sudden a library of wonders was revealed; a rich cache beneath the withered trappings of winter's last charme. What a frivolous waste of prying eyes.

When had it gotten so dark?

Distracted, he didn't even react as the match burnt down to his fingers, removing skin and fingerprints alike.

He lifted the lantern before him, ignoring the flickering flame as his arm struggled to maintain stability before it slipped from his grasp, and the black returned like a cloud of ink.

~

Dawn

Edgar awoke stiff as a board, though with twice the shine.

Something was looking at him. It had been all night

He looked around, recalling his surroundings as if for the first time, the pieces falling into place like an impossible puzzle made of half-light reflections and a grey penumbra split between itself and the world without.

"Should have taken the suite", he muttered to himself, awkwardly moving to his elbows.

Absurdly, beside him, the fireplace burned brightly. It was probably the only reason he was still alive.

Flickering in the intermittent light, a small, fine glass cabinet adorned an occasional table towards the rear of the study. Within it lay a bedraggled crow, nestled into a pile of parchment and shivering quietly.

Edgar wondered if he had ever seen a crow shiver, but the thought soon bored him and he dismissed it out of hand.

Uncomfortable with introductions he loomed over the taxidermy at which point the creature choked out an all too human cough.

Edgar cursed profusely then, before abruptly removing his cloak to throw it over the cabinet, table and all, distancing the creature from his mind.

He slumped back down again by the fire.

"You startled me…" he muttered quietly, almost to himself. "And I'm afraid to admit, I may have just soiled myself"

Chapter IV
Grey Bastard

In that frail place, Edgar gingerly pulled back his cloak from around the cabinet.

There was no subtlety to it; no pomp, no ceremony. But as he drew back the veil, he swore he saw the thing change.

"My Halidom...", uttered Edgar, incredulous.

As he moved closer it seemed to back away from him, yet confined to its four walls there was nowhere for it to go.

Edgar peered into the cabinet, his sense of cold, hunger, thirst... all but forgotten.

There was something other about this thing. It didn't look at him like a Crow should. It looked at him like Crowe.

And before he knew it, he had unlatched the case, short breaths frosting the glass, imperfections to create the impossible, and a doorway to the unbelievable...

"I guess you are free to go now..." said Edgar, solemnly. But with no obvious response forthcoming, he had a hard time ignoring a peripheral earworm...

Go where?

He was jolted back to a more lucid state by the unceremonious tapping of Crowe upon the opaque keys of a ruined piano.

He had no idea that birds could play piano, much less those that shouldn't exist.

Each key sent up more cold dust and before long a gentle melody spread itself like a soft curtain over the room, in delicate defiance of the elements, once again lulling Edgar into a place where he had been before but had no desire to be again.

He slumped into a mouldering wingback chair; the thing swallowing him up like it meant to devour him, the cool leathern membrane clinging delicately to his skin.

Decent chair.

Discord and harmony found a way to him then. What he saw filled him with dread. He knew not how to dance. But when it came to the bow there was none finer.

And as the notes played out the winds died down, and all about him apparitions of varying shapes and sizes made themselves known; some familiar, some less so. But that might just have been the wine.

He told himself it couldn't be happening; a frozen illusion, somehow different from the one before... No chance of knowing conclusion, having not yet begun... He told himself it couldn't be real.

But when a box beside him moved and crunched against the frost that lay within, he knew what he saw was true.

~

Edgar peered inside the box with eyes heavy from long-lasting torpor.

Eyes gleamed back at him. And there were fingers, too. They trembled.

Crowe fluttered around, back inside in his case, startling Edgar.

Eventually, he returned his focus to the box.

A head peeked out from the darkness. And with that the head turned into a face, gaunt and on the verge of frostbite.

And far too young to be there.

Stranger still, the box was full of coins. The Chylde was quite the little hoarder.

"I see you helped yourself to some coin," said Edgar as brightly as possible, though it came out as drear as the persistent joy of inevitable horror...

The Chylde just looked at him.

Edgar cleared his throat. "Would...would you like something to eat?" It was a hollow gesture. Edgar had no food. In fact, he half-hoped the Chylde had managed to scavenge some and was rewarded seconds later when some stale bread and crisp apples were offered up before him.

Edgar sat crouched on his haunches and bit into an apple, idly looking around him, before abruptly his attention returned to the Chylde.

"Do you have a name?"

Edgar could almost perceive him speaking. But it was a deception. It came from somewhere else. A place he had no desire to explore.

"Here...take my cloak"

As he held out the offering the boy made no motion to accept it, but merely looked back to the apples he had given up.

"So, you *are* hungry..."

Edgar rolled one back and the Chylde joined in the feast.

At that Edgar uncorked the wine and was about to share it out, before he realised what unlikely and un-enjoyable company he had.

~

"Well, we can't stay here", Edgar concluded. He stood with his hands on his hips like a caricature hero; more a parody than anything else. The Chylde stood at his heels, mute as usual, clutching onto the glass cabinet that contained Crowe as though it were his favourite toy or lunch-box. Either way, his knuckles were white with more than just cold.

They stood in the creaking doorway of the keep and Edgar's eyes swept the horizon for anything that resembled a landmark.

Everything looked the same. There was just too much snow. Bone white bluebells on a vista so bleak, you can practically smell the desolation.

The only difference was that the box that Edgar had found the Chylde in was now free of coins, and his own travel bag brimming.

A thought occurred to Edgar then, but it was a tedious one, and he considered it for a long time before committing to the idea.

He drew out his Sack of Ire and placed it on the ground. Into this, he shovelled a small amount of the snow piled around his feet at the edge of the doorway.

It did nothing. And reclaiming it was next to impossible as it melted and sank through the hessian cords like...Well, like water.

Edgar frowned and briefly considered smothering himself with the sack.

As he glanced again at the pitiful vision of the Chylde gripping onto the strange, shivering Crowe, his bitterness mellowed and he lowered his shoulders.

"Well, that didn't work" he responded to the expectant look the Chydle was giving him.

He cast around the castle one final time.

"Hmmm...I am no stonemason. And this is not the season for learning new skills. We should leave this place".

He took a few steps across the bridge with the Chylde and Crowe in tow before swiftly turning and dipping into a low bow, followed with a flourish, before his family home of so many years.

"Farewell you stoic, grey bastard!" he said, before turning on his heel and leading the trio off onto the bleak horizon.

~

The next few days were some of the worst Edgar had ever known.

He was half-blind from snow, completely lost and, to cap it all, he'd managed to almost all of the gold in some indefinable pit whilst stopping to rest. It was only by sheer luck that the three of them hadn't walked onto that exact point themselves and come to an untimely end. Considering how much gold he had just lost in a short space of time, Edgar didn't rule out the possibility of that fate being the lesser of two evils.

Still, he was alive, if it could be called alive, and well. And by well, it meant favouring the blissful warmth and euphoria of oncoming hypothermia and starvation.

Delirium was en route. But he waited and waited and waited, yet no one ever came calling.

Chapter V
Sterling

Edgar washed his face in the clear water of a nearby spring. It was a strange thing not to feel cold for a change and as rivulets of water ran down his gaunt frame he considered how much weight he had recently lost.

Yet his appetite had diminished.

He looked up and saw the Chylde talking to Crowe and couldn't decide if this was a good or bad thing. Sure, it was nice for the kid to have a friend, but a re-animated stuffed bird in a glass case?

Oddly, the Chylde behaved as though it were actually entertaining intellectual conversation with the thing, as of someone when left alone with subconscious for company.

Edgar frowned. It had never spoken to him. He had no judge of its character, yet he considered the malleable mind of a child dangerous ground for the seeds of ill words to be sown. But then, why not dream a little bleaker?

Still, at least it gave him a break from having to answer yet more inane questions.

Ever since they had struck camp the Chylde had felt confident enough to start asking about every subject under the Moon. It was all Edgar could do not to slit his throat. Yet there was something familiar about the situation and so he let the Chylde rant, content to ignore his questions and offer the occasional grunt in response to appease him, as well as the odd crust of bread.

Sadly, the last of the liquor had run out days ago which did nothing to ease the situation and meant with each passing minute Edgar's headache grew worse, and his patience shorter.

As he pushed his face back into the water he considered holding it there and being done with the whole nightmare, but couldn't quite be bothered.

Sat there, watching the clouds roll in, it dawned upon him that there was another squall inbound.

Edgar scrambled to his feet and donned his shirt.

Grabbing his sword on the way he sauntered over to where the Chylde played with Crowe, the creature stiff with rigor and no more alive than since the last time he saw it.

The Chylde looked up.

"Storms' coming" stated Edgar, offering his hand. He took it, not forgetting to pick up the cabinet as well.

Quickly, they moved off in search of shelter as the clouds rolled ever-thicker overhead, like ink in still water, and by half-light across a plain of amaranthine verdure.

The once charming valley now gave way to bogs and midges with a few complimentary leeches thrown in for good measure, something which Edgar quickly discovered after dropping his sword only to pick it up along with what looked like a gauntlet of burnt sausages.

They weren't.

For a short while, they had managed to shelter under a small stand of trees, whose thick canopy lessened the persistence of the rain, though not completely. Still, it was a relief from the ferocity of the storm which had, in Edgar's opinion, become an overzealous affair.

Annoyingly, the Chylde had slept through the whole thing.

"Might as well hit the road again", suggested Edgar, after a while, paying no attention to whether the Chylde was listening or not. Unceremoniously he nudged him awake before loping off at a brisk pace to try and find some semblance of a trail amidst the muck.

And just before nightfall, they had reached a place that Edgar deemed appropriate to spend the night. It was a welcome sight compared to the other accommodation on offer; a muddy puddle or hard rock. There was a third option of passing out in a damp shrub but he'd tried that before, albeit a few years ago whilst leathered on some strong wine, and didn't fancy repeating the experience.

Evening spectres drifted shyly in, before the rains began again in earnest, preceding their query and their thirst.

There loomed a ruined tower of dark stone, unremarkable behind the modest shroud of coming night. Strands of pale flame broached the dusk with delicate fingers, highlighting a structure slick with olde moss and rich with ivy; a relic of worse times, where the sun shone throughout skies of graveyard blue and the earth bore its weight without care nor apology.

The corners of Edgar's mouth twitched into the approximation of a smile.

The Chylde looked up with apprehension.

"Here?" he asked, quietly.

"What of it?" replied, Edgar, taking in the looming façade.

The Chylde said nothing but clung into Crowe all the more tightly.

Leaving both at the foot of the steps Edgar moved toward the tower. Thirteen steps lined the way, a foreboding number for some, but Edgar cared not for the superstition, instead focusing on removing an errant leech that had somehow become attached to his codpiece, refreshingly on the outside, this time.

He took up his sword as he approached large doors fixed upon solid brass hinges, strangely untarnished. And as the rain beat down he considered the portal in silence. Crowe and the Chylde looked on with mute concern.

But as Edgar raised his fist to issue the first knock, the doors simply yawned open.

"Just like in the books", Edgar muttered under his breath with the beginnings of a wry grin.

He turned to beckon Crowe and the Chylde.

"A warm welcome!" he called, but was still on an in-breath when a strong hand reached out of the darkness and dragged him inside.

He found himself moving through the air before connecting awkwardly with damp flagstones, blessedly adorned with soft moss. His throat was then summarily met with sharpened steel and he stiffened up, quick as a limpet.

Dim candlelight flickered about the vestibule and danced off dull, rusted armour; the kind found on an abandoned battlefield or at the bottom of a well.

A mailed fist wrapped around his throat, momentarily lifting him a little from his feet.

"…And who are you?" asked a male voice, rich with tones that spoke of high standing, but also with a kind of grit that spoke of many years shouting over the clamour of dying men. And there was something else...

"Blacke…" Edgar rasped. "Edgar Blacke" His voice sounded like a comedy sketch of a man trying to talk whilst chewing a half-foot of leather.

The figure dropped him like a hot rock.

"…I know that name", the voice replied, seeming to relax.

Armour creaked and groaned as the figure shifted his stance before continuing.

"The name's Sterling, Richter Stirling. Or *Sir*, Richter if you wish to be pedantic about it. But let's not get bogged down in honorifics. They mean little to me these days, much less to others".

He offered a hand and pulled Edgar to his feet.

Edgar brushed himself off, relieved that his windpipe was still functioning, though it would probably be some time before he could sing a soft lullaby again.

"Now… What brings you to this place?" inquired the knight.

"I would have thought that was obvious", said Edgar, dripping onto the flagstones.

"And them?" asked Richter in a brusque tone, gesturing to the two forms of Crowe and the Chylde peering through the open door.

Edgar said nothing.

The knight sighed deeply.

"This is the very worst place you could have come" he stated, turning away as the candles flickered and spat.

"I don't think that…" Edgar began but was quickly cut off.

"Bring them in", said Richter, without conviction.

Edgar stood at the top of the steps and gestured the Chylde in from the rain, who carefully crossed the threshold and picked their way over the slippery stones without, and those within for that matter.

Behind them Richter closed the doors, in a perhaps overly ominous way for Edgar's liking, the motion bring to mind the death-rattle of a slaughtered cow. The knight obviously had an eye for dramatics; that, and the fact that he had probably lost no small amount of marbles somewhere along the way.

Richter lay his sword aside. And as it gleamed in the candlelight Edgar realised it was the only part of the knight's gear that was not left to rust.

"Look, the rules are plain; you stay down here and keep as quiet as a crypt gone midnight, else this may well become yours. You can stay out of the rain, spend the night, but then on the morrow... you need to leave"

"But what if it's still raining?" piped up the Chylde.

Edgar raised a brow.

"I'm sorry" replied Richter, mournfully. "That's just the way it is"

And with that, he seemed to sag in his armour before shuffling up a flight of cold stone stairs and into the dark beyond.

~

The candle was now a third of its former height, and the glass half empty.

Edgar continued to stare at the painting. It was the most intricate thing he had ever seen.

He looked at the oils on the canvas as though he could see the very base components of their making; each stroke, each colour, each choice – A dance upon the page of woven fabrics. He could tell here and there where the artist had repainted over some error, or when tears had been shed on a lonely night.

Strong mountains of maddening height loomed above, while below strange creatures and places of misery fought for clarity amidst the darker oils.

Edgar's eyes fell upon it all, until eventually he was drawn to an area depicting a knot of warriors strewn across a desolate plain. He could almost feel the ache of the moment; the discord and the horror of loss, and his cold figures fell upon the oils like braille.

In his minds' eye, he found every sword and spear, broken lance, and fallen helm. The slaughter was relentless and here the oils crude. Eventually, pieces fell away and left scars upon the earth. The greys and whites were first to yield and it was then that Edgar's nail caught upon a ridge within the mass. Somewhere the artist had removed the brush, a fraction more paint, a memory of the error. Here he picked away upon a glittering helm by the hand of a fallen knight to reveal a cup, rich in design.

Edgar let his hand drop.

~

Several hours later it was still raining. That being said it was little different to being inside. Edgar regarded the puddle he lay in and struggled to stifle a sneeze.

At first, he had tried to nap, but that didn't happen. Then he had attempted to explore their surroundings further, but he could barely see anything. In the end, he settled for the idle conversation within his own mind.

The Chylde was asleep.

There was a groan from upstairs. It sounded like Richter. At length he shambled down the steps, his sword arm hung limp. He seemed… Different.

His head held low, Richter found his voice.

"Edgar, I…"

Their eyes briefly met before the candles began to give up entirely. With grim expediency and little mercy, the deep colours ran unto themselves until there was no telling the beginning and no sight of the end.

"They heard you". And with that, the darkness deepened still.

Edgar felt the Chylde squirm beside him. Out of instinct, his hand searched for the hilt of his rapier.

"Richter, what…"

As he stood up, Edgar's nose pushed against wet flesh.

Instantly he recoiled, frantically, and was rewarded by cracking his skull against the unmoving stonework behind him.

There was a clatter of steel followed by a flash of light.

Goode grief...

But how he had wished that light had never come upon him then. That its spark had gone to visit some other hall in some other, distant place; Instead of this. He might live another lifetime and still, of all the depraved curses he would utter, or of all the ill-will and tainted luck to ever befall him, that moment was the worst.

So cruel was the visage, he would have traded his good sight for the memory to have never been made.

He had no idea if the Chylde had seen.

He had no idea if he was even still breathing.

Before him, they were there, and They numbered nine.

Gradually, a dull lantern came to life, its once welcome light now an abomination. Richter lay prostrate upon the floor.

Edgar stared as his mouth worked in silent denial and put up little resistance as the figure before him stuffed a handful of what appeared to be sloughed flesh into the gape of his already be-slackened jaw. And as he gagged on the morsel Edgar's rapier fell from his grasp, clattering to the floor like a clarion.

In the corner, Edgar thought he witnessed a grotesque form with folds of skin that slapped around the edge of his mouth. Fat of frame and devoid of features it sat quietly; observing, waiting, slavering; part human, part beast, tending to macabre fauna in a world bent by shadows.

Edgar turned away and tried to regain his wits, but the putrid meat falling from his lips made him gag once again.

Seconds later he found himself retching with abandon over the antique armour of Sterling.

His hair was then grabbed and his head forced back before another festering mound of flesh was portioned out and compelled upon him.

"Eat", rasped the fat figure as one of the Nine mouths of peripheral vision shaped the words. So grotesque was its neck that the voice sounded like it came from a bowl of salted porridge.

Edgar began to hiccup, but as fast as he spat the flesh out more was proffered up. A steady stream of bile and half-chewed meat spilled from his mouth all about him, raining down with gracious viscosity.

There was also laughter. And it came from all directions.

On all fours, he rolled over to find the Chylde missing. And then, with no small fortune, his hand brushed against the cold steel of Richter's sword and he claimed the weapon before rolling awkwardly to his feet.

Spitting, again and again, Edgar soon found some courage.

"What is this, then?", still not quite sure who, or what he was addressing.

Another flash.

And together, The Chant.

"The Groak...The Groak..."

Numb with fear he staggered. What lacked in light was made up for in hunger... and never felt the teeth sink into his flesh.

~

Edgar found himself in a pool of blood and with a head that felt as though it had been dehydrated and stuffed into a leathern sack before summarily being tossed onto a cobbled street.

It hurt.

As for the blood; a few moments later and he was able to ascertain that it, well most of it, wasn't his. However, he wasn't quite sure if this was a good thing or a bad thing.

As his hearing came into clarity he was dimly aware of the unmistakably jarring sound of a crying baby accompanied by whimpering from above. Furthermore, this was punctuated by drops of the ever-present rain finding its way through cracks in the keep's less than sound infrastructure.

They didn't build them like they used to.

He was half-blind in the darkness and fumbled about in the gore until his hand fell upon a large mushy form. He didn't want to think about what it might be. He didn't want to know.

He could hear voices above and eventually managed to find a way leading up.

As he scrambled about on his knees he spiralled round and round until at long last candlelight began to penetrate the gloom more readily once again.

Reaching the top the sounds became increasingly acute; a baby's cries, a child's sobs...

A grown man's voice.

He stood and braced himself on a wall, his head swaying, and through twice-clouded vision he could make out three forms, with perhaps a fourth upon the floor.

The dull glint of Richter's armour was unmistakable, and his sword was stained a deep red.

Huddled in the corner Edgar could just make out the Chylde cradling an infant, terror was written upon their face as the knight moved towards them.

Richter halted as he noticed Edgar at the top of the stone steps.

"Look away," he said in commanding tones.

"What...?"

But before Edgar could finish a second word the knight strode forward, stepping over what now appeared to be the butchered body of a woman, and mercilessly tore the baby from the Chylde's grasp, the sob's turning into shrieks of protest.

The infant continued to cry as the Chylde uselessly battered bloody hands against the armour of Sir Richter.

The knight swatted them away with one hand, sending the Chylde clattering into a ruined bookcase, rank with rot, whilst raising the baby in the other.

Edgar's mind reeled and he felt overwhelmed and nauseous.

He staggered forward, reaching out to no one in particular, and eventually met with the Chylde, throwing a protective arm around them. As he glanced about his eyes fell upon the face of the body on the floor.

No...

He recognised the mouth. That hideous mouth...

Richter raised his voice, but it cracked even as he spoke.

"I said look away!"

And then the crying stopped.

It was dark; too dark...But not dark enough. And in the presumed half-light of the moon above, Edgar was overwhelmed.

All that was left to punctuate the sudden silence were several sounds very much akin to each other, though horribly different in their revelation.

Blood.

Tears.

Rain.

Chapter XI
Taprooms and Tantrums

The tavern bristled with all manner of folk foaming at the mouth with ale. Kegs were being drained at an alarming rate and a mild panic came to the fore as a band of travelling louts had arrived and proceeded to drink the place dry.

It was only the middle of the afternoon and the brawls had already begun, resulting in six broken chairs, four broken limbs, and here or there a good deal of broken pride. Not to mention a broken stool bucket that leaked freely in a far corner. But nobody paid any attention to that.

Elsewhere in the tavern things were less offensive, though hardly much quieter. Folk were enjoying various stews and beverages, and some of the regulars merely sat idly playing chess or breaking wind.

In a far corner sat a middle-aged man, beak-deep in a wide array of heavy books from around the globe. He was shrouded by the thick smoke that filled the room, clinging to him like a robe, his long, dark hair concealing most of his features but doing little to hide a second chin jostling for position beneath the first. A small goblet of fine red wine sat on the table beside him and remnants of cheese and bread be-speckled a silver platter.

He flipped aimlessly through the pages of a large tome before him as though they were nothing more than a cheap sample pallet for next year's furnishings.

He tore off and summarily stuffed another hunk of bread into his mouth without thought, crumbs raining down like confetti to land upon the floor and page creases besides.

But even his eyes turned when a bedraggled rake of a being, dripping with rapidly melting snow, fell through the front door and stumbled through the boot room like a man half-cut on yesterday's discarded dregs.

All conversation died down. The only sound remaining was that of the door banging in the wind and the crackle of the open fire. This was, of course, punctuated by the occasional flatulent augmentation and giggling fool.

Edgar stood in the doorway until the barkeep found his voice.

"Close the door, would you?"

Edgar slowly obliged.

The room seemed even quieter than before now that the elements had been shut out, braced against a winter that never seemed to end and a spring that would never come. The burst of fresh air had at least done wonders to relieve some of the built-up stench. The inne smelled like a fine meadow in high summer now, compared to mere moments before, with its aroma of plague cart and bottom.

Edgar took a few unsteady steps forward into the bar area and wrinkled his nose. "Are you sure you don't want me to leave it open for a while longer?" he inquired.

Another cough was followed by further silence.

Edgar swallowed, parched, his cloak gradually causing a slip-hazard. "Ale...and stew", he finally uttered.

And the conversation returned.

Looking around Edgar discovered precious little seating available to him. Indeed, the one available spot appeared to be opposite the erstwhile scholar. And while Edgar didn't fancy having to stomach a bowl of stew whilst watching a man dig crumbs out from under his own neck rolls, it would have to do.

He picked his way through the throng of inebriated revellers and unceremoniously sat upon the bench.

The man opposite appeared to pay him no heed, continuing to flip through pages at an incredulous rate, but Edgar tried not to make eye contact all the same. Many of the guests seemed to be spoiling for a ruckus, and who knew what this large intellectual could be capable of.

Edgar looked around uneasily.

At length, the scholar looked up from the book he was scrutinising to regard Edgar.

"It's hardly clement out there. Why don't you bring them in?" His voice sounded as though he was gargling a dozen eggs.

For a moment, Edgar feigned confusion, but they both knew the man spoke sense.

Edgar felt defensive.

"Who?", he asked unconvincingly.

The scholar's smile faded and a vein began to protrude from his forehead, looking like some fat worm in a freshly ploughed field.

Just then, a woman came to join them, though little could be seen of her person. A dark robe and hood covered her every visage, and a strong perfume clung about her as of late autumn, with its rich smell of fractured limbs half bound by cold steel.

Something seemed amiss.

She leaned over the books of the scholar and whispered into his ear, keeping half an eye on Edgar.

He caught a glimpse of a single tear run down her cheek.

The scholar sighed, downing the rest of his wine and collecting up his books with barely concealed effort.

"All yours" he nodded reluctantly toward the crumb bejewelled table before leaving swiftly with the woman.

Edgar felt himself relax and picked at a left-over piece of stale bread.

He was in a world of his own when a steaming bowl of stew slammed down on the table in front of him, spilled over the edges of the bowl, dribbled along the woodwork and eventually onto his groin.

"Thanks for ours", said Richter, irked. The Chylde was shivering beside him, clutching onto Crowe.

Edgar stammered, trying to find his voice.

"Wha…What happened to you?"

"If you'd bothered to look you'd have seen we were lagging"

Edgar nursed his ale, vaguely embarrassed. The truth was that once he had finally pulled ahead of the pair he was loathed to give up the solace in solitude.

"Sorry…" he muttered without much conviction.

"Let's just get some food," said the knight resignedly. "My stomach is as empty as last night's jug"

~

Edgar let his gut distend. As usual, he had over-done it. One by one he had unfastened the buttons of his shirt until it looked like he was near enough wearing a cape.

The tavern had begun to thin out and they soon found themselves situated nearer the fire.

Watching the angry flames and nursing their ale, Edgar and Richter reflected in mute horror upon the previous events in the tower.

It was as though speaking of it would make it real and so in silence they had travelled. And now in silence, they sat.

The Chylde absent-mindedly took to carving shapes in the table with a piece of broken glass. At the moment, it looked like they were drawing something that resembled some sort of unfathomable creature; a foreign beast ...And as it stood amidst the others as they stared and stared it tried to form reason. Had it done something wrong? Had it arrived too soon? Was it where it wasn't wanted? It would never know its own beauty. And things would never be the same again...

Edgar shook his head and stared into his ale.

The fire popped and spat, seeming louder with each minute of silence passed, and before long Edgar felt as though he was stood next to an inferno. The Chylde's newly enthused carvery did nothing to lessen the incandescent cacophony either.

And then, without warning, Richter broke.

"I forgot who I was" he replied, forlornly, his voice cutting through the atmosphere like a bark against the night.

His throat seemed dry and the knight drained his mug, taking a deep swig without batting a lid. The resulting gulping sound was entirely unnecessary.

His eyes glazed over.

"Go on…" Edgar urged.

"The Three…They… They have a cruel sense of humour. For many years I was their puppet. And all for the want of the impossible", He paused.

"…Yet possible" he added under his breath.

Edgar didn't think this was going to be a simple conversation and so took a long draught from his own tankard, prepping for the predictably forthcoming charade.

"Foolishly I was alone, one spring evening. My spirits were high as I quested for a gilded cup, last seen in a forgotten tower much like the one in which you and I met. A strange man ordained me to seek the trophy, but instead, I ended up on a path to nowhere, approaching starvation and without a steed to carry my burdens. Eventually, I found a ruined hovel set back from the road and populated by a family of nine, all-female, ranging from the new-born to the crone. They fed me, furnished me with a fresh mount, and indeed gave me new information on where the cup I sought had likely come to rest. I lapped up their words, as well as their stew, and by evening those of age had taken what they wanted from me and in turn, I had given them everything I had. That was my greatest mistake. But a man is a man and a knight, no matter how holy, is subject to the same temptations as the common peasant. Those who can claim otherwise will have already found madness"

He looked up at Edgar.

"Once they had a part of me, they had all of me"

He shook his head as if to clear it.

"I slept for perhaps a day and a night and for the longest time I actually believed I was dead, doomed to walk upon this earth for all time in a perpetual limbo-like state"

He paused.

"Of course, I wasn't but I didn't know that. For days on end, I wouldn't eat, couldn't eat. Then I slept little, if at all; the world blurring in my false eyes so that I never realised the passing of time between one day and the next, despite the rise and fall of the soft, pre-summer sun"

"But you lived", Edgar commented, leaning in.

Richter shook his head once again.

"No. Three of the group, in particular, did their best to sustain me as I became a deadly marionette for their macabre wants and devious needs. But you could hardly call it living".

Then he paused for a long time. In contemplation, it was some minutes before words next shaped themselves upon his lips.

"Knowledge cost me perfection. And I fell victim to an illusionary seduction..."

He looked back down into his empty mug.

"So many died by my hand..." He drifted off.

"I returned from my quest and promptly battered the strange man with the very chalice he bid me find. And I merely watched as the Three took turns to sup his blood from the vessel, before giving it to the Others, as I've come to think of them, to clean"

"At the commotion, my olde comrades in arms came running and stormed into his chambers. But with unnatural strength bestowed upon me, I slew them one by one, without remorse, all so that my jailors could achieve their selfish needs"

Somehow his head hung lower than ever before, resembling a sunflower broken in the wind.

"A Brotherhood is for life. Our vows are sacred, our friendship strong. You don't understand...I cannot remember any of those who used to be my friends. I...I cannot remember their names"

He paused.

"I am a long way from sunlight, between the chalice and the jaw, the last of a long line and the end of a memory..."

Edgar leaned forward and laid a hand on the Richter's shoulder.

The knight seemed half the size he had been when Edgar had first met him in the tower, though it looked as if a heavy weight had been torn from his shoulders with each word of confession.

"What happened in the tower,...I don't think you are nearly as dead as you think you are", He trailed off. "But I think we will move on tomorrow."

"Where to? I cannot go home"

"Well...", began Edgar, before pausing to sigh deeply. He placed his mug on the table.

"I'm sorry if I seemed interested. I'm not..."

~

That night Edgar and the mysterious Chylde remained in the common room, huddled under a blanket loaned by the innekeep himself. Rooms were sparse, but floor space was ten-a-penny and Richter had passed out in front of the fire, sprawled in all his armour, no less.

Thoroughly thawed and with a full belly, Edgar's mind now wandered as his eyes followed the merry dance of the flickering flames before him.

He had hoped to find the Chylde's guardians or someone who knew something about them, and now found himself strangely reluctant to abandon the youngster.

Astonishingly, as if reading his thoughts, the Chylde spoke. *A rarity.*

"I'm scared," he said, bundled up in the blanket like priceless goods on an overseas journey.

It was a pitiful sight to behold, and with no one else around to offer comfort other than a few regulars who had fallen asleep and slumped in situ, Edgar found himself the reluctant and unlikely voice of comfort.

He looked down at the Chylde. "We are safe enough. Don't let Richter's tales disturb you. His long shadow follows *him*"

The words sounded foolish to his own ears, but he had hoped that they did something to comfort the Chylde nevertheless.

As it turned out, they didn't.

"But I'm not scared of the stories...*Or* the shadows."

Edgar raised a brow, not knowing how to respond. He had never been good at this sort of thing and his eyes drifted back to the fire.

Annoyingly, the Chylde tugged on his arm.

"What is it?" Edgar asked, starting from his reverie and feeling mildly irritated.

"I'm sleepy..."

"Then go to sleep", replied Edgar with all due tact.

There was a moment's pause before the Chylde replied.

"I don't want to"

"Why not?"

The Chylde turned to look at the fire himself, the constantly moving orange glow taking away the worst of his pallor, yet still leaving an eggshell radiance.

"Because I'm scared"

~

The following morning greeted Edgar with a sense of foreboding.

Something about the way the Chylde had spoken the night before stayed with him throughout the night and, as a result, he'd slept poorly. Fragments of the night came and went, but parts seemed missing, vague recollections between the pitch of somnolence and the blanch of manifest.

He was just easing into consciousness when a tankard slammed down on the table beside him, most of the contents washing over him like a cold slap to start the day.

Richter wore an expression so grim that his face resembled an upturned walnut glazed in honey.

Bleary-eyed, Edgar looked around, taking in the scene. It was obvious someone was missing.

The tavern was surprisingly quiet and, although it was morning, he had at least expected to witness some commotion. Instead, he laid eyes upon the long-cold ashes of the fire and the void behind the bar.

Richter slumped violently into the chair next to him, almost breaking it in his effort.

Edgar knew then that the Chylde was gone.

"They are gone" uttered the knight, at length, staring in into the empty fireplace.

Edgar looked around, his eyes eventually falling back on Richter, who was nodding even as he sat.

"And why are you so exhausted?"

Richter laughed a mirthless laugh, then, the sound of it making Edgar uneasy even as he supped at the dregs of the freshly spilt tankard of ale.

"What is done is done". His stare never left the fireplace, as though his eyes bore through the ash and into the structure below.

"What's that supposed to mean?" asked Edgar, irritated. He shrugged out of his chair and sauntered over to the bar to refresh his drink.

As he reached the taps his attention was drawn to a dark smear leading towards the cellar hatch. He thought nothing of it until around halfway through his decanting when he looked again.

Richter watched as Edgar rigidly returned to his seat, slumping into it much as he had done not long before.

Edgar drained his tankard in one and ran a hand over his face, ending up looking like a sad mime without makeup.

He stared into the dark fire.

"There's no chance that what I saw was real, is there?" he asked into the ashes.

Richter rightly took that question to be aimed at him.

"Edgar… Something happened last night; something grim"

Edgar exhaled deeply, having held his breath without knowing. Ash went everywhere to provide a shroud between his reaction and the reality.

It was Richter's turn to fill his tankard then, and he returned with a hessian sack.

He dropped it at Edgar's feet.

"I don't know where the Chylde has gone, but I'd wager it isn't to a good home"

He stooped then to examine a coin by the door. Turning it in his fingers he muttered to himself.

"Two sides of the same coin and the fortune of seeing both...And with a third face soon to be spent, though no less valuable..."

He turned back to Edgar who sat staring at him.

"I think I know where the Chylde might be. The question is, do you want to find them?"

Edgar continued to stare.

"What's in the sack?"

Richter straightened.

"Bones"

Chapter VIII
Crepitus

Edgar stood beside Richter on the edge of the Endless Meadow, so given its name by the rows upon rows of flowers that stretched as far as the eye could see.

That was then.

Now, the fields were riddled with myriad unmarked graves, necromantic inversions upon a choked, alluring plain, half-drowned in ceaseless rain. Some flowers still remained; the brown-ed husks of bleak memoriam.

In the distance, a fire burned; a thin wisp of white smoke climbing towards the black clouds above. Beside it, a figure in tattered robes lay bent double and arched in agony.

"And I was expecting so much more", commented Edgar as he surveyed the scene.

Richter set his jaw in disgust. "If anything climbs out of one of those graves, I'm leaving".

Edgar nodded, slowly, and pulled his sodden cloak about him that little bit more.

"Are you sure you want to go through with this?" asked Richter. "You could just pretend none of this ever happened".

Edgar looked up at his strange companion and shrugged the sack on his shoulder.

Then he took a step forward.

An arm shot out to block his path. It was the knight.

"What now?" complained Edgar, irked.

"Look" Richter pointed ahead.

In the distance, six withered men-at-arms lounged about filching items from the graves and picking the heads off dry daisies.

"I know their kind" added the knight. "They'd sooner your use your anus as an ashtray and your skull as a spittoon than let us pass unmolested. We'd do better to wait".

"As long as it's not the other way around", replied Edgar taking another step forward. "Besides, I'm tired of waiting…and it's getting dark".

Richter turned to look at him. "There is no reason to believe that light shines between here and there…"

He shrugged again. "But look at where waiting has got us", he added.

It was hard to argue against the grey misery before them.

Richter regarded the scene, the rain running off his piecemeal armour and down the back of his neck, his eyes falling again upon the dead monk by the fire. He set his jaw once more and slowly drew his sword.

"Then let us search"

He paused, then added. "But give *them* a wide berth", gesturing to the men-at-arms with a finger so long it bordered on comedic. "There's no need to burden an additional grave, no matter how gaping".

The words were carried away as the wind picked up, causing the fire in the distance to flare and accent the grimace on the dead monk's face.

Edgar made his way forward, taking a swig from his skin of wine so sour it reminded him of bile. Who knew, Edgar mused, maybe it was. Perhaps the crone who had given him such a gift had merely removed the gall bladder from some unspeakable beast and capped the end.

He cared not.

Richter's cold, dead eyes looked as grim as Edgar had ever seen a man look, though he seldom had access to a mirror.

Darkness crept in like a thief and so the pair soon found themselves moving toward the familiar comfort of the seemingly ever-burning fire they had seen from afar earlier on. Despite finding themselves shin-deep in mud at times due to the rain, the stalwart flames showed no sign of receding.

As they approached, the details of the bent monk became clear.

Dead he was not. But alive wouldn't have been quite the right word either.

The man displayed all the hallmarks of rictus and was contorted awkwardly, half sodden, half bone dry from the fire. But there was no mistaking the fresh tears in his eyes.

There were no sobs. There were no words; just a gentle liquid secreting from behind quivering lids.

About him lay a dozen ruined parchments, a selection of gemstones and a mortar fashioned from a human skull, stuffed with damp herbs.

Richter knelt down and drew a dagger across the monk's throat without preamble.

Before Edgar could speak, Richter interjected.

"Save your pity. This man was a charlatan clad in ill-gotten cloth. No holy water can save him now"

The knight sheathed his steel and exhaled deeply, examining his own hands.

Edgar knelt by the corpse, watching the tears wash away in the rain.

He held up one of the jewels to the fire to better see it, static colours cast upon the ground in mock subjugation to the deluge above.

"These stones…", began Edgar.

Richter's look was dark. "Leave them"

Edgar's hesitation to put back down the stone caused an awkward silence between the pair. In the end, Richter's brow furrowed so much it began to collect rain. At which point Edgar conceded the point and released the jewel.

The knight scanned the horizon. "This is no place for us. Find what you came here for and let us be gone; the sooner the better. Any later than and we'll end up six feet under and without a blanket.

By now dozens of crows had begun to flock home to roost, taking up residence on any number of the gaunt, lifeless trees and crumbling stone about them. By nightfall, the Endless Meadow would play host to a carpet of black, the birds drawn to its epicentre by a strange rancor and a longing for the macabre.

Edgar's eyes glazed over as he continued to look at the flames through another gemstone he couldn't resist fondling.

Shapes came and went; visions, nightmares, from one form to another. With gradual persistence and with no small wonder...

"What did we come here for?" he replied, distractedly.

Richter looked up and laid a hand on Edgar's shoulder. "Let's move".

The scavenging party that they had spied earlier had apparently noticed them and were now making in their general direction. Flocks of crows parted in their wake, heralding their approach.

Edgar threw down the stone and drew his rapier.

"Put it away" hissed Richter.

"We want no trouble!" Richter called out. "We're mere mourners, come to pay our respects to the..."

It soon became apparent that the rogues were something Other.

"...Dead", the knight finished. "This is the *Monk's* work!"

He grasped Edgar by the arm. "Come!"

There was another flurry of crows as the pursuers picked up their pace. They moved swiftly, as of tumble-stones upon the river bed. It was then that Edgar comprehended their reanimation.

"Shouldn't they have fallen when you cut the throat of that monk!?" cried Edgar in between panicked breaths.

"Worse", Richter replied. "It doesn't work like that. They are now free of their bonds. Now there is no one to control them, if it could ever have been deemed that anyway".

Edgar riffled through his own mind of what he knew about such things, searching for something to use against them, should it come to it.

It was then that Richter stumbled and fell; clattering and folding like an olde tin can under the wheel of a heavy-laden cart. It was only a matter of time before one of them did, the landscape being a patchwork of broken masonry and forgotten relatives.

Edgar followed suit moments after, losing a foot down a shallow grave and having it lodge in the ribcage of an unsuspecting cadaver.

He lost his grip on both sack and rapier and they promptly sank into the mud, and it took him precious moments to retrieve them lest they become relics of an uncertain future.

At the edge of his consciousness, he could hear the heady sound of swordplay as Richter lay about him in defiance.

Edgar was struggling to free himself when the space before him parted into an unbroken void and he crawled towards it, dragging the skeleton with him. As he reached the threshold he could feel a dull tingling sensation coupled with a gentle pressure.

And then he was through.

~

The rent closed behind him almost as suddenly as it had appeared.

Edgar lay prostrate for a few moments, one hand reaching out.
Silence.

Wearily, he progressed from the muck onto his knees and took a moment to catch his breath, as well as remove the ribcage from around his ankle.

A modest, stone gateway loomed before him, steeped in mystery and flanked by two stone columns upon which sat a pair of idle crows punctuating the silence of an otherwise reticent courtyard.

He had no clue as to his bearings, but the familiar feel of rain on his skin offered some comfort; something for his mind to cling onto.

Edgar got to his feet and took stock. He was utterly, forgivably alone.

He looked up and let the rain fall into his eyes before pulling his cloak tighter around him and moving on.

It was then the shadow approached, unseen, unheard, but omnipresent all the same.
He could feel it.

And as he stepped forward through the pillars he paused to reflect on how, even now, he could recall no grimmer place.

Chapter VIII
Laughter on the Wind

Edgar took a deep breath and looked ahead at the entrance to the catacombs before him. The stairwell was as slick as an abattoir window and into the gloom, it disappeared beyond sight. Beside the portal lay a sarcophagus, cold to touch.

Some small minutes passed before his eyes focused on the worn inscription on the stone.

Someone was watching him.

It was hard to contend against the Grey. Yet there remained a revenant upon the stygian black, argent by midnight, void by day...

A half-perceived movement from behind sent prickles along his neck and deep down into his spine, culminating in a twitch of the sphincter.

Turning with a flourish he was met with nothing; just carrion on the stones and laughter on the wind.

And then, as the persistent droplets that distorted his vision cleared, the spectre before him morphed into something more coherent.

"Herbynlocke…", uttered Edgar

The man lounged casually upon the nearby sarcophagus. And for once he was fully clothed.

Adorned in tattered black rags they blew fervently in the wind as though applauding some unseen spectacle.

Edgar couldn't help but stare until the sage's eyes fell upon the sack in Edgar's forgettable, limp grasp.

He laughed again.

"Bones, Edgar?"

"Memories"

Herb stood. He was taller than Edgar remembered with straight black hair that fell almost to the ground.

"You know what's down there, don't you?" said the sage, glancing at the stone portal, his hair catching a gentle breeze.

Edgar took his time before responding.

"Bones", he said at length.

Herbynlocke chuckled once more, clapping leather-clad hands together upon which a withered rose appeared swiftly within his grasp.

Gently he laid it upon the sarcophagus beside him as the rain battered the fragile petals from the stem and left only leaves and thorns.

The sage inclined his head. "For Richter".

Edgar moved forward, extending a hand.

"He…"

"Yes" replied Herbynlocke. "But he is free now, a man under his own rule. His work is done.

Edgar knelt by the stone.

"Your life was bought with his and now you must find coin of your own, else be indebted for eternity"

Edgar pressed his head against the side of the sarcophagus and took up a handful of dirt.

"Farewell", he said softly to the ground.

"He left you this", said Herbylocke, looming over him, idly wiping the item with his cloak.

He held a grim broadsword, the hilt encrusted with assorted jewels and the blade notched in several places.

Edgar got to his feet and took it from him, the sudden weight causing the tip of the blade to drag across the side of the sarcophagus.

Herbynlocke was laughing again. "Scarred then, even in death"

Embarrassed, Edgar hefted the blade and turned towards the steps leading down. On the brink he hesitated, squinting into the darkness.

The sage watched him with close interest. "There are many things down there, Edgar. None of which require light"

Edgar started forward once again, before glancing back at the wizard in his damp rags.

"Then I'll be right at home"

Herbynlocke raised a brow as he caught Edgar's gaze lingering on the grave of Sir Richter.

"You've been given up before, mayhap many times. You've gotten used to it. Perhaps you think it commonplace. And you would do it again"

Edgar elected for a silent riposte, picking up the bag of bones and taking his first step out of the rain and into the gloom.

~

Inside the catacombs the smell of death was palpable. But there was also a sense of peace and Edgar welcomed the silence. For a brief moment, he forgot what he came for.

And then the cold hit him.

Whereas outside was wet and windy, inside was just plain frigid. With each step descended the temperature dropped perceptibly and it wasn't long until he uncorked the reserve spirits.

He'd just motioned to take a swig from the vessel when movement somehow caught his eye; a deeper pitch against the black.

The click of fingers.

It was the loudest dual-fingered snap Edgar had ever heard since sliced bread, and the motion reverberated up the stairwell and along the corridor ahead.

Torches abruptly flared along the walls and a lone figure became outlined upon the bottom step.

Gaunt, with long hair matted with dirt and powdered with dust, clad in black and in desperate need of a shave, the figure was everything Edgar's mother had told him to avoid in life. Well, maybe not quite *everything.*

"Greetings", rasped the figure in a tone that was akin to a death rattle, or words worked around ancient rust, before disappearing down a corridor.

Edgar gave chase, almost slipping on some ice towards the bottom steps as he went.

He arrived just in time to see the figure vanish down another corridor to the side, and then repeat the move once again when he had reached that one.

The whole process went on for what seemed like hours but was, in reality, only minutes. Still, the result was much the same. It was tiresome.

Edgar had become lost and was now relying on half-seen glimpses of the strange man to lead him further and further into the crypt.

Impossibly, even when he ran right on his heels, Edgar found that the man was always already looming at the end of one of the long corridors, his fingers steepled together, before he got there. It seemed to him like some game, played by two and enjoyed by only one. And Edgar wasn't enjoying it.

Breathing hard, Edgar eventually found the man stood straddle-legged in a doorway, and ran directly into him, inadvertently brushing up against the man's clothes in the process.

It was then that he discovered that the flickering shadows had kindly masked the attire from afar and now garments fashioned from strips of what looked to be skin, possibly human, were clearly visible, lending the man a more grotesque visage than before.

But he had come too far to be dissuaded by be-shrivelled giblets hanging off an unlikely host. One man's nightmares were another man's garments. But at that point in time, Edgar reasoned, he was no man.

The figure's mouth motioned in mute response, and the torches faded away, leaving only half-light visions upon an inadequate canvas formed of deep fabrics not yet known of felt.

An unseen vacuum pulled him forward, and for a moment Edgar thought he would find himself once again pressed up against the strange nonce before him, looking down at strips of flesh as of jerky upon the tree.

But there was no longer anyone there.

And when the vacuum ceased he found himself before an iron door fixed to the stone. A faint glow emitted from a fine grill on the front and the gentle echo of sobs from within met his ears.

Edgar pushed against the door, the tang of damp, rusty metal making itself known to his olfactory senses, and the lock sprung, causing Edgar to fall into the cell before him. The contents of his sack spilled onto the bare ground within, be-marked as it was by some strange design.

As bones clattered about him and he fought to regain his balance, it became apparent that the sobs came from no guest of this most inviting room, but were a mere conjuration, the light a product of base sorcery.

And in the doorway, the man.

"You mean to deceive me". It was not a question. The figure's brow was furrowed and his eyes piercing, yet he made no move against Edgar.

Even so, he took up the sword Richter had bequeathed him and felt the jewelled hilt embolden his resolve, the hard gems settling into the soft palm of his sweating hand like a crown upon a velvet cushion.

This only seemed to amuse the man. "Richter's precious sword," he said with a gentle chuckle, garnished with disdain. "How noble", he added, the words echoing down the hall. "Would that you had brought the olde knight himself".

"I brought you bones", said Edgar, gesturing to the remnants about him.

The man furrowed his brow further, so much so that Edgar was assaulted with memories of Richter doing similar, yet for much less reason. Or so he thought.

"You brought me nothing!" the man snapped, barely letting Edgar respond.

As he backed through the door he flicked a gold coin into the room before the portal closed and an iron bolt clamped shut behind him like a long nail in the coffin.

And then the black returned.

On this side was a nightmare; an ire and a fractal exaction. On the other; nothing.

Edgar heard the coin strike the ground beside him and his ears followed its direction. He sat for a moment considering what had just happened.

After several moments of contemplation, he came to the same conclusion, and to no one in particular he voiced a single word.

"Bugger"

~

It wasn't a good night's sleep for Edgar, alone, in that dark place. It seldom ever was.

The lack of room service was unnerving, but then he was in an oubliette.

The absence of light brought the presence of hunger and the hours began to eat away his resolve, if not his excreta. Early on during his imprisonment, Edgar had examined a floor grill that he had located towards the edge of the room, but a strange, continual squelching sound made itself known whenever he went near the thing and he had since given it a wide berth.

At least the place was peaceful enough. He had hoped for something more but found only stale crumbs upon a concrete mattress...Yes, it would be as good a death bed as any. And as the flesh slowly sloughed off his body at least he wouldn't be bothered by anyone.

Minute by minute he finally started to drift off, gradually visited by visions of grandeur, made real in slumber...thoughts of other kinds of denizens within the void, though he knew not their presence, nor their purpose.

He felt every breath keenly then, and his very pores soaked up the qualities of the air. There, energy found its way to him; through him and out of him, the fragrant undulations of distant paradise...

He was only two-thirds worthy of rest, but one step closer to death he felt more alive than he could remember.

Eventually, a kind of sleep came like fingers running freely through hair and he let himself be taken away from the hard stone walls about him. The Endless Meadow blurred as an unfinished painting caught in heavy rain and the forests surrounding it faded like sunset behind mountains turned to lines of laughter about the eyes of a care-free man.

It took a day and a night to become corporeal.

An act of will.

An act of Geomancy...

"Edgar…"

"If you dream of someone enough, does that make them real?"

"Edgar…"

"It doesn't matter who you are,
Sometimes the right tragic ingredients will make you a monster…"

"Edgar…"

"If you lust over someone enough, does that make them yours?"

~

Mole-eyed, Edgar sat up on his elbows.

A woman was at the door holding a lit torch.

She wore black, gilded with silver, her pale arms and face appearing to float in the night. A long hood covered her features and strong perfume clung about her, reaching him even from where she stood, like a feast upon the senses. And in that shrouded place, the banquet was endless. And it tasted like wilderness and afterthought…

But something seemed amiss.

She stared at him then, circling the room, each step a distorted reflection, the ladder of light.

Her gaze bore through him as though deciding upon his very makeup.

"A quiet place to lay thy head, close to the earth, close to the dead…", she uttered at length, having come full circle.

She smiled slightly before turning to disappear down the corridor.

The door had been left open.

Edgar scrambled to his feet, kicking bones about the place as he did so. When he reached the threshold he called out to the woman.

"My lady, your *name*!?"

As she drifted down the hallway and disappeared into the darkness she called back.

"Rain"

"My name is Rain…"

Chapter IX
Goode Coin

Edgar stepped through the doorway.

A sparse selection of torches lit the pathways of the catacombs seemingly at random. Since he had no real recollection of his route in, he had no reservations about proceeding in any direction in search of a way out.

That was until something else caught his eye.

In several places along the ground, the unmistakably shy glint of gold presented itself.

Edgar blinked over-exaggeratedly as if to test the fabrics of reality, when the tips of his fingers came into contact with what seemed to be good coin.

Before he had even finished drawing breath or considered what he might spend it on, particularly when lost down in the catacombs, he pocketed the meagre sum and said no more about it.

His footsteps echoed in the hallways as he moved slowly forward in the dust, idly fingering the coin.

And then he saw another.

"And they say there's no luck left in the world..." he muttered under his breath as he stooped to acquire the gold.

It wasn't until he had found his fifth or perhaps sixth coin that a pattern began to emerge and realisation started to form; that, and the now semi-tumescent nodule jutting from beneath his codpiece.

Edgar followed the trail of coins, filching them one by one as a matter of course. He cared little if the trail was leading him out or deeper into darkness. And as his fists overfilled with gold he couldn't have been happier; that eternally stooped man beneath the Endless Meadow.

But no sooner had he run out of room in his fists and codpiece combined, he found himself at the foot of a stair.

The strange stone seemed far older than that of the rain-soaked steps he had previously descended, and a wide array of mosses and lichens had taken up residence as a result.

He stood and looked up. The coins continued up into the light.

Reluctantly, Edgar dropped a handful of gold to take up Richter's sword and tore through the vines before him.

But the last thing he expected to see when he emerged from those musky depths was the olde knight himself sat upon a crumpled form by the exit.

He was caked in mud, blood and his armour was dinted in so many places that the texture resembled pumice.

And he looked olde, too olde.

How long had he been down there?

He stared at the knight for a moment, incredulous.

"You look tired", Edgar exclaimed, awkwardly.

"More than you know", rasped Richter.

Edgar looked up and held out an upturned hand.

"And it's stopped raining".

Richter said nothing.

"And who's this?" he added, gesturing to the heap the knight was sat upon.

"A friend of yours, I believe", replied Richter, standing with visible and audible effort. He groaned so much during the motion that he sounded like an olde treasure chest out at sea, before being informed that it had washed up on the wrong island, devoid of gold.

As he moved the heap complained, and it was then that Edgar recognised him as the same man from within tomb. He looked different in the cruel, unforgiving light of day.

"You"

"Yes me!" the man snapped, regaining some strength.

Richter put pay to that by placing an armoured boot upon his back and forcing him firmly onto the ground once again.

"Fuck you, Richter" the man spat. "I own you!"

Richter pushed harder, this time driving the man's face into the mud.

The knight loomed over him.

"Tell me, what authority do you have under my boot?" He looked around. "What demands can *anyone* make of me now?!"

"Sterling, you fucking arse..." the man choked around soiled lips. He spluttered once again, trying to rise. "You are bought and paid for. It doesn't mat...".

"Was", the knight interrupted, tossing down a golden-white chalice which embedded itself into the earth beside the man's face.

He had clearly spent a long time out of sunlight but somehow, in that undignified moment, he managed to turn a shade even paler. On any given day Edgar would have mistaken the man's flesh for bleached parchment or antique porcelain.

An earthworm crawled between the chalice and the man's jaw as he summarily writhed and wretched on the ground.

Richter turned to Edgar.

"This man wear's charmed garb - Obscene, but rare".

Edgar looked on, blankly.

Richter stared at the gold still clutched in Edgar's fist.

"His breeches... fashioned from reams of human skin..." He thrust a mailed fist down into the restrained man's gusset, withdrawing it to produce yet more gold. "...can bestow an endless flow of coins on the wearer"

Edgar looked down at his fist, then over to the man in the mud, his tattered trousers hanging off him like a wet towel.

Richter continued.

"With flesh gleaned from some poor soul, upon death they can be crafted with all due care and no small element of sorcery. Exhumed, the dermis must be taken whole; from nave to crack.

Naturally, a coin taken from some olde widow must then be well placed within the remnants of the scrotum, along with a sigil of some sort, penned in fine, fast, and unfailing ink"

Richter let several coins spill through his fingers.

"Once worn, the wearer would never want of gold on the non-negotiable assumption that the first coin remained wholly untouched"

As if to reiterate the point he added.

"Endless Riches"

Unable to process the meaning of such an artefact, but rigid all the same, Edgar returned Richter his sword.

The knight solemnly stretched out and took it.

He looked down at the man struggling on the ground.

"What do you say to a…a fistfight?", the prone man hastily gasped.

But without preamble, Richter upturned his sword and drove it down into the base of the man's neck.

A brief judder and then nothing.

"Quickly", urged Richter, gesturing to the man's trousers.

The pair bent down and unceremoniously stripped the fresh cadaver of all below-the-waist accoutrements.

As the trousers slid off a flood of coins poured out about their feet, which Edgar fell over like a beggar upon scraps.

Richter exhaled and turned away, seeming suddenly fragile, and removed a few pieces armour.

Looking into the sky without having to blink for a change, the withered knight laughed bitterly as he slumped back down onto a large rock.

"I'm done"

"What?" Replied Edgar, his looting interrupted. Carefully, he put the trousers aside and moved closer.

Richter was rolling a small disc between long fingers.

"Do you know what this coin means, Edgar?" asked the knight.

"A good meal at the next tavern we cross and ten to twenty mugs of extra-strong ale?"

Richter laughed bitterly again, but this time with less strength.

"If only…"

He glanced over. "That sack of shit on the ground was the worst of them", he spat.

Edgar regarded the man in the mud, naked from the waist down, a coin pushed up his anus for good measure.

"What do you mean?" he asked.

Richter merely sighed, staring up at the clear sky as he lay upon the rock.

"I think you'll find what you are looking for. But try not to rake up olde graves…"

Edgar moved a touch closer.

The knight turned slightly towards him, his breathing shallower, but his focus on something in the distance.

"Richter, what do you see?"

The knight licked his lips and it was a long moment before he replied.

"Have you ever felt like you missed something so deeply, so profoundly that you can feel the hope in your veins dissipate to nothing, and your heart fall from a branch already too low? It sends shivers down your spine and forces tears behind your eyes. And so you light a candle with the vain hope that its unfailing incandescence might guide you out of the fog and back onto the road once more"

He took a deep swallow.

"And yet you find yourself back right where you started; where the moon shone brightly through crystal walls and the world grew a little colder, crystalline formation caught between tangent motions, covetous fields of frigid emerald...

Torn from the inadequate grasp of free-form perfection, what nightmares break away and fall over each shoulder. Far gone, then, recollections of bitter sunrise; a look away from beauty, a thought away from grace...

Segue toward serenity... Yet neglect not the rot..."

And then Edgar watched quietly as the golden coin fell from those same fingers and sank slowly into the mud.

He looked up.

"… A wet day without rain"

Chapter X
Last Man Standing

It had been a long time since Edgar had eaten.

And for that matter, it had been a long time before he had even properly drawn breath, for the chill in the air drove daggers into his lungs and thick perspiration from his mouth.

A sleet rain drove through from above, though no matter how cold it got, the perpetual gloom of the wood and the dense thatch of never-ending branches were nothing if not insulating. And for that reason the river still flowed; flowed onward like gentle tears upon the cheek of a newborn babe; and not the gouts of blood pulsating from its throat like he wished it were.

His mind was a phalanx of greed, lust, and ire; the latter of which was a General at the helm of the assault. And beauty…If beauty were a pendulum, it could hang as far as he was concerned.

Clutching the Sack of Ire within the folds of his cloak Edgar trudged on, the ceaseless babble of the river constantly nagging at ears long wrought sensitive from too little rest.

Peripheral visions of olde parchment and withered veins encroached, aberrantly brought to focus by a calculating winter sun. At least it remained blessedly behind an unbroken blanket of threatening cloud, though threaten is all they did. It was as though the sky didn't even have the common decency to either rain or snow, but instead insisted upon a stark backdrop noted through chance openings in the canopy above.

Edgar jumped to catch and break a low-hanging branch, quickly fashioning it into a crude walking cane. For the first time in a while, a smirk chanced upon his lips.

And then he heard singing.

As the mountain pass curved out of sight, Edgar could tell the source of mirth was coming his way. Through laden branches, he caught the flash of gilded raiments and kindred entourage.

Before he even had the chance to look for a suitable spot to leave the path, two men on horseback hoved into view.

Edgar quickly regarded what seemed to be a minstrel and a second man clad in worn leather and a ruined tabard; The tattered carmine finery of a vagabond upon the road, A spiked club hung by his side.

The minstrel sang merrily and appeared to swagger in his saddle, if that was even possible. The ruffian did likewise, though he sagged a bit, a bottle of some vile liquid clutched within a large, grubby palm. He was also notably out of tune with the minstrel who was, by his own estimate, at least worthy of fixing into some stocks and pelting with an assortment over-ripe fruits, vegetables, and bed-pans.

As they approached, the minstrel slung his lute over his shoulder and casually slipped off the side of his mount, leaving his witless companion to tend the horses.

The man was clad in all manner of colours, many of which seemed to be torn strips of various banners from around the realm. He also wore fragments of armour, littered about his person, as though he expected neither battle nor parley. But most noticeable of all was the strange, ornate codpiece that he displayed proudly without one iota of remorse.

The piece appeared to be fashioned from the basket guard of a swept hilt rapier and the stuffing acquired from some plush cushion or toy.

Edgar couldn't look away, though the purse of monies hung from the man's leathern belt and the cornucopia of foodstuffs and strange reagents in the saddlebag of his horse did steal some of the attention.

"Road's closed," said the stranger, thumbing over his shoulder.

His words emerged with what could only be described as a thick, regional accent, though that could have meant anything. Perhaps the man, as many minstrels were wont, had simply stayed in so many places over the years that he had developed a truly unique lilt to his words and mangling of language in general.

At Edgar's silence, he tried again to broach the tedious subject of introductions.

"Name's Kemp," he said, spitting on the ground by his boot. A wad of black and brown burnt through the white crust. He held out a soiled mitt as if to shake hands.

Edgar obliged. "That's err…a nice codpiece you have there" he blurted; clearly ill-at-ease with the small talk.

A bark of laughter from the drunk on the horse embarrassed Edgar further.

"Oh, err…yeh…thanks…" replied Kemp, clearing his throat.

"Well, the lout behind me is Duke. He's err…a bit down on his luck at the moment, shall we say?"

Duke's horse began to urinate.

But it was only a short matter of time before both Edgar and Kemp realised the urine was not of the horses' making.

"Bloody 'ell, Duke. Use the damn trees", Kemp scolded before distractedly muttering further curses beneath his breath.

"Kemp", said Edgar, touching the man's arm and pulling him around. "You… You said the road is *closed*?"

Kemp scratched his head. "Is it? Well, nobody told us? Duke and I were just…" He trailed off, turning to tend the horses.

Edgar let out a small sigh and looked up to the dripping branches above. Cold droplets ran down his brow, across his lips, and found a place within his beard, now decidedly bushy with neglect. He brushed his hair back with a damp hand and approached the pair.

"Kemp" he started again.

A further bark of laughter from Duke heralded another inane comment. "How…how do you know his name?" Duke managed to remarkably slur.

"That's right," said Kemp, turning, the tone of his voice rapidly beginning sour. "How do you know my name, eh? Been following us have you?"

By now the horses were pointing back up the hill in the direction they had just come from.

Edgar wasn't sure how to respond. "Err…" he began, but was cut off.

"Thought you might follow us? Track us to the cave, slit our throats in our sleep and take our spoils did you?" said Kemp, un-shouldering his lute and smashing it violently on a nearby rock.

"Fuck!" he cried as the minstrel threw sharp pieces of broken lute at him, like knives or unbroken horse chestnuts.

"Did that fucking hermit pay you to double-cross us!?" cried Kemp.

"Well, I'll tell you this, I'd sooner eat that shit for breakfast than give it over to the likes of you… No, too much has gone into finding it, all of it…"

"What shi…", began Edgar, but was cut off.

Hastily, Kemp grabbed at the pack of reagents slung off his horse's saddlebag.

"A simple taste and we discover just how shallow-a-grave this truly is…"

It was by this point that Edgar came to the realisation that Kemp and his companion had clearly lost what was left of their minds a long, long time ago and the twitchy look in his eye explained why he was out in the middle of nowhere rather than attending court at a king's table. They had probably been out here for years, though how Kemp had ever acquired such an exquisite codpiece Edgar would still never know.

Duke fell from his horse, fumbling for his spiked club, but Kemp looked as though he simply wanted to wring someone's neck, namely Edgar's.

He bolted.

Before Duke and Kemp could even react he had already gained good distance on them, his long legs stealing through the snow like a partially handicapped gazelle. He figured he had a few minutes before Kemp would manage to manhandle Duke back into the saddle, but by then he planned to be off the road and into the sunset, if such a spectacle could be seen.

As he ran it was as though every breath applied fresh thorns against his lungs. The air was thinning, the temperature dropping further and further until at last, the rain turned from sleet to comforting snow.

And then, as fragments of rock gave way underfoot, Edgar found himself hanging to the edge of a ledge like an icicle, a rivulet of shit trickling from his arse to his ankle and out into nothing.

The wind was strong now and his fingers ached, but he lacked the strength of arm to pull himself up. And so there he hung for an indeterminable amount of time.

It felt like forever.

Below he thought he could see a pack of wolves circling, but perhaps it was just wishful thinking.

But his surprise was absolute when the neck of a lute appeared within arm's reach. Without thought, he took it and was hauled back onto the side of the mountain. And it was almost as though he could hear the angelic voices of some unknown entity on the wind. It certainly wasn't Duke's singing.

He found himself face to arse with Kemp's horse, the lute neck being attached by a length of rope. Kemp himself seemed to have calmed somewhat.

"You owe us now", said the minstrel with a smile. And within that smile, a gold tooth caught the light, like stained glass in a makeshift chapel, supplicant to a midwinter framework and a dash of natural hue.

"Your grin is worth more than your horse, song-smith" Edgar replied, sarcastically.

Kemp seemed to ponder something for a moment.

"Well, never mind," he said, at length.

"But I could use some company up the mountain"

"And Duke?" asked Edgar.

"Err…Duke 'ain't exactly what you'd call company. A…liability, maybe, sure… But straight-up company?..."

He let the thought hang much as Edgar had moments before.

"I've always been meaning to ask," said Edgar, dusting himself off. "I thought you already came from up there. Did I miss something?"

"Yeh, err…Can't say we got very far, if I'm honest, which incidentally I am"

"Oh no, and why's that?" he was beginning to tire of the conversation by the second.

Edgar was loathe to believe him but decided that keeping up the pretence of friendly banter until he could find another moment to escape was prudent to his current survival. He didn't need company like this on the road, or indeed off it.

Kemp looked uncomfortable.

"Come on, you said you were going that way anyway, and you can have a turn of Duke's horse. I'm sure he'll let you do so *willingly*". He cleared his throat.

Edgar arched a brow. He smelled something rotten about all this, and he wasn't referring to the contents of Kemp's codpiece. But the road beckoned…

"Fine", replied Edgar. "I'll join you. But I want to remain unmolested for the duration and my possessions unsullied by your lackey"

"Done" snapped Kemp, his gold tooth glinting once again as he grinned. "Let's get back to the road"

~

An hour later, and against the vast backdrop of the remote mountain pass, three unlikely figures could be seen. Upon closer inspection one could note that the figures were not alone, a dozen smaller forms shadowing their route with interest, a palette of shallow embers and delicate pantomime.

"Did you say something?" Edgar asked Kemp. They had been silent for some time, especially since the minstrel had destroyed his lute. With no instrument to keep him on key, he sounded more like a child working his way through puberty than any real bard, though Edgar hardly found that surprising.

At this Kemp looked mildly alarmed, though Duke said nothing. The drunk was walking now, having relinquished his steed to Edgar at Kemp's behest.

"What did you hear?" asked Kemp in hushed tones.

"Oh, nothing really" replied Edgar. I just thought you said something"

The wind raced past once more and Kemp was beginning to act strangely again.

"Let's move" he suggested, putting the heels of his boots into his horse and forcing Duke up to an uncoordinated jog.

For a moment Edgar lingered behind, confused.

He thought the air smelled like more rain, but…

"Wait up!" he called out, before urging on his own mount to give chase.

Yet as the trio passed under a low hanging branch something spooked the bard's horse, sending him hurtling to the ground in a pile of needlessly flamboyant attire and equally obnoxious expletives.

Faded apparitions of a night-time so long ago came and went, there within the Monochrome Overwood.

And as he floundered in the snow, Kemp glared at Edgar as if it were his fault.

Duke seemed distracted by something as the wind bristled still further, tearing at Edgar's cloak.

"Listen, I don't want any more trou…" Edgar said holding out his hands.

He never finished the sentence before a series of shrieks assaulted his senses and Kemp was taken bodily from the pass before his very eyes, as though some force of the wind had stolen him off the mountain. His first instinct was to check if Duke had indeed broken wind, perhaps even soiling himself in the act, but pleasantly the brute was also harried by some force other than the result of a fourth plate of beans hastily consumed at last camp.

And then Duke was gone too, his spiked club peeking out of the snow like a rattle.

The quiet tittering of a female voice disappeared into the aether.

Edgar took a moment to compose himself before scrutinising his surroundings, dismounting his distressed-looking horse. Letting go of the reins he stood back from the beast. "Well, go on then…" and watched it trot off back down the pass until the torrent of falling white flecks removed it from his vision.

He cast around to make sure he had left nothing behind and then realised that perhaps he should.

Taking the time to select a fine specimen he pulled a ripe, shiny onion from The Sack and placed it carefully upon a large stone, which he cleared. A second thought caused him to take a bite of the thing himself before he fled up the slope, ever upwards, ever alone. Somewhere at the back of his consciousness he still heard the shrieks.

~

In many ways, Edgar preferred the silent trail. Kemp and Duke had provided the kind of inane company he could easily do without and, to be honest, without trying to be too harsh, he hoped they were frozen solid at the base of a ravine somewhere. And if he was feeling malicious he would have also added eternal damnation and an unmarked, yet regularly defiled grave into the bargain. And that's before he had gotten to know them.

Another hour as the day wore on and Edgar once again considered the cruel joke that was his life. How many times had he walked this path?

It never got any easier.

Pulling his cloak tighter about him and securing his hood against the elements he trudged on.

Breathing heavily, Edgar watched the air in front of him condense and disappear. It had been long enough. He stumbled and picked his way over rock and through drift, never seeming to gain an inch on his destination.

Is this it then?

Something struck him on the head and fell to land by his boot; half an onion.

He stooped to collect the remnant, casting an eye about him all the while. Pushing back his hood and, in turn, his hair, he scrutinized the landscape.

Then he saw it; a small alcove naturally cut into the side of the mountain. He'd almost passed it by, so it was half-hidden in Cimmerian shade. The pouch of reagents sat calmly by the entrance, awaiting his arrival.

"But what do I know about luck?..."

Chapter XI
Grimm's Kitchen

Edgar found the entrance to the cavern as described.

There were other orifices too, but these were choked with the bones and remains of previous visitors who had got caught short when the rains came, a common occurrence, so there was no time like the present.

He peered into the opening until he felt himself about to topple. Moss and slime lined the edge and glistened wetly, winking like hundreds of regarding eyes, maybe thousands, each with its own agenda or suspicion in iridescent apprehension.

Edgar placed the leathern pouch of reagents by the lip and sat down with his legs dangling freely into the small chasm. It was then he noticed the furrows in the rock and the glint of gold below. A king's ransom in efflorescence, left out in the rain... A fortunate find for impatient eyes and restless hands.

And so, hand under fist, he began to descend.

But all too late Edgar realised that the coins were but monetary offerings given to mourn the dead, and as his pockets brimmed to bursting yet another fell into the precipice before him.

He blinked up stupidly as though awakening from some blessed sleep. Beyond the rays of light given from above, a dark totality prevailed.

Edgar grubbed around for some more minutes until his fingers ran lightly across a cool metal almost flush against the stone; a crescent.

With a gentle push, he was through and a warm red light presided over him, complemented by a faint hum, barely audible in the background, yet enough to permeate his flesh.

Why swim when you can drift?...

The words were felt, more than heard. They came from nowhere.

An endless pool with shores comprised of jewels, and with air as of a charmed perfume greeted him from a bank of which shells were worn from the twisted cartilage of myriad species, forgotten in time. Large stones sat stoically within the water, offering a delicate path and the surface was like a mirror; an oily abyss in which one could lose themselves forever.

Edgar picked his way across the stones, as careful with the last as with the first.

When his feet met with sand once again a brown door with a silver star lead him onward to a dense forest with gnarled trees and sumptuous, flamboyant fruits. The smell was inimitable. A cloying sweet on the verge of decay, but gentle enough to leave the mind confused and wanting more.

Edgar moved towards the fruits plucked one from its host. A single bite left him delighted in its sweet finish and immaterial texture. The rest were forthwith given to the Sack of Ire and lost forever.

And further on things got no better.

Door after door and cavern after cavern took their toll on Edgar's sanity, such as it was, and he could no longer remember a time when he wasn't searching for the hinges of some secret portal, only to find another shortly after. The rooms, peaceful at first, had turned nightmarish before eventually petering out into a sort of void, all the while climbing steadily upwards whilst appearing to be leading down.

The imperceptible ceilings had been shaped to an opposite, downward gradient and as such when Edgar finally emerged above the clouds it was all he could do not to scream.

Edgar looked back at the last room he had journeyed through, its portal still lay open; herald to a reign of purple minarets and unbidden slumber. He felt then a reluctance to turn away from that subtle illusion, of unmerciful charms.

Eventually, he turned and faced his path once more, holding up a hand to ward his eyes. Mountaintops stretched in all directions, and their beauty was maddening.

~

It had taken eight long days for Edgar to reach the top of the mountain each room with its own perception of time. He had lost about a stone in weight and managed to stub not just one, but all three of his big toes, which was a shame since he had always considered them one of his finer features.

Furthermore, during the endeavour, he had soiled himself. Not just once, but thrice.

To be honest he was beginning to get bored with the number three. Ever since the age of three, he had been fed up. And now that he had spent eight days in a mind-bending cave only to reach an unremarkable summit with trousers full of week olde shit he was thoroughly fucked off.

He sighed and squinted into the flat sunlight, hands on hips.

Before him, a modest hut stood proud on the mountain crest. How it ever survived exposure to the vigorous elements Edgar would never know, nor care. Still, it had a certain charm, if only for the potential firewood it presented this high up in such a cold, barren place. What a beacon it would make, what a pyre against the night.

Edgar pulled his Cloak of Misery about him and edged forward towards the fine establishment, muttering to himself about the unabashed pretentious nature of today's common Sage.

And yet upon arrival, he was met with another door. This he kicked open with gusto, sick of them, leaving splinters on the mat and snow upon the floor.

Inside, however, the hut was enormous; far out of proportion to the size without. Mirrored glass stretched out before him in all directions, perhaps an explanation of the apparent size, and the floor ebbed as though it were made of magma or warm urine mixed with flour.

Edgar sighed before double-checking the contents of his pouch. The reagents lay dormant, waiting. In that leathern darkness they held no charm or place in the world.

But combined…

He was interrupted when a slender figure presented himself before him.

"I say...Would you mind covering that up?" Edgar asked.

The man reached for the pouch and then for the sack, covering it up with a length of gangrenous moss plucked from within.

"Now you can see why I was in such dire need of some of these ingredients", the man said.

Edgar sighed immediately.

Why could he never meet anyone normal?

Hesitantly Edgar reached out his hand. "Might I have your name, sir?"

"Indeed you may. I am Glahzeer, as it please you"

"It would please me more if you could furnish me directions to the nearest privy, and poste haste at that", replied Edgar. "I would hate to extrude for a fourth time"

"Or indeed, a final time", replied Glahzeer. "Come".

With that he strode off, leaving Edgar to match him lope for lope and wondering how the naked man could cope with the cold winds up on high.

The hallways were full of all kinds of curios; from long spent matches to shrunken heads adapted for use as doorstops, scrolls within scrolls, herbs within herbs and candles, stones, dirt, and leaves. All had their usual homes, and at the back a stuffed bear stood upright, a tray of imperial mints offered up from a hand draped in flannelled cloth.

They walked for some time, to the point in fact where Edgar became doubled over trying to restrain his bowel movements.

"Please" he gasped. "This is getting silly"

Glahzeer stopped, pulled up a chair, and spread his arms.

Edgar stood awkwardly until Glahzeer bent down and removed a wooden cover from the icy floor.

A hole gaped in the ground before him and a strange musk issued forth.

"Bottomless", winked the Sage.

Edgar peered into the hole and thought he could see the distant yet unmistakable glisten of fresh faeces.

"I don't believe you" he responded.

Glahzeer looked incredulous "I've been shitting into that thing for years now and it still hasn't backed up"

Edgar did not humour him. That was a long time to shit.

He shook his head "Doesn't mean it's bottomless"

Glahzeer pulled an annoying grin. "I'm older than you might think"

"How fortunate, then, that your bowels are still in good, working order", replied Edgar, sarcastically.

It was at this point the thought crossed his mind that he'd made a big mistake - A fool's errand just to exchange pleasantries with a naked madman about filling a mountain with human waste.

Great.

~

Half an hour later and half a stone lighter, Edgar found his way to 'The Pantry', an area Glahzeer had suggested that he could often be found frequenting deep within the Cold Mountain.

The room was full of basically everything, as well as bits and pieces of something else.

Many phials and jars lined crooked wooden shelves, and excrement of all kinds decorated the walls with a fairly contemporary motif.

Components from strange creatures, desires made whole, and reagents that would never be found again all had their place in The Pantry.

Glahzeer spun on the spot, a sack of something clutched tightly to his chest.

"Ah, Edgar. Glad to see you looking so, er…trim."

Edgar patted his stomach. "Well, let's just say that someone may have to re-measure the height of this mountain"

The sage grinned. "Well, quite".

He paused. "But still, why not choose a bottle?" he added, gesturing towards a selection of vessels from around the globe.

The choice looked like so much effort, and so Edgar just took the first one he saw and handed it to Glahzeer; It was square-shaped, but with rounded corners and sported unremarkable, black cork.

"Right. Let's get this over with"

Glahzeer looked at him quizzically, in a way that Edgar had not yet seen. "You really want this stuff?" He asked, waving the bottle.

Edgar merely nodded.

"Then follow me"

~

After a steep climb up some narrow steps, they arrived at what was affectionately known as 'Grimn's Kitchen', though where Grimn himself had gotten to wasn't so clear.

But that wasn't the only logic behind the name. The place was rank with detritus and general chaos from several generations of reckless butchery and wanting cuisine.

Edgar ran his eyes over the place for a good minute. It looked like the world's last abattoir.

Glahzeer caught Edgar's look of horror. "Our chef has no stars, but this high up in the mountains you can have as many as you like". He winked.

Of all the smells that Edgar thought a truly good kitchen *should* smell like, a cesspit was not among them. And the enormous pipe leading directly into the roof where the mountainside latrine would roughly have been didn't fill Edgar with a great deal of confidence about what would be the evening menu. Or indeed, any menu.

He choked down some vomit. The last thing he wanted to do was eat yesterday's meal *again.*

~

That evening passed slowly, not least in part because Edgar had awoken to relieve himself during the night, resulting in several hours spent with the inner rim of his anus stuck to a cold rock at the very edge of 'The Pipe', slick with ice.

He stood watch while the others slept. The perfect guest; the perfect gentleman.

As he dozed bolt-upright, wondering if he would ever get back to bed, he caught instances of strange noises emanating from below. And it wasn't just his supper repeating on him.

Echoing up through the grotty aperture were a wide array of aural fascinations through the mundane to the magic.

Half-awake, such sounds conjured curious images within his mind; a withering soul, crunching leaves, the sound of water. Another time; laughter, abruptly quelled; a shocking revelation made known by sporadic droning.

And the rich smell of burnt earth and petrichor...

As the time passed...

And the stars wheeled overhead...

And Night drew down...

~

The next morning Edgar awoke haggard, hungry and, annoyingly still alive.

He found Glahzeer meditating in a small, wicker hut next to a cluster of bare trees. As Edgar approached the Sage wasted no time in presenting him with a clear bottle, full of a strange amber liquide.

Edgar un-stoppered the bottle and inhaled deeper than he perhaps ought from the vapours of some unknown substance... and the world seemed darker for it. A general sense of ill-omen descended over him.

But the sensation passed quickly and Edgar motioned to take a sip.

Glahzeer interjected; those sharp eyes and bent shoulders far above the Bleakening Realme.

"Careful with that, Edgar. Remember what's inside"

He stared at the sage one last time. "You don't need to remind me"

And then he necked the lot, smacking his lips before wiping them clean on the cuff of his shirt.

"It's what I came for"

Chapter XII
Everlasting Autumn

Richter stood over Edgar's slumped form, his keen eyes scanning the forest while he slept.

A snap in the branches beyond drew the warrior's attention, though he moved not. Only his pale eyes dared rove in search of the disturbance.

It was nothing.

Looking down he stole a glance at the unconscious Edgar. Even during slumber, his features remain rumpled, though by day he masked it from most. Richter saw through the masquerade.

The morning dragged on.

When would he wake?

The knight found himself riffling through his own memories with swift fingers and choosing to open but a select few. Reminiscing was a luxury he could ill afford right now. Thus, he pushed the thoughts aside.

The skies turned grey and with them came an unmistakable smell.

Great, rain. That ought to wake him.

Soon enough, Edgar stirred as droplets of water fell through the forest canopy and onto his body, gradually soaking through the well-worn cloak which he had draped across him.

He woke to find himself on a mossy bank somewhere deep within a forest. He didn't know which forest, because he didn't even remember getting there. And it was not the first time that it had happened.

He was thoroughly damp but otherwise unharmed, and as he sat up a stout bottle fell from his limp grasp and onto the leaf-strewn dirt beside him.

Casting his mind back he was met with a fugue replaced with lucid and tactile recollections of high places, stars that begged to be touched and cold as he had never felt before.

But, of course, it had to be a dream; like the embers of an ill-tended fire, gaunt and misshapen they hold stubbornly fast with what life remains them. But in the end, dead things fall...

The warrior bent down. "Finally...", he said quietly

Edgar looked around, blearily.

"I've lost him, Richter", he said, blankly and he struggled to stand up.

"What do you mean?" replied the knight.

"What do you think I mean!?" screamed Edgar out of nowhere, his voice causing a murder of crows to take flight like seeds thrown to a field.

Richter stood uncomfortably in his armour, unsure of what to say.

Edgar pulled up the hood of his cloak before turning deeper into the woods.

"Edgar!" Richter called after him, but to no avail.

Edgar's mood had settled in an instant and he had become deaf to the world, consumed by his own thoughts and intolerant of everything and anything. Idly, he crushed a small scorpion underfoot as he made his way through the dense woodland.

Dappled with spots of light, some areas of the forest played host to bright, pink flowers, proudly reaching out towards the sun, or as much of it as they could get. But Edgar was in no mood to tolerate their presence and summarily tore up one bunch, stuffing it haphazardly into the Sack of Ire.

The forest vista de-saturated once again and Edgar sighed. Before him, mute greens, dark browns, and soft greys were all that remained.

"Edgar!" Richter's voice was trailing off now, lost amongst the trees.

Good.

"Asshole" cursed the knight, more under his breath and to himself than anything, but it cut through Edgar's aural defences like a knife through cold butter - It took a while, but got there in the end, sticking to the edge and forming clumps as it went.

He stopped in his tracks and slowly turned on the spot to face the dull shape of the knight through the trees. If he was trying to look threatening it didn't register with Richter, but the knight decided to humour him and took half a step back, his metal skin piecing the unbroken sound of rain upon the ground like a beggar's last meal.

Edgar strode back towards him with a purpose and vigour that the olde knight had not seen before.

Only when he was within a few feet of Richter did Edgar relinquish. His close proximity to the knight reminded him that he was un-armoured and untrained. Still, he harboured enough anger and indeed frustration to continue to yell unreasonably in his face.

"What do you want!?"

Richter allowed a moment's pause for Edgar to calm down before his reply.

"I just thought…just a thought, mind, that if I were the Chylde and I found myself out here in this wilderness I would probably go there"

With a mailed hand he extended a finger to point through the trees, past the bark and the leaves.

The pair hadn't noticed it at first due to the fog, but now it was plain for all to see. On a hill above the tree-line, a large castle loomed, silhouetted upon the horizon, and sat without apology upon deep foundations. Grey towers stood against grey walls, and a grey keep stood behind it all.

"That is where I would go" affirmed the knight.

Edgar squinted, following Richter's gaze, his irritation transmuting as his eyes took focus. And then, almost as suddenly as it appeared, it was gone - Like some trick or conjuration. And he was left feeling foolish.

As comprehension set in, Edgar threw back his hood. Beneath it his was grinning.

"Let's face it," he said, cheering right the fuck up "Whether they are there or not, we're taking a look".

~

The castle was further afield than it had appeared at first and it was nearly two hours before the pair got within reach of the sloped path leading up to it.

More than once Edgar had sworn they were being observed by a hooded figure, set back against the trees, but whenever he looked to Richter for confirmation the vision was gone - Nothing more than an apparition in a lost man's mind.

As they broke through the top of the trees Richter announced that he could see movement towards the castle.

Edgar shrugged and continued on. Even so, Richter loosened his longsword in its scabbard and maintained wary eyes.

They briefly encountered a belt of low-hanging mist, blanketing the forest about them like a still lake. But nothing prepared them for what was beyond.

Set in front and to the side stood a gnarled tree, long dead and complete with an olde, twisted swing; an unlikely place for such a novelty, but curious nonetheless. And it was not empty.

A shiver went up Edgar's spine and Richter unconsciously tightened his grip on the hilt of his sword.

A skeletal form rocked back and forth, tangled in the ropes of the swing, assisted by a mild breeze. Rain ran down it's down its bleached bones and a light mist blew across their path to fully punctuate the scene.

As they approached, the figure, upside down as it was, did nothing to address them, but seemed to duly follow their progress, almost turning a head with eyeless sockets in their general direction as they passed. And it looked strangely pleased with itself.

"Couldn't be happier" muttered Edgar under his breath.

Tall gates loomed before them, bringing their progress to a halt. Richter promptly knocked thrice with the pommel of his sword but he would have had just as much luck throwing cabbages over the walls instead. The result was the same; nothing.

Several attempts later and still the pair stood before the gates patiently awaiting entry. But the place seemed long deserted, all but the swing and its tormented soul.

Edgar sat upon the ground, bored and weary from their journey up the hill. He leant against the gates, idly watching the skeleton as one might a piñata.

Weirdly, it was still looking at them, never once missing a stroke as it gently swung back and forth from the broken and twisted branches above it.

Edgar rolled his shoulders. "Any bright ideas?" he asked Richter.

The knight shrugged. "Nobody seems to be home, if you can call it that. Or if they are we don't appear to be welcome. Still, at least we are not *un*-welcome; else we might have boiling oil running down our arse-cracks by now"

"Boiling oil would be a luxury compared to what I imagine that fellow had down his arse crack to end up there like that" replied Edgar jutting his chin towards the skeleton.

It was still smiling.

"Who do you suppose it was?" asked Richter.

Edgar shrugged. "Who cares? But I note your non-committal use of 'It' in your reference"

Richter sighed. "I'll be honest; he looks how I feel, minus the smile"

The knight approached the tangled figure on the swing.

It was unabashed at Richter's approach and strangely preserved eyes rolled perfectly to regard him hungrily.

Richter leaned forward, trying to ascertain some recognition in the thing's 'eyes'. There was nothing.

"Hail!" said Richter.

Still nothing.

Richter looked back at Edgar and shrugged before turning back to the main gate.

"I say, greetings!" He hollered.

I say, greetings...

The sound was ethereal, as though on the wind. It came from somewhere dangerous... Somewhere beautiful... It came from the bones.

Further shivers ran up Edgar's spine like gentle fingers as he stood up, pulling his cloak tighter about him for comfort.

The thing had not moved.

"Did you…?" he began, but Richter cut him off with a raised hand.

The knight looked intrigued.

"I am Richter Sterling, a sworn knight. We seek young squire believed to have come this way. Have you seen them?"

Nothing.

The knight appeared frustrated.

"Have you seen *anyone!?*"

Nothing.

"Are you even really there…?"

And still, the figure rocked.

And still, the figure smiled.

Annoyed, Richter strode forward and grasped the rope of the swing.

Stopped so abruptly, the bones fell apart before the knight could react, and tumbled onto the ground like a heap of cheap crockery.

"Shit!" cried Richter, looking troubled.

"What is it?" asked Edgar.

"Some…Ill favour upon this contraption" uttered the knight, incredulous.

Too late he had realised his mistake, but by then his second hand was affixed to the other side of the otherworldly rig.

Edgar moved forward to help.

"Don't touch me!" blurted Richter causing him to recoil. "I'm…I'm in the shit here…"

"What… do you want me to do?" asked Edgar.

Richter was breathing heavily, clearly trying to stop himself from panicking and making things worse. He closed his eyes for a good moment, trying to think.

Edgar motioned forward again as if to help.

"Keep away from me!" screamed the knight, becoming angry.

In his armour he could not even articulate his body properly to sit upon the swing and so remained spread to the elements as those he was waiting to be searched.

"At least we know what happened to the last poor soul who thought this a welcome spot for idle frivolity", said Edgar.

The knight twisted his head to face him and then looked to the gates.

"Maybe someone inside can help," he growled.

"Find a way in."

~

An hour later Edgar returned to Richter with ill news.

He had skirted the perimeter of the castle no less than twice and found no way in other than the solid gates before them.

A small postern gate and a sewage grill were possible options, but the gate was stuck fast and the grill oozing with excrement. And whilst crawling up a pipe of raw sewage was tempting, he couldn't bring himself to try and squeeze through the gate.

Richter was starting to sweat and cramp given the awkward position he was stuck in and Edgar felt his bowels betray him. For all they knew, he could be stuck there forever.

Feeling decidedly glum, Edgar took up the discarded skull from the ground and tossed it over the castle walls; its familiar glare and endless smile spinning over and over until it was lost to sight.

Idly he sat at the base of the tree that Richter hung from so at least the knight could look down at him easily enough.

Richter grimaced. "Well, this isn't exactly ideal…"

Edgar wasn't quite sure what to say to that but felt he should say something at least.

"Good job you've got me here for company, then. Instead of… I don't know, some sort of rapist"

Richter just looked at him.

But as time drew on and the skies darkened, the oppressive gates behind them inched open with a sigh; lachrymose aural offerings drifting out across the mists.

Edgar looked up at Richter.

"Huh…Well, there we are"

Chapter XIII
Wanderlust

Edgar craned his neck around the corner of the huge castle gates.

Inside there was nothing, but beyond the gates, it was still raining, an all-pervading night-time filling the courtyard. A huge, singular cloud hung overhead, warding off sunlight from above.

How such a phenomenon could exist Edgar could only guess, if he could only be bothered. He considered it a pleasant environment but, without Richter by his side, his confidence to explore was shot to pieces, fragments, and shit.

Meekly he called out, his voice barely carrying at all, somehow absorbed by the aforementioned miasma.

"Hello?"

He shook his head. All he could hear was the rain drumming upon his cowl and so he lowered it now, letting damp hair fall about and soak up the moisture like a wick. He'd seen people adopt this pose under waterfalls before, but never in a bleak courtyard. He considered it a first.

Carefully he picked his way across the flagstones, looking for signs of activity. Someone had opened those gates, he'd state his reputation on it, or his name wasn't Edgar J. Blacke.

In the centre of the courtyard stood another curious tree, only from this one hung a dozen lit lanterns fighting a feeble battle again the sucking gloom, offering the only illumination within the confines of the castle walls; fragments of the night, a fraction beyond darkness.

Upon the bark, a limp parchment hung from a long, rusty nail. Some faded scrawl was upon it, penned with a rough hand.

Edgar approached and squinted to read the text.

What is Spirit but pursuit of our desires; to leave the mind to wander?

What then when dreams turn to nightmare, broken, stuck forever?

When left alone with subconscious for company, it's irresistible to you.

So take this gift from my hand. But if it pries your head in two remember;

Lust has made you mad.

Edgar snorted back grim laughter. The last time he had found himself lust over anything it involved a length of rope, a fast-flowing river, and a heavy stone.

He snatched the note off the tree with a flourish. It had been some time since he had had decent toilet paper.

Next up was a visit to a large, iron-bound door at the other end of the courtyard. He could just make out its shape in the distance but decided to take a lantern from the tree as a memento.

He nearly tripped on several piles of *something* on his way but decided not to dwell upon the specifics regarding that. Ignorance was bliss.

But by now ignorance wasn't enough. His eyes fixated on the door ahead, leading his body like an automaton, wound a revolution too tight and with an edge approaching all too soon.

Someone had opened those gates. Someone had written that note.

Of course, simple curiosity had won out. It had nothing to do with answers, the Chylde or, indeed, the erstwhile Sir Richter. Edgar just wanted to know.

And as he approached the door and extended a hand with which to turn the latch, a whole firmament of groans and moans issued forth from the other side of the woodwork. It sounded like a human abattoir.

Edgar muttered beneath his breath, his hand hovering about the handle. He couldn't be sure if they were the sounds of agony or ecstasy.

He waited, poised, for a length of time he could not remember, but soon found himself re-reading the note from the tree in the courtyard, the small lantern still protesting against the unnatural night.

Something seemed amiss, but he felt as though his brain wasn't working properly. A fog hung about him, befuddling his thoughts; a mental representation of warm toffee, cooling molasses or tar.

Light fades like a half-remembered song, leaving only the remains of failed endeavours,

And a breath held too long...

And by the wayside, as if the broken ribs of some unknown beast,

Lays the key to an Everlasting Autumn...

Edgar shook his head.
What?
"I am no detective," he said to himself out loud, looking around.

He stuffed the note back into his pocket like a used tissue. "But how did I end up here?"

He lifted the lantern. It was like the darkness was suffocating him, snuffing out his thoughts. But not his desires...

The light hurt his eyes and he lowered it again. The sounds from behind the door met his ears once more and his hand returned to the latch.

"Did you find anything yet!?"

The voice was Richter's; Faint, distant, thin.

But it was enough.

Edgar blinked rain from his eyes, staring at his hand.

Slowly he released the latch, regaining his senses.

"Not yet!" he called in response to Richter, almost automatically, his own voice sounding hollow to his ears.

He assumed the knight had heard, though he gave no indication.

Edgar backed away from the brothel-come-abattoir and looked around.

On the eastern wing of the courtyard, some olde stone steps caught his eye. Spiralling up they disappeared into a round turret shrouded by mist. As before, with the castle itself, if there was anywhere Edgar wanted to go at that moment it was there. The place simply smacked of intrigue.

Upon reaching the top Edgar found a smirk creeping across his face. He could see beyond the murk and over the walls which afforded him a fine view of Richter trussed up like a sack of meat at market.

"The state of that…" he muttered to himself.

He took a moment and a few breaths to scan the courtyard, but only shadows remained.

Cautiously he entered the turret. The lantern held before him did little to permeate the gloom but it was enough to stop him tumbling to an impromptu death, although there were times when he considered blowing it out.

To his right, a small landing was revealed and played host to a crossbow and a case of bolts beside an arrow loop worked into the masonry.

Edgar stooped to examine them and soon realised that they were coated in a thick layer of dust.

To his dismay, he also noticed that his own passing had left faint footprints in the very same grime upon the stone floor.

So much for shed skin…

And that was when he heard footsteps other than his own…

A second lamp cast flickering shadows up the stairwell, bobbing in the dark like an angler fish. Edgar dropped his own lantern in terror, plunging his corner of the landing into darkness.

Mutely, he drew his rapier as carefully as possible and hunched back into the shadows, waiting as the presence slowly approached. Cold steel in trembling hands seemed foolish but it was all he could do not to bolt. Something held him there.

The steps became louder, each one a hammer blow in the night.

And the nearer it got, the slower it moved.

Austere and unerring, the light was lowered... There was something there.

Edgar held his breath, straining to see.

The other lamp went out.

Then the unmistakable resonance of boot on stone moved toward him, step by drawn out step, as a cold breath made itself known in the darkness; The Shape.

A short, but shrill sound pierced his left ear and he cowered away from it, lashing out with his sword.

The steel met only stone, but the action had emboldened him. Trapped, fight or flight instincts kicked in and Edgar found himself calling in hollow tones.

"Who are you!?"

He swung again, meeting only fresh air; a flash through shadow.

Moments dragged on like hours as he listened to the blood pumping through his ears at an alarming rate.

And then the presence just left.

"Fuck" Edgar whispered to no one, a cold sweat crawling down the side of his face like a spider down a web.

He worked the stopper on his hip flask and took an ample swig.

If the Chylde was in this place then things had reached a sorry state of affairs indeed, and hope remained but an illusion.

Edgar groped his way down the stairs to a place where an archway spilled out into a corridor through to the castle proper, the remnants of a dozen candles nearly choking out their last flame.

Sparse in furnishings, the owner clearly had wealth. And the place was not as decrepit nor as abandoned on the inside as it had seemed from without.

Along the hallway, occasional plush sofas augmented floors replete with thick carpets and well-swept flagstones. Dimly lit, it was Edgar's best guess as to where to go next, or whether to retrace his steps.

But he couldn't go back the way he came. That *thing...The Shape*, might still be out there.

Edgar was continuing to recover from the encounter with the apparition when he was met by another door set into the wall.

He pressed his ear against the oak and thought that he could make out the heady sound of torture beyond, at which point he gave the room a wide berth.

Shaking his head he moved on, only then realising that he still had his rapier drawn.

A lot of good that served him…

Rounding the corner he emerged into a well-lit antechamber lined with opulent statues wrought of marble and assorted gems from around the globe; a trove of rubies and diamonds laid out against the cool palette of a pale-lapis vault.

A man sat in the corner, idly plucking upon the strings of a seasoned lute.

It was Kemp. He looked up briefly from his playing to regard Edgar before continuing, head down.

Behind him, Edgar felt a presence. He didn't bother to turn, assuming it was Duke.

And at the end of the hall sat a third man; one that he had yet to meet.

This man was dressed in a blend of expensive fabrics and had an annoying smirk plastered on his pudgy face. Edgar found himself wanting to stuff a soiled rag into that oily mouth without even having heard him speak.

He could hear the meaty *thwap* of Duke's cudgel meeting an upturned hand behind him and came to the conclusion that he was, indeed, finished.

The fat man sprawled on a large, gilded oaken chair like he'd had his spine removed and been flayed.

Slowly, he reached for a pipe that was smoking nearby and took a long draw. His eyes rolled back briefly and then focused on Edgar.

"Oh dear"

He carefully replaced the pipe onto a tray by his right hand.

"Not what you were expecting was it?"

Edgar cleared his throat. "To be honest, I wasn't really expecting anything".

"No?"

Edgar shrugged.

The man clicked his fingers then, and the room spun. Edgar felt like he was going to be sick but, as abruptly as it had begun, it ended.

In the centre of the room was now a large dining table, strewn with spent matches and lit with a dozen brightly burning candles each in their own ornate, pewter candlestick.

Edgar recognised the table. He could see his name carved into the side of it from when he was a boy. He had taken a caning for that, or a leathering, he forgot which.

Idly he scratched his lower back.

"Impossible" he uttered under his breath, standing up straighter.

The fat man laughed heartily before taking another draw on his pipe. The room was stuffy from the smoke, but nobody seemed to care.

The room spun again, this time to reveal Herbylocke flanking the man's throne. He wore a pained expression on his face and his mouth worked in mute harmony.

Another puff and again the room turned, this time to reveal an open grave sporting a withered rose under a clouded sky. There was a man upon his knees beneath a hangman's noose; a castle in ruins, flames, so many flames…and a tarnished cup within the mud.

"Enough!" screamed Edgar, vomiting up his breakfast upon the open floor.

And as he looked up there was the Chylde.

The man drew once again from his pipe and placed a ring-embellished hand upon the Chylde's head.

"Leave him", spat Edgar, numbly, drawing his rapier as he regained his footing.

But before he had taken three steps Duke had hold of him, twisting his arm so that the sword fell from limp fingers to clatter definitively upon the cold stone floor. As much use there as it was likely in his hand.

"Get off me!" demanded Edgar, wrenching free of the grasp.

The fat man held up a hand.

"Now…" he began, but got no further.

"Deleriant!" screamed Edgar, the nearly incomprehensible exclamation echoing off of walls only partially bedecked. Even Kemp momentarily looked up from his playing, the metre of his song passing briefly out of time.

The fat man sat up in mock confusion. "I'm a… What, now?" he asked with feigned interest.

"Hand him over", demanded Edgar, extending a hand. It was a simple gesture, but the cold, dead, look in his eyes reflected true hostility held at bay only through lack of skill.

The man sat back, casually. "I'm afraid I can't". He paused. "You see, if I do that, then all this goes away" He gestured arbitrarily around him.

Edgar looked around and when no retort was forthcoming the man continued on.

"I don't think you quite understand"

Edgar strode forward, taking the Chylde abruptly by the arm and dragging him across the hall. He seemed half asleep.

Duke stood in the doorway.

He glanced around for another way out and thought he saw something; large drapes hung above an alcove. Dragging the Chylde with him once again he made a beeline for it, but was dismayed only to find it bricked up and no longer providing access to the adjoining room.

Keen, amused eyes followed their progress.

"There's no door there…" voiced the fat man as he watched Edgar tear the drapes down in frustration, entangling both himself and the Chylde to the sound of mocking laughter.

"Calm down. Relax and I will tell you what's going to happen" He took another draw on his pipe.

Edgar visibly sagged until he resembled a deflated balloon stuffed with mince.

"Fine".

Taking up a position between the man and the Chylde, Edgar tried to calm himself.

Issuing forth yet another puff of smoke the fat man regarded him once more.

"Tell me, if you could have anything,…*anything*, what would it be?"

Stubbornly Edgar stood mute.

Annoyingly, the fat man smirked again and continued.

"Allow me to hazard a guess; some decent matches, some proper candles, one less hole in your belt... Stop me if I'm being too ambitious"

Edgar squinted.

What?

"Now stop wasting everyone's time and sit down to dinner"

Edgar thought he saw the Chylde's eyes twitch as if in deep sleep, though it might just have been the smoke. But before he had time to dwell on the matter a fine banquet was laid out before him like it was a midsummer festival. Not that he ever celebrated that. One less hour in the day was more than enough to appease him.

The meal had all the trimmings; a dozen roast meats, fine ruby wines, fresh breads, butter and honey, and a selection of over-cooked, grey vegetables.

No onions…

The fat man leaned forward and struck a match, lighting the candelabra beside him before taking up a large silver fork and thrusting it into a nearby haunch.

"Dig in"

Edgar sat as a chair was abruptly pushed beneath him, whilst Duke promptly carried off the Chylde like a sack of yesterday's olde corn.

Transfixed, Edgar scanned the spread before him, eventually trying the fish, which had been burnt and tasted of leather and ash.

He looked around once more, trying to lay eyes upon a more appealing dish, but the results were lacking.

Eventually, his eyes fell back to the sack of shit that sat across the table before him. He seemed to be thoroughly enjoying whatever he was eating and in between globulous mouthfuls he briefly looked up from his food, gesturing with a fork.

"Oh, I forgot to mention; that pathetic knight you befriended? His jousting days are over"

The noise as he worked around the food in his mouth to form the shapes of the words he was trying to say sounded akin to a man trying to extract a boot from a muddy field in mid-winter.

Kemp chuckled at the quip whilst he continued to play in the background, grinning without looking up from his lute.

Edgar regarded the minstrel, vowing to someday shove a rapier up the man's anus to the hilt. It was either that or thrust it down his mouth and then out through his anus. One way or the other, it was going to be steel-to-sphincter.

"Not hungry?" asked the fat man, idly.

"Who *are* you?"

The man stuffed another portion of meat into his already oversubscribed mouth.

He grew then in stature, a darkness falling over his eyes. The room seemed colder and Edgar knew he was evil.

"Just a man with a vision... As are you"

He finished chewing over a fresh quaff of wine and holding up a ringed finger he continued.

"I'll tell you what I'll do. You are free to leave here, this place, so long as you can do so without temptation" He grinned. "You can even take the little brat with you..."

Another puff of the pipe revealed afterimages of Herbynlocke and the hooded stranger in the throes of ecstasy, not a thought spared for anyone else.

Oddly, Edgar felt his stomach churn.

The man laughed heartily.

"Lust will make you mad, Edgar."

Edgar swallowed through a dry throat.

The drunken blob began to laugh even harder amidst roils of smoke. Turning purple, Edgar thought the man was going to soil himself.

And then it began to rain.

Despite being within the castle, some charm gave way to the precipitation without. The very walls, so strong beside him, seemed to thin and tear apart, revealing the forest beyond.

And still, the man laughed, though the motion seemed more ethereal now.

Yet there they dined under lightless moonlight, embraced by broken rain. And, as the candles spat and guttered, a deep vision came to the fore.

Beyond, one building held true. A banded door barred the way, and Edgar scooped up his rapier as he ran over.

Shattering the restraints, he burst through the door thinking to find the Chylde locked away or under guard by Duke.

But instead was met with something other.

A vaulted ceiling and thick walls played host to an elegant, pewter-framed stained glass window depicting a lone knight beneath a tree. Beside him a woman in black stood with a broken heart holding his hand, what showed of her pale features depicted an expression that was somewhere in-between sadness and sorrow.

"I gave my soul to you, in pieces. Will you hold them for me?"

But none of these intricacies concerned Edgar, for ahead lay a small series of steps leading to a raised dais upon which lay, half-hidden; a form in the distance. Obscured by vapours, marred by twilight... the largest oaken chest he had ever seen.

"Sweet Halidum..." he breathed, his pupils dilating even as he spoke.

Something, then, pulled at his consciousness but he couldn't look away. And carefully closing the doors behind him the room became silent as the grave.

Slowly, he approached the steps and took them one by one until he found himself before the chest, all other thoughts and concerns forgotten. A single-minded approach to the vision made corporeal.

Reverently he knelt and lifted the lid, savouring the groan of the hinge as he did so.

Within he beheld a king's ransom in gold, jewellery, and gems as well as other exquisite tokens and trinkets besides; an encrusted fortune, a miser's hoard.

And if he knew how, he would have wept.

Chapter XIV
Reflections

Richter entered the ruin to find Edgar draped over a large rock and his pockets stuffed with pebbles.

"Help me", Edgar managed to say in muffled tones, his mouth and cheeks pressed up against the coin.

The knight slowly sauntered over, his sabatons chinking on the stone floor with slow recession.

As he approached the dais he looked up to regard the cracked glass, a grim expression upon his face.

He stopped by Edgar's form, affording him a skewed view of his greaves.

For a moment Edgar said nothing, breathing heavily.

"They're gone," said Richter, finally, his voice reverberating away much as his footsteps had. He didn't sound amused.

Edgar didn't reply.

There was a long pause, broken suddenly.

"All night I was out there!" bellowed the knight, at length, his words bouncing off of the lofty, broken walls in deafening array.

When no response was forthcoming he looked down at the slumped form before him, bent double and half-buried in stones.

"What the fuck are you doing?" Richter asked, incredulous.

Edgar swallowed, trying to nurse some moisture back to his lips.

"It's exactly what it looks like," he said.

Richter sighed, his ire evaporating like water off a hot rock.

"Edgar…" he began, offering a hand.

"No!" snapped Edgar, hugging the chest as though to let go would be his undoing.

Richter wrapped strong arms about his waist in an attempt to pull him bodily from the artefact, but he clung on stubbornly.

"Fine. Have it your way", said the knight. "But know this; thanks to you, we've lost... *You're* lost"

He then slumped onto the cracked steps himself. "I'm lost...", he added under his breath with finality.

And together they sat there in that indefinable hall. And as the fabric of the walls broke down about them the rain beat upon their withered forms. Glass cracked and colours ran, stone faded and dreams disappeared...

And all for the want of a little restraint.

~

As the sun rose behind distant clouds Edgar found himself in loving embrace with a boulder as long as he was tall.

Richter was frozen stiff, his armour coated in a thin sheet of ice and his mood lower than an insult after injury.

The knight raised his head, groggy from his impromptu hibernation, and ran a mailed hand through crisp hair, looking over.

"Edgar..." He muttered quietly, to no avail.

He took another breath and repeated himself.

Edgar's eyes cracked open; a smirk above the rim of solitude.

"We can't stay here forever", added the knight.

"And why not?" replied Edgar, still hugging the boulder, his voice heavy with fatigue.

Richter sat up a little straighter, groaning with the effort.

"Because after all the battles I've fought and lost, I don't believe this to be the place where my olde bones retire; another tome upon a dusty shelf, given over to neglect and compromise. No, for me this is no way out. I shall fall on the sword or be torn in two, drown in wine, or choke on the fragments of some wild feast. For me, to end here comes too easily and for you too readily. This is but a skirmish against the dark when we have a fight ahead against the true, clear ringing of steel and the quality of each man's courage"

He paused before adding a final thought.

"No, we do not give up"

"But…the *chest*", uttered Edgar between ragged breaths.

Richter stood, the action taking him minutes instead of seconds. It was like trying to form a loud of himself against the will of gravity, each moment pulling him down until his legs quivered in earnest.

He stumbled over to Edgar and looked down upon the man; the defeated man, the shell of a man.

"Look at yourself"

He knelt beside him then, and through the rough, distorted reflection of Richter's worn armour he saw the dark apparition of a man long since lost to resignation.

He didn't recognise the man that he saw. He didn't know the face. And it wasn't just the convex design of the knight's breast, or the pallor of his own skin, but rather the look in his fractured, haunted eyes. There was no one else to see it, but he knew Richter was right.

Look at yourself. He had said, and of that sack of shit staring back at him. It didn't matter how bad the mirror was, the reflection was always the same.

Edgar exhaled deeply, his breath fogging up the metal. And then he looked away.

"I need to take a shit"

Chapter XII
The Eye of a Needle

Edgar sat bundled up in his cloak, hunched as any man had any right to be under the age of seventy. Rain filtered down through broken branches to fall upon him in irregular endearment.

"I'm a what?" he asked, incredulous.

Richter adjusted a rusty spaulder as he reclined against the tree, exhausted.

"The olde legends didn't lie", replied, seeming vaguely excited. "I knew I wasn't alone".

Edgar shook his head. "Spare me the history lesson, what just happened in there?"

"The Chylde!" laughed Richter, seemingly to excess. Edgar began to wonder if the whole ordeal hadn't finally cracked the man.

He'd had enough of the banter and got up to throw stones into the moat, wishing that each one would stir up some foul creature to devour him wholesale. But he was not spared, and Richter continued.

"They are some sort of demiurge, Edgar... I see that now. We've been so blind and for so long! And, if that's the case, well, that would make you a very important guardian indeed, a Tutelar, even. It's been a lifetime since their like has walked the ground around us. And now here we sit. Here *you* sit. And...well...well, we've lost them"

His face turned glum.

"That word again!" snapped Edgar, turning to fling a stone at the knight, who caught it on the vambrace where it spun off into a bush.

"One that serves as a guardian or protector" Richter replied, calmly. "Try not to be too disappointed".

Edgar sank to his knees in frustration, cushioned by the soft mud as far as the eye could see.

"But you know that I lead a solitary life. I only found the Chylde by chance. Any man would have done the same".

Richter nodded.

"Any man would have"

Edgar thrust a fist into the mud before smearing it over his face and tongue.

"Why are you doing that?" asked Richter, baffled.

"I don't noooo…!" whined Edgar.

He then spent the next few minutes spitting and using his damp cloak to clean his face.

"Got that out of your system have you?" asked Richter.

"Fuck you", spat Edgar. "You don't know what it's like"

The knight stared at him. "Oh, but I do"

He let that sink in.

Edgar then proceeded to deliver a performance worthy of a six-year olde that had just had realised the rest of their life lay before them.

~

When he had calmed down Richter shared a simple meal with Edgar, cooked on a damp fire and almost guaranteed to have them shitting through the eye of a needle within hours. Still, it didn't taste half bad.

"A demiurge…" Muttered Edgar with disdain.

"A maker or creator", offered Richter.

"Right…"

"I suppose that it explains why our 'friends' have shown such interest in the Chylde. Certain faiths would believe such a person to be a heavenly being…almost godlike. I suspect they seek to use or harness that 'gift', although you and I both know it is nothing short of a curse.

"This can't be real", exclaimed Edgar, feeling sick. "One minute I leave for some fresh air and the next I find a life sentence carved out for me in the stale excrement of a madman's desires".

Edgar pushed his meal aside.

"I don't know what's worse; the fact that I'm supposed to be looking out for *Them* or that you're supposed to be looking out for me. To be honest, I could do without a six-foot killer staring over my shoulder every time I go to sleep. And for that matter, every time I wake up. Go away"

Richter smirked, taking up Edgar's meal and tucking into it himself. "I'll take that as a compliment", he replied.

"You'll take it as nothing!" Edgar snapped, frustrated. He stood up abruptly, his cloak fanning out with dramatic effect, and then un-fanning. Pulling up the hood he stared at Richter through the flames. "I never asked for this".

Richter went quiet.

"And what's up with you now?" asked Edgar.

The knight shook his head. But when he looked up he was smiling.

"For the first time in my life, I feel as though I'm doing the right thing". He looked to the sky, realising that it had stopped raining. His smile turned into an unbroken grimace and he seemed to be holding back tears, though it was hard to tell in the shadows.

"For years I trained" continued Richter. "So many years..." he trailed off, his hand making a fist within the gauntlet. "And for what?" He stared directly at Edgar now, and the look in his eyes was unnerving.

"I would sleep with my sword, wake with my shield. Sometimes I would even bathe in my armour..."

Edgar regarded how ironic this was. Since he'd known him he'd neither seen the knight sleep nor bathe. Yet, given the amount of rain these days he would have happily bet not a thrifty sum of gold that he was rusted into that armour by now. He tried not to think what the man's gusset must be like, though the thought did occasional cross his mind.

Richter went on, idly touching the chest of his plate "The Tutelary Order. We were sacrosanct...for a time. I never questioned any of it"

He paused "But whilst others sang songs, courted women, feasted into the night...I butchered men..."

He shook his head again. "All my life I wondered to what end…" He sighed and spooned some tepid stew into his mouth, spilling half of it down his chin.

"…And now I know"

There was a long pause this time whilst each man reflected on recent events and the potential ones to come.

Edgar was lulled by the sound of the diminished flames and the omnipresent raindrops striking the floor arbitrarily around him.

Eventually, Richter broke the silence, with a guttural belch, well-endowed in girth and gifted in longevity.

"I've been thinking. There is only one logical place the Chylde could be by now, and if you want him back we're going to have to go there"

Edgar lifted his head. He had been dozing and his stomach didn't quite feel right.

"But we're going to need help" he winked. "And I know just where to find it"

Chapter XVI
Abattoirs Are Us

It was night.

Richter nudged Edgar in the ribs. "You knock", he said quietly through gritted teeth glittering like dice in the twilight.

Edgar reached up towards the rotten door, olde paint flaking off even as breathed. His hand paused near the wood and he looked back.

"Why me?"

The pair had gotten leathered in one of Slaughter's finer watering holes. And, by finer, it meant that the place offered second-hand, rusty pales to vomit into after a hard-won fistfight or during morning hours when the stout on offer still tasted like oilcloth stuffed into jars of milk. It meant that the chairs had four legs, the wenches two, and the dog by the fire simply went "woof"

It also meant that the place was rife with scum.

Indeed Richter hatched the idea that they might seek help from a mercenary band who used to operate some years ago, and at one time he had even fought alongside, during some of the lengthier, less honourable battle campaigns he'd been involved with.

After Edgar had managed to embarrass them by accosting a trio of local minstrels with shaved heads, the knight had made a point that he thought it best if he made the enquiries from now on.

But now the moment approached, and Richter's resolve had disappeared as quickly as his last pint. *Abattoirs Are Us* were not known to offer particularly affable company, and dealings with them were often shrewd. The knight had no idea how they might respond to a pair of drunks turning up on their doorstep after hours.

By day the mercenary band masqueraded as a simple butcher's shoppe, offering up wholesale rates to both merchants and consumers alike.

Reports were that their meat was of good quality and that their prices were next to reasonable.

By these principles, it seemed likely that the other side of their business would operate likewise, mused Edgar.

But now, down a dark alley after lights off, the only thing that seemed likely was getting beaten up.

Dark figures shuffled past them in grotesque fashion, displaying all the trappings of first-rate delinquents and second-rate politicians.

Before his milk-white knuckle had even connected with the woodwork, Edgar was met with the grizzled features and extensive vein neck-work of a large man in the doorway.

He wore a string vest and displayed a wide array of scars upon his shaved head, as though someone had cracked and partially fried an egg on it. His neck looked thicker than a normal man's thigh and Edgar realised with dismay that both his eyes were made of glass.

He just stood there breathing.

"Good evening?" Edgar croaked, pre-pubescently.

When he looked behind him, for support from Richter, he touched cloth, noticing that the knight had promptly fucked off.

Edgar fixed a grin on his face, for some reason, and backed slowly away as if on a conveyor.

He found Richter by some bushes a short way down a cobbled street towards the end of the alley, shaking off the remnants of some recently excreted urine.

"This isn't going to work," spluttered the knight, before hanging his head over a bin.

Feeling annoyed, Edgar flared. "I tell you what's going to work," he said, accosting Richter by the shoulder. "You're going to draw that fucking giant sword of yours, march right into that butcher's shoppe, and tell those men that you want their services or you'll be adding extra meat to the menu, like it or no".

Richter swallowed down a mouthful off sick and regarded Edgar with a raised brow. "That sounds a bit... odd", he mocked.

Nevertheless, they returned to the butcher's shoppe poste-haste under the guise of a duo of wandering mercenaries looking for work.

"We're looking for Quinne", said the knight to the doorman, their disguises lost on him, who promptly stood aside before looking back out into the street, peering into the darkness left and right.

Weirdly, there was a beetle-browed man at the counter with dual, heavy cleavers, pulling apart some kind of offal. He seemed unsure of Edgar, however, and "Went to get something from the back", which resulted in him returning with a sword at his hip and a fresh nugget of gristle clinging to his moustache.

Edgar swallowed and began to stammer an enquiry until Richter spared him.

"We're here for the performance," said the knight, flatly.

Chonk, went the cleaver, a jet of blood and a gizzard flying across the counter to land neatly by Edgar's left boot.

Chonk.

"Erm...I say, my man. We seek Quinne"

Chonk.

Chonk.

Chonk.

Unnervingly Edgar noticed the man was now only forcing his cleaver into the woodwork, the meat long since pared.

Chonk.

The pair looked at each other.

Another customer entered the shoppe, build like a brick shit-house and sporting a beard that he could buff his shoes with.

Edgar gave this man room.

"Where the fuck, is he!?" said the man, aggressively, leaning over the counter to accost the butcher. He cared not a jot that he had jumped the queue, jostled Edgar and Richter, and arbitrarily spoiled any meat that got in his way, his beard dragging over the surfaces like a frayed towel.

The butcher's response was withering.

Chonk.

"We'll be leaving," began Edgar, adding a mock bow to enhance the farewell and made for the door, Richter tailing him like a marionette.

But when they turned to leave they found the way barred by a man-mountain. And he didn't look in the mood for sausages. Well, muscled, grizzled, and chiselled he wore a flowing beard and long dark hair adorned with rings and flecks of oil.

Edgar sighed before sliding back into the room. Richter loosened his sword in its scabbard.

Chonk.

The man looming over the counter did likewise.

"You two... You can use the rear door, over there", the butcher nodded to Edgar and Richter.

"And as for you..." he cracked his knuckles, staring at the man-mop.

Edgar and Richter nearly tripped over themselves in their haste to leave the room, and once the door had shut behind them it was a quiet as the grave.

Just what was that door made of?

They had ended up in what appeared to be some sort of recreation room, as far as Edgar could guess, but the choice of sport seemed unorthodox.

In the centre of the room stood an iron contraption and an overturned keg, whilst from the walls and ceiling hung a wide array of fine manacles and chains, strategically rusted for good measure.

And in the corner; a bucket of shit, urine, pus, bile, and blood brimmed to the point where it was a marvel that the meniscus had not yet broached to wash the floor in assorted gore, a veritable cornucopia of bodily detritus.

The pair regarded the scene in horror.

"Well, these guys know how to celebrate, at least", said Edgar, breaking the silence.

"Yes, I'd say that's a bit of an understatement" replied Richter, tight-lipped. "I've seen midden heaps in a better state than this common room. And that's not a sentence I thought I'd ever have to say".

At that moment, the huge man from the shoppe front burst into the room, mopping his brow and showing a gold tooth through a slight grin.

"Gentlemen", he paused to shut the door behind him, throwing the heavy bolt across - it was as thick as his wrist. In that brief moment, Edgar thought he briefly heard something escape approximating the sound a man might make when trying to gargle a mouth full of blancmange, but he couldn't be sure.

"Allow me to get you a drink"

~

Edgar and Richter exchanged glances, holding gingerly onto their drinks; topped so full that they couldn't drink them or risk spilling the contents; an awkward position to be in, and ironically much like the slop bucket in the corner.

Their host had introduced himself as Mullet, pronounced *muhlay*, and the man reeked of anger and salt beef.

"*Sir* Richter Sterling..." he began with some amusement, the gold in his teeth showing in the dim light. "This is *the* Richter Sterling? Hero to some, saviour to but a few...? Surely not...?"

The olde knight breathed in to reply but was cut off forthwith.

"Save it. I know exactly who you are and why you are here. And you're just in time" He downed the rest of his drink, pausing for a moment. "You know, Richter... it's a shame you never joined us. We could have had such fun"

There was a pause before Mullet laughed and got up to pour himself another drink, splashing in the puke and gore about his feet.

The meniscus had broken then.

For a moment, it looked as though he might slip on something that resembled a pair of lips, but he regained his footing and continued with the liquor.

"But what I don't know is who *you* are," he said, gesturing toward Edgar with a leading, well-muscled, finger. "In my line of work I find it important to know who I'm…working with" He swirled his drink, raising a pronounced brow.

Edgar swallowed, the action audible in the quiet room. He drained the rest of his own drink and felt a false courage descend upon him.

"Me? I'm nobody"

Mullet looked around.

"Ok, so I already have your name"

Edgar licked his lips.

"I had heard that you provide…"

"I asked who you were"

Edgar felt himself becoming increasingly annoyed at Mullet's tone and struggled to reign in his attitude. After all, he was under this man's roof.

But he couldn't help himself.

"I'm nothing"

Mullet moved to a cracked and spattered mirror on the wall that looked more like a shiny painter's palette than a true mirror and touched up his beard.

"Maybe so," he finally replied. And then he burst out laughing.

Edgar and Richter exchanged further glances, but when the man stopped his wild mirth the energy in the room became tangible.

He moved towards Edgar and came close to his face. He could smell the liquor, the cigars, and the rot.

"I want to show you something"

And with that, the door burst open and the blind doorman from before entered with the limp body of the ring-adorned, muscled behemoth, whom was then summarily stuffed into the iron chair and manacles in the centre of the room.

Moments later, at the back of the room, a burgundy curtain that Edgar had not noticed yet drew aside to reveal an exquisitely bedecked man, cradling a finely worked lute as though it were wrought from his own blood.

He took slow, measured, steps to the centre of the room and Edgar took note that Mullet had held his breath.

And, note by note, inch by inch, the room filled with music.

~

An hour later and Richter sat with his chin resting on his hands. He and Edgar had followed Mullet back out into the butcher's shop not long after the musical performance had begun and the man fixed to the chair had started screaming.

The pair were pleasantly surprised to find the place clean and empty at last.

But the meat cabinet was full, a fresh layer of ice keeping the produce chilled and an astonishing range of giblets and other portions of meat on offer. Again, Edgar was impressed at the competitive prices.

The butcher stood idly sharpening his knives and cleavers behind the counter, a light sweat upon his brow glistening like crisp morning dew upon the downs.

"People say I'm a cheat, a scoundrel… a charlatan. But they always come back for more", Mullet was saying as they waited.

"And you know why? The taste" He chuckled to himself. "Always the taste…"

Edgar and Richer exchanged glances.

"So fresh…" His voice trailed off.

"What exactly did we witness in there?" Richter finally ventured to ask.

Mullet had instructed them to remain quiet for the duration of the "Performance", which he considered strange, as they were no longer in the room.

And yet…they could still vaguely hear the music, if not the screams, despite the door having blocked all sound from the other side. This left him confused.

However, since Mullet had broached the silence, he thought a simple question couldn't harm their situation.

Mullet held up a hand.

At some point, the music had stopped.

Daylight now poured in through the window, highlighting a glistening wave of red – The recent produce.

An unassuming customer was making the extra effort to head towards the shoppe, presumably for her evening's liver and onions, but Richter stepped in.

"Food's off. Come back tomorrow," he paused as the crestfallen lady turned away, slumping like an olde leather purse.

"Actually, better make it next week," he added.

The back door opened and out emerged the minstrel, his shirt damp with sweat and his lute having broken a dozen strings.

"It is done", he said to Mullet, before turning his eyes to the strangers, offering a slight bow.

Mullet stood. "Quinne, meet our new customers, Richter and Nobody".

Edgar motioned forward, his hand extended.

"Actually, my name is Edgar"

Quinne made no move to return the handshake.

"Pleased to meet you"

He regarded the hand. "I am sorry; I cannot touch the hands of another" And at this he seemed to sag.

Richter stepped forward. "Can you help us?"

Quinne looked to Mullet, who nodded. "They say they have the coin…"

Quinne turned his attention back to Edgar, who was unconsciously cupping his inner thigh.

"I can revel in the madness behind the eye, turn the night against you, and smile when you leave. Early morning endeavours of which sweet nectar made worthwhile, then but a taste, but a banquet in time…If you wish memories of fabrication, for a song beneath the shadows… To make the nightmare seem real, then, I can certainly help you"

Edgar looked at Richter who stared unrelentingly at Quinne.

"How much?"

Chapter XVII
Music & Mayhem

Night fell without warning. But it was not unwelcome.

Edgar and Richter had set out to seek the Chylde and, at all costs, free him from the maddening regime so cruelly forced upon him.

Neither was under any illusion as to what they might face and Edgar had spent the last few hours bent double in a bush or draped over a crude trough, bringing up his anxiety in addition to his last meal: literally and partially metaphorically.

As he focused bloodshot eyes on what looked to be a pile of assorted gizzards brimming over the edge of the vessel, he pitied any animals that might drink from it that night.

Richter sat by the fire and watched with wry amusement whilst he honed his sword on a whetstone pilfered from one of Duke's own saddlebags. His sword was so knocked and pitted by now it was starting to resemble a flamberge. Still, it was his sword and the familiar weight and comfort of it in his hand was worth more than any other. He considered this fact fortunate since they were near neither smith nor smithy.

Looking sorrier than a milkmaid after sundown, Edgar trudged back to the fire. His pallor had taken on new levels of grim and grey, and his shirt looked like it had been wiped around the inside of a bedpan.

"Are you certain your message got through?" he asked for the sixth time, wiping a nodule of sputum from his upper lip.

"Edgar", replied Richter, prodding the fire. "If you ask me that again I am going to stuff some of these hot embers into my own ears" he paused. "And then *your* ears"

Edgar remained mute, looking like he was going to throw up again.

Richter softened. "Listen. I am certain the message got through. Quinne will not fail us"

"It's not Quinne I'm worried about", muttered Edgar into his sleeve before running off again.

Richter shook his head in disbelief. Not so long ago he could never have imagined the man becoming so worked up over, well...*anything*". Yet there he was doing his level best to bring his own lungs up out of his throat and deposit them on the cold dirt.

He sighed, pulling out the bottle of mead that he had also found in Duke's packs. Since the task ahead of them was so delicate he had considered a sober approach was best. But now, looking at Edgar, he wasn't so sure. The man didn't have butterflies in his stomach so much as a plague of locusts.

"Ah..." muttered Richter in satisfaction, uncorking the sweet, honeyed wine. The smell lingered pleasantly in the air and he took a swig, followed by another, longer draught before calling out.

"Hey, Edgar, look what I found!"

~

Meanwhile, back at the Abbey, Quinne began his evening's work. He had been playing throughout the hallways all week now and he saw no reason to cut his run short at the annual feast that night.

If all went as planned, he might hang up his lute and live entirely off of his loot. That is, if all went as planned.

The song he had penned was incredibly...specific, and gone were the days where he enjoyed simple ballads that could be easily embellished on a whim or had short, boisterous words that any drunken, toothless fool could sing along to and come out sounding like the King's own courtier. At times he even indulged himself with some quick-fingered lute work that only a select few minstrels and nobles could appreciate, or even comprehend.

But tonight he found himself hoping his words rang true. This time, there was no room for flamboyance. No room for error. No room for drunken, toothless fools.

The timing had to be perfect, else their plans were forfeit, as would likely be their lives.

A pleasant selection of simple refrains, to begin with, followed by some cheerier numbers mid-feast would take the diners on a pleasant aural jaunt as they masticated their way through dish after dish of fine culinary delights.

But by dessert...

Quinne checked the tuning on his lute, straightened his shirt, mussed up his hair, and tested his voice.

A small tankard of dark ale lay nearby which he promptly sank in order to take the edge of his nerves.

And as the Cloth took to their seats and were served rich wines and sweetmeats, he began to play.

~

A heavy mist blanketed the Abbey like a silken dress, cast aside in haste and forgotten for a while.

Edgar and Richter hugged the forest outskirts, reeling from their binge only hours before. What had seemed like a good idea at the time had turned into an impromptu roister that had the pair staggering uphill and down dale, until they finally reached Bleakenstone, so named after the stark grey stones of every structure. The Abbey there was no different and it stood cool a dark against the soft night sky with its ethereal roots.

Richter had suggested that they dunked their heads in a nearby stream to relieve some of the grogginess laid upon them, but that idea had only served to adorn their faces with fresh leeches and, peering out from the trees; Edgar plucked one from his neck before casting it aside like a spoiled olive.

"When do we know?" he asked, idly checking for more leeches.

Richter looked on intensely; his furrowed brow and slight squint making him appear ancient in the early evening gloom.

He shook his head. "When the time comes, we will know" He paused, laying a hand on his companions' shoulder.

In the distance, they could hear the clarion of a large bell, its deep resonance a sound of ill omen.

"Edgar, are you ready?"

He took a deep breath. "What choice do I have?"

Richter opted to say nothing, instead turning his focus back to the Abbey.

Was the mist stirring, or just a trick of the wind?

Somewhere a blue haze augmented the uniform vapours before them and a brief parting of the mist was all the indication Richter needed. The glint of steel was unmistakable.

If I look too long do I risk losing focus?

"This is it", whispered the knight through thrice clenched teeth, his words dragging Edgar's mind back to the present.

Taking his hand in a firmly mailed grasp he wished him good fortune in a hollow gesture.

Edgar nodded in response, the weight of his part to play cutting through the heady reprieve given by the mead.

"Let's go".

~

Edgar rummaged around in the undergrowth for a short while more, finding it difficult to locate the cellar hatch in the fog and darkness, but he dared not use a light.

As he groped around, his fingers brushed up against thick webs that he chose to ignore for sanity's sake and he chanced that he could just make out the faded edges of a grim sepulchre in the distance.

He rubbed his face, the remnants of the mead hanging on. He needed to focus.

Or...he could just walk away.

He sat there for a full half-minute, but eventually, his hand found the cellar door.

A strong musk came from within as he carefully eased the doors open.

A colony of bats took the air, startled by Edgar's presence. His plan was to start low and work his way up through the Abbey until he located the Chylde. In theory, working in this systematic way, he shouldn't miss them. However, it also meant his chances of bumping into someone else were also increased.

He spared one last thought for Richter as he went off in search of his doom. If Quinne's spellbinding song had worked its magic the knight shouldn't have a problem.

And when he closed the hatch behind him the blackness was complete.

"Is someone there?"

Startling him, the Chylde's voice was quiet but clear.

Edgar felt a small trail of urine make its way down his inner thigh. He had not expected that but should have known better. When would he learn to wad-up?

He edged towards the voice and reached out a hand.

And as his fingers embraced the source he found himself holding onto nothing but dry ash, the pieces slipping through thoughts upon the unspoken aether.

A certain chill ran along his spine and he found himself retreating back towards the cellar door. However, unlike his bowels, he found it now immovable.

Panic began to set in accompanied by an unnervingly instantaneous cold sweat. Vast palpitations and distorted perspectives took hold.

"Fuck me", Edgar whispered under his breath. Then he drew his rapier and edged forwards once more. There was no turning back.

~

At the feast Nastute sipped gently upon his wine, supping each drop as though his last within the cradle of inebriation. It was a subtle vintage, brought out for special occasions. The legends were that the grapes were borne of olive groves, an enchanted soil turning the bitter to a sweet, and adding a richness unmatched by all other suitors.

Nastute considered it both fact and fable. After all, he was in control.

He drank from an extravagant chalice, needlessly utilised in heathen fashion; to quaff some from such a cup and at a mere banquet – the very idea... And he pursed his lips upon the rim. He had an uninvited guest.

Without drawing too much attention to himself he summoned a tall man in bronzed armour who had loitered nearby all evening.

"We have intruders"

The man gave a curt nod and disappeared forthwith. He was immeasurable in his metal skin, but he moved with precision.

Nastute then returned to his wine and, of course, food, a mixture of both jostling for position within the folds of his chin. And as he chewed upon a morsel of tender brisket his eyes fell upon Quinne.

The minstrel quickly averted his gaze.

Carefully laying down his silver-gilded knife and fork he wiped face upon an errant drape before standing and addressing those dining.

"Gentlemen... Apologies, but if you will excuse me I have... Indigestion"

He punctuated this statement with a belch from within that hung in the air with stringent tenebrosity.

There was a general muttering amongst those seated but on the whole, no one really cared. And as the wine continued to flow, Nastute slipped quietly from the table.

~

Richter strode forward with both menace and purpose. Two perimeter guards were brutalised in swift fashion as they stared at the miasma before them.

Herbynlocke emerged through the portal like a mannequin draped in a bedsheet, his usual flippant look this time somewhat more severe. Behind him a dozen knights followed without comment and without pause.

The magus confronted Richter.

"You don't have long".

Richter nodded in acknowledgement before turning to the assembled knights.

"Follow me", he commanded in deep tones before striding forth once again.

And as the mist parted in his wake the heavens opened and made themselves know, falling with the irregular endearment given unto cut-rate adornment and with twice the shine...

The knights fell upon the guests as of wheat in the field, and by the time the congregation knew what was upon them the place was awash in gore; myriad colours upon a field of grey, punctuating current existence as a carpet might absorb fine wine, inexorable and without one iota of remorse.

Richter's eyes scanned the faces before him. He passed over Quinne without recognition until his gaze fell on the empty chair.

Shrieks of terror rose up from the guests as the knights awkwardly continued to cut their way through the room like a living procession of woe.

Tables and chairs were thrown arbitrarily aside and wine was spilt with abandon. One man cowered feebly in the corner of the dining hall behind a large font, hoping to escape notice. He was crying into his lap when Quinne appeared beside him and garrotted him with the G string of his lute.

"No holy water can save you now", he uttered as the monk fell forward with an unceremonious clatter.

And then the tall knight returned with a detachment of well-armed men at arms, not the bungling milksops assigned as common ornaments at most social gatherings. These men knew war and they wore it upon grim faces with downturned smiles.

He sneered, taking a step back as a volley of crossbow bolts sped past him to find new homes in several targets.

Richter caught a quarrel on the vambrace and winced as the barb dug in. Several others of his knights bore shields that thundered with the sound of bolts slamming into them. Others were not so lucky and found themselves embracing newly formed cavities which offered a puff of grey as their corporeal forms broke apart, the enchantment undone, leaving empty suits of ruined mail and discarded weapons upon the ground.

Richter danced through the melee scoring many kills before his party was driven back outside and into the courtyard.

Quinne desperately fumbled with his lute, hoping that perhaps his notes could reinforce what magic was done. But as the battle raged on beyond he realised with dismay that he had neglected one feature in his song. Never once had he mentioned the rain.

~

Nastute eased open the door as of the pantry gone midnight. The Chylde had a room of their own lit by a single, unwavering candle. That night it seemed almost blinding.

The room was sparse, containing only a small font and a stone plinth which served as a bed. Too much comfort would lead to sleep too deep, and then the subconscious would not be open; would not be malleable.

Nastute entered and quickly, but quietly, closed the door, wincing at the momentary swell of commotion that drifted through the portal until the thick wood shut it out.

Inside you could hear a pin drop. The priest moved across the room with satin slippers crafted for just such an occasion, though the feel of them irked him somewhat, resembling the texture of crushed flowers.

Looming over the sleeping form which twitched and muttered before him, Nastute listened carefully and was astonished to hear words that were far from his previous design.

He clenched a fist until the knuckles were almost opaque.

Quinne.

Quietly he whispered into the Chylde's ear before moving over to the font to refresh his senses.

Before the water had even dried upon his face, he had slipped back out of the room.

~

Edgar made his way through one of the inner hallways. The place was far bigger than it looked, a surprising amount of it underground.

From the cellars, he had passed through what he could only imagine was some sort of archive. In the gloom, it was impossible to tell, but the tang of damp was unmistakable.

Well, the monks needed somewhere to store all their grog, he mused.

He had not encountered another soul on his journey thus far and as he padded along his mind returned to Richter. He chanced he could hear the sound of some distant skirmish but couldn't be sure. Down there the tunnels and alcoves made for confusing acoustics, much like the last time he had been moaned at for drinking all the ink after a ridiculous night out. The immovable dark dribble flanking his chin had been punishment enough without the verbal scolding.

He continued on, hoping to find some clue as to the Chylde's whereabouts.

"Where are you?" he whispered under his breath, which followed him for a few moments before fading into the black.

He entered one room, wreathed by a stone archway, and was met with the smell of death. However, and most intriguingly, there was no sight of it.

An ornate window in the ceiling cast moonlit rays of muted colours upon the scene.

A large maroon flower the size of a table with, and with a phallic epicentre, took pride of place amidst a halo of low-burned candles. Edgar covered his nose and cleared his throat a couple of times to no avail. The reek was oppressive.

"Why is this even here?" he thought out loud, scratching his chin.

"Enchanting isn't it?" the voice behind him crept in. Nastute loomed behind him, arms across his waist and tucked into voluminous sleeves.

He stood with a slightly off-kilter smile, his enormous conk making the seriousness of the encounter seem almost comical in the half-light madness.

Edgar turned slowly around, affording his codpiece a brief courtesy fondle to ascertain unwanted leakage before confronting the man.

"Some call it the Titan, others, The Corpse or some other imaginative name" murmured Nastute with disdain, his eyes glazing over as he gazed at the gigantic triffid. He made no attempt to move.

"I often like to visit this room, when compared to many of the others in the Abbey, since I find the fragrance so familiar, so…" he breathed deeply. "Uplifting"

"Most of my life I have lived here and have only laid eyes upon its blooming twice in all that time. And now here I stand for a third, and likely final, such time…"

"Sometimes I find that if I can't sleep at night, just lying here on these cool stones beside this beautiful specimen can be most comforting. And then come dreams of subtle purple on a field of green; nothing more than the rapidly fading memories of an astral foray. And by morning, they are gone...Of course, the scent is not to everyone's taste but let me ask you this; in a place so devoid of anything…who wouldn't prefer the smell of rotting flesh?"

Nastute closed his eyes and breathed deeply for a moment more before fixing Edgar with a stare, his look eventually softening and glazing over with moisture.

"You really have no idea do you?"

Edgar raised his rapier until it met the sagging flesh beneath Nastute's rumpled chin. The thing now resembling a hessian sack filled with clay (the chin not the sword).

"You're not human", taunted Edgar.

Nastute darkened then.

"It doesn't matter who you are, the right tragic ingredients will turn you into a monster".

And then he merely smiled as Edgar circled around him until his back found the opening out of the suggestively necrotic chamber.

He ran down the hall.

~

Many doors presented themselves over those frantic minutes whose count Edgar could only guess was more than fair. Either they were locked, or the rooms were simply empty. But as sweat began to bead upon his brow Edgar began to wonder if he had been playing a game he was destined never to win.

He did not have to wait long for an answer, rounding a corner to find a room under guard. This had to be they were keeping the Chylde. That or it was the entrance to some boudoir. Either would have sufficed.

The man filled the doorway nearly flush to the frame, and Edgar pondered his options.

It was then lulling notes drifted down the corridor, catching the man's interest, and he plodded off down the hallway like a caricature following the scent of a particularly well-baked pie.

Edgar made a mental note to thank Quinne. So much had hinged on the man's participation in events Edgar could not quite believe he would do so even vaguely willingly, despite the coin involved. He must have known Richter a long time.

As Edgar entered the quiet room he was astounded at how cold it was, as though a tomb.

Then his eyes found the Chylde and his arms did the rest. Hoisting them onto his shoulders Edgar felt himself crown and wish that he had not had a second helping of Richter's 'Special stew' that evening, despite having thrown most of it up. That man really didn't know how to cook.

Taking a moment to look around he ascertained that the only way out was indeed the way he came in, and from there the way was closed to them.

I'm not strong enough for this.

Edgar lay the Chylde down onto the floor but they barely stirred.

"Wake up", urged Edgar, but they seemed to be in the throes of some deep dream, some further nightmare.

Wearily he moved over to the font to clear his head.

Of course...

Flicking water onto the Chylde's face Edgar had hoped to rouse Them, but the act only seemed to cause pain; a fact reflected by impromptu contortions of the face. His own visage began to burn in synergy and Edgar flung the font aside to shatter upon the frigid floor.

Crackling and condensing to ice even as he watched, Edgar looked on as myriad rivulets made their way through imperceptible channels, pale patterns like nature's woad revealed under nocturnal duress.

And behind the sconce supporting the ever-bright candle they disappeared.

Olde foundations were forced apart and grey stone gave way, enough parts to make a diorama. Enough time to create a scene.

Edgar's breath misted before him as the candle guttered and failed to reveal a hidden aperture beyond and beside him he felt something stir.

The Chylde had woken.

Chapter XVIII
Vanitas

Edgar's mind drew back into focus with the Chylde shaking his arm like a length of rope.

Quinne was standing next to him, a set of lock picks in one hand, the other clutched around a bolt in his leg. He looked pale and not long for this world, but he had enough wherewithal to give Edgar rough directions in hushed whispers and melodic tones.

The Abbey was in an uproar, he heard. They could probably blend in with the kerfuffle and be halfway into the Night before anyone even noticed.

Of course, Quinne was doomed; Nastute had spent the last hour scouring the grounds for him after learning of his ruse and he had only just managed to reach the chamber in which they now stood.

"Many more minutes and they will be here", Quinne said with thrice-laboured breath.

Edgar grasped his hand, "And Richter?"

Quinne shook his head. "I don't know…Maybe if you can get to the winery…the cellar's…"

The Chylde reappeared with Edgar's cloak and, indeed, his sense of dignity.

"Quinne, thank you" replied Edgar, but the minstrel was already dead, slumped over the oaken chair, a mop of hair muting the strings of the lute by his side.

The world had lost another song.

~

Edgar and the Chylde found themselves at the end of a long hallway. Olde paintings hung upon every inch of the walls. Towards the far side, one stood out in particular.

Edgar squinted, his lashes coming together like a portcullis. *It couldn't be...*

The hallway was lit every couple of meters or so by a sconce, but the paintings on the walls were unnerving, even to Edgar's tastes, which was rare.

Several depicted mass orgies with bodies piled so high that lower participants appeared dead, yet were being used anyway.

Others depicted ancient heroes and strange beasts, apparitions, and other things.

And the third sort, the austere faces of a hundred men and women that he didn't know. And one that he did.

Oak and pewter framed, his Father's portrait hung heavily on the wall. Grim and noble, his expression was severe at best, and from there he watched Edgar keenly as he escorted the Chylde down the hall.

Dark flagstones comprised the floor and their footsteps echoed along the walls, announcing their presence to anyone with an interest and to those with none.

Tapestries punctuated the gallery portraits as the pair advanced and the Chylde looked on in wonder, eyes wide at the richly framed depictions of a frozen world.

But even as they moved forward they progressed no further.

Some malice hampered their every step and before long the pair found themselves separated.

"Stay there!" Edgar called out as he found himself once again at the beginning of the hallway and staring back at his Father's portrait.

The Chylde turned on the spot to regard a curious painting depicting an olde man peering into a looking glass, which in turn depicted a younger man peering into a looking glass and so on.

"Just, just wait..." Edgar called again, becoming frustrated as once more he took one step forward and three steps back.

After the fourth time, he stopped.

What was this place?

He moved to the edge of the hall, trying to creep along the corridor and this time he seemed to be making progress. But within a few feet of the Chylde he was gone again, only this time he had moved forward. The experience was becoming bewildering and, despite the corridor appearing plain, he now felt lost.

It was tiresome, having taken the last straw, bent it neatly in half, and wedged it firmly under the slightly short leg of a well-worn taproom table.

The Chylde stood mute, still staring at the painting.

"OK, now come to me" beckoned Edgar.

The Chylde turned and moved towards him.

Within four steps he was returned to the start of the hall and Edgar cursed in frustration.

Another step and Edgar was right back with him.

He felt as though every eye in the Gallery were watching them, willing them to fail; mocking them.

And why not? This was not his place.

They started over, this time more systematically, Edgar taking the Chylde's hand in his own.

He took a moment to try and puzzle out the phenomenon under the watchful gaze of oil upon the canvas.

A pattern was emerging.

He tested the theory and was rewarded when they ended up back where they started.

A laugh emerged from his lips, a bitter one, certainly, but still a laugh.

Again they moved forward, along the wall this time. But Edgar made a point of counting each flagstone as they progressed.

Every time they were thrown into an undesirable location he tried to remember which stones they used to get them there.

Progress was slow, and often Edgar would forget his count or the Chylde would distract him by staring at some odd painting, but eventually, by inches, they made the end step and held their breath a few moments before they felt they could adequately relax.

Edgar looked behind him. In the last ten minutes, they had only moved a hundred feet. The thought was withering.

But before the feeling fully could set in, Edgar's eyes glazed over. He was met at close distance with an olde painting depicting a skull and a raven sat casually around a spent candle.

He took a nearby sconce off the wall and held it near the picture. Flakes of paint were missing but the piece was unmistakable.

Edgar lowered the flame, turning away in disbelief.

Slumping against the wall he slid down until he was sat upon the cold, hard floor.

~

Somewhere on the edge of his consciousness, Edgar was aware of a battle; the dull ring of steel on steel and the screams of men as they were butchered and burnt.

He felt as though he were flying as he made his way from one courtyard to another, slaughter all about him.

His mind held on to glimpses of boots in thick mud as the rain drove down around him.

Flames rose up and shouts filled all the air, the ruckus resembling a busy kitchen at midday meal.

He tried to ask questions. He had tried. But a heavy hand had beaten some of the sense from him and he had soon learnt his lesson. Resigned to his fate he followed the only words he could remember; the words of a song.

The hour was late and it would soon be too dark for battle. The trouble was no one had anywhere to spend the night.

Chapter XIX
Out of the Ashes

The oaken door looked and sounded like a breached hull.

In a queer sort of way, Edgar regarded that it would come as somewhat of a relief; the militia would burst through, the Chylde would be torn from his burnt hands and a knife drawn swiftly across his throat.

Done.

All he would have to look forward to then were his bones being thrown to the dogs or in an unmarked grave, and his name cast into ignominy forevermore.

But that was not to happen.

He could open the door, yes. But he wasn't about to.

Bang.

"Hand him over, heretic!" called a priest from the other side of the wooden slab.

He was in the Abbey cellars, large flames rising up about the outer walls, making him wish that every cask of wine contained cool water, which wasn't his usual preference.

He had fled there since the truth of the Chylde had been forsaken and he had been readily swept up in the proceedings as a scapegoat, his relationship with Richter frowned upon, the burdens of the populace attributed to him.

It was thin reasoning, but that's all they had. And that's all they needed.

Within hours he had gone from plush furnishings and fine wines to one of the worst seats in the house; bunging up a forgotten corner of a half-empty cellar.

Edgar had rolled a few kegs in front of the doors, but he didn't hope that these would hold out for long, and soon dark splinters were shearing off the door as the men without forced their way in.

The Chylde remained surprisingly mute throughout the experience, and for that much Edgar was grateful. The last thing he needed right now was the screams of an infant incessantly nagging at the edge of his consciousness.

The timbers of the winery began to catch alight and odd bits of debris were making themselves known, falling from on high about them with explosive disposition.

Edgar threw an arm around the Chylde and shrank back to the far end of the long building, drawing his sword. He removed his cloak and soaked it in wine before draping it over them. They didn't need to see this.

And it was there that they awaited the inevitable.

Edgar's mind began to wander then and, as the flames licked higher, he wondered about Richter, of Herbynlocke…of the hooded woman.

It was then the door burst open and the soldiers piled in, with Nastute at the forefront of the column.

"Search the place!" he commanded "They're in here and I'll drain every keg in the place until we find them!"

It wasn't long until they were spotted. Edgar got to his feet and held his sword out before him in weak hands.

It was no use. In seconds he was disarmed and smashed round the face with a mailed fist.

The world spun but he kept his feet.

Had they noticed the cloak?

"Where!?" the priest screamed Edgar's face, spittle flying forth freely to array itself upon Edgar's forehead like morning dew.

That answered that.

Another fist sent Edgar's face in the return direction and he barely held on to consciousness, teetering on the brink.

"Answer me!"

The words sounded woollen as another voice interjected.

"We need to get out of here, now…This place…"

Rough hands took Edgar by the scruff and under the armpits, dragging him from his nest and out of the building.

A half-focused glance afforded him one last look at his crumpled cloak at the back of the winery. Seen for the last time; the image, but an afterthought...

They never said a word.

~

The door.

Gaping pupils withdrew to pinpricks as light from the hallway streamed in like so much fallout, revealing rents upon the walls. Trapped between worlds, each mark an heirloom; each moment a maddening charade.

Footsteps made their way towards him, harsh as tin pans after a hard night of debauchery and gross consumption of ale.

"Edgar, how do you fare?"

There was a sad quality to those words.

"Look at me, Edgar"

Obliging, his eyes adjusted just enough to make out the unexpected shape of a woman... There was familiarity there. There was understanding.

But that moment went by, moving swiftly, as of smoke over running water.

She held forth out a canteen, half full as it was, and Edgar drank deeply.

As though bargaining with some unknown force in the aether, Edgar looked around, his eyes eventually settling on the woman.

"I sent my soul to you in pieces. Will you hold them for me?"

Silence.

The torch guttered and waned as a draft crept through. Scant moments were left; all too little, all too late.

The woman spoke.

"Meet me where the parts divide and existence becomes a fragile thing... Cry not into the night, and hide not from the Rain..."

And as she looked back one last time, the failing light limned what was left of the prisoner. There Edgar sat hunched, seeking something, yet finding nothing.

And then the book fell from his hands…

~

At dawn Edgar was summarily dragged starved and naked through the castle dungeons and up to the courtyard where a sturdy gallows stood proud before a rabble of onlookers.

Grimly, Edgar looked on as he was strung up and presented before the gathering like a puppet.

Within seconds he was caked in all manner of detritus thrown at him by members of said crowd that probably didn't even know what he was accused of, but cared little since it punctuated their mundane existence with some unnecessary brutality, which incidentally put a smile on everyone's face.

The dross slid down as the heavy rain cleansed his body, but the unsolicited offerings kept on coming.

Still, at this final hour, his mind turned to things he would miss. The list was short, worryingly short, but there were at least a few items that warranted his thoughts and, at length, his sadness.

He could hear in the background the executioner addressing the masses, but it was a muted sound either to do with the leather around the man's face or the foggy sensation upon his own mind.

Far more keenly could he hear the rain, his own breathing, and the rhythmic drum of his heart; each beat closer to its last, quickening towards finality.

He had refused the blindfold and was surprised when a second figure was brought up to the gallows beside him.

Small in stature it was hooded and stood with quiet dignity.

How many more will join the spectacle, to enjoy his last moments?

The faint voice of a priest found his ears and he knew his Last Rights were being uttered.

No one else came to join them.

And at the last, strangely, Edgar's mind turned towards the mysterious woman he never quite got to know. For a moment he thought he saw her dark visage amidst the crowd, but it couldn't be...

And then the floor dropped from beneath him and pure fire assaulted his neck. A pounding, ringing sensation ebbed and flowed and his vision began to dim.

He was aware of the crowd's excitement and as he writhed he slowly spun to face the other body.

It too was swinging freely upon the rope.

"Heretic, Heretic, Heretic!"

Why call me that?

Shadows started to form. The body beside him had already stopped moving. He was dimly aware of something *other* touching his face.

"Edgar..."

Oh, and the rain...

Part II

Chapter XX
Visions

A seemingly endless cliff-top path extended toward a point which stood firmly out into the ocean. Grey skies and driving winds offered a dreary sight in contrast to the lush vistas far beyond. Several figures stood gathered in stern conversation.

As the tide came in and stole fragments of the rock face it was, all the same, a reminder to those on the cliff of the relentless effects of time.

A narrow path, dashed with shale and sand, snaked up beneath the meet-place. A small cluster of figures could be seen picking their way carefully along it. The path eventually merged into a more desirable track, beyond which various plains stretched out inland and beyond.

At the gathering, a man, tall in stature and mature in age, appeared to be doing most of the talking, though half of his words were no doubt lost to the wind.

To a woman he spoke. Cloaked in black, dark hair flew about her like an ebon flame.

"Tanera, we have decided that *you* are to go"

The woman lowered her head "I will do as you wish"

"I know…" the olde man said quietly.

With keen eyes, he looked up.

"Go now", he said.

And without further hesitation the woman reluctantly left the company of her people, looking back often as she hurried along the coastal path.

Once she had rounded the cliff and was out of sight from the others, the path broadened out and it was here she sat to let her tears flow. Slowly they came, and with gentle grace fell upon the sandy path even as the wind dried them from her face.

But before she could break down completely, six figures arriving from the other direction moved towards her.

Tanera seemed little bothered by their presence and made no effort to walk on and meet them.

Each with long, fair hair tossed about violently in the coastal winds, the figures came gradually into view. The glint of faint sunlight shone off armour worn with age, yet no less in splendour.

"You summoned us" replied the tallest of the group. "We have been travelling for some time, yet it seems we are too late"

His gaze disappeared behind her into the distance, to where the group had once stood.

On the pinnacle of the cliff-top smoke rose on high and was carried swiftly across the sea, leaving behind its point of creation and with it the souls of the few who watched.

Tanera glanced over her shoulder.

"No. He is just waking up"

~

"Introspection leaves no room for the living..."

Edgar hit the leafy ground firmly as he and Tanera's embrace came to an end. After a few moments, he noticed his surroundings and the slack rope around his neck.

It had stopped raining and somewhere behind him embers smouldered as the low winter sun disappeared below the trees, casting long shadows as night drew in.

Edgar groaned.

Everyone was gone.

He turned to the woman.

"Time to go", she said taking his arm.

Edgar didn't know what to say and followed without thought.

What do you say when you make it to the next day, having never thought about what to say?

And together they slipped away...

~

A small tavern on the edge of town played host to hushed conversation that night. And words that Edgar never expected to hear we spoken not just at him, but *for* him.

For the first time in a long time, he nursed his drink.

The woman had brought him his clothes and belongings, but something was missing.

She dragged out the Sack of Ire and heaved it onto the table.

"This is getting heavy" she commented.

Edgar spared the thought no more than a second and promptly placed the remnants of the noose into the sack as well. He could breathe easily again.

He had remained mute for almost their entire, short journey, other than to enquire as to what had happened, with which he was met with solemn silence.

Finally, he gathered his thoughts and leaned forward to address the woman.

"You are from my dreams" he stated.

Or were they nightmares, delusions even?

Turning from a half-heard conversation, dark hair covered most of her face. But one golden eye peered out to regard him.

"Herbynlocke sent me" she looked down and swallowed. "Richter is lost…"

Edgar drew breath.

The olde knight.

But the woman continued.

"But Edgar, the Chylde is gone"

Edgar idly rubbed at his neck and blood drained further still from his face.

"How?"

It was a question void of emotion.

The woman smiled, but the effort seemed to pain her and darkness clouded her eyes, shifting them to amber, then to brown, and over to grey.

"Nothing you could help"

Edgar let that sink in, taking a sip of his wine.

After a few moments, he eventually mustered enough courage to attempt a simple question.

"When you say the Chylde is gone…" he trailed off.

The woman brushed her hair back.

"I am afraid no map can find him now. His nightmare is over"

The world seemed to shrink for a moment then, and cold fire burnt in his eyes as if someone had put hot sand behind them.

"Why...?"

"Find Richter" the woman avoided. "He needs you"

She got to her feet and in the process draped a burnt cloak over the back of her chair. It seemed all too familiar.

She read his face then.

"The guilt is not yours to bear, Edgar. But time moves away from us now. I doubt we shall see each other again"

And she turned before he could speak, leaving him with the charred remains of a failed endeavour, and the scent of cinnamon on the air.

Chapter XXI
Window

The world was cold now; colder still in the shaded ruins of the Olde Abbey. Only now everything was gone.

Edgar stood bathed in a hard light that forced its way through a cracked window, arched and beautiful in its neglect.

Tanera's words from the night before played on his mind like a gentle harp, but it wasn't a tune that he enjoyed.

He was done now, ready to leave it all behind. As far as he was concerned he had utterly failed.

Idly, he fingered his cloak where it was burnt and singed at the edges, watching solemnly as flakes fell upon the ground.

A distant noise assaulted his senses; the relentless hammering of so many parchments being affixed to doors, trees, and sills.

They all said the same thing.

Wanted. Renegatho. Gold.

Word had gotten out then...

And that wasn't the only thing.

The potent gust he had let loose mere moments before promised potential for a further bout of plague. But he pushed it from his mind, that is, after he pushed it from his anus.

As he listened to the parchments going up he wondered if he cut a fine image in the artistic depiction or if it was simply another generic sketch of some ruffian who hadn't shaved in weeks.

Dust motes sparkled gently before his eyes, causing them to focus and un-focus alike.

It was time he left.

Footsteps from behind made him start, but he dare not turn to meet them.

Pulling his cloak up around his face, as if to ward off the errant ash still clinging to the air inside, and by air he meant methane, he knelt in mock prayer before the window; either waiting for harsh words or swift execution.

"Who goes?" he inquired, softly.

"You know me. I've been here before", said the voice, simply.

The voice was not unknown, yet still, he erred on the side of caution, keeping his head down and hood raised.

Edgar cast shrouded eyes around as if taking in his surroundings for the first time.

"This place? So have I…"

"They tell me you are quite the magician" the voice continued.

"Do they, now…?"

"Not everyone comes back"

Edgar wasn't sure how to respond to that.

"I am tired", he said, at length, his breath hanging on the air. "And wounded", he added, absently rubbing at his neck.

The voice spoke again, with a timbre so familiar it was all Edgar could do not to turn around.

"And yet you wear your scars like a garment".

Edgar looked down at his hands.

The voice, noticing the motion, continued.

"You are no swordsman, perhaps. But you have won battles".

Edgar was beginning to bore.

"Are you not cold?" he asked, trying to change the subject.

"Quite", the voice replied, matter of fact.

Then there was a long silence before it continued.

"Richter…"

More silence.

"They tell me he was the fiercest knight they'd ever seen. A sword incarnate; both blade and hilt"

Edgar could almost feel the face behind him, and he could certainly see the breath on the air.

"The Grey Monks have him now. He will be given the very worst kind of burial."

The footsteps began to recede before stopping once again. "Quite a few knights ended up in their hands over the years. Or so I'm told…"

There was a metallic sound before a coin came to rest by Edgar's foot.

"Move towards serenity... Neglect not the rot"

Abruptly he turned and flung his hood back to catch a glimpse of to whom he had spoken, but all he saw was the figure disappear through the endless ash and rays of sunlight.

Edgar's head swam. He had been holding his breath the whole time.

~

Edgar fetched up at the steps of an olde ruin on the outskirts of Bleakenstone, overlooking a small sham of a hamlet named Ire. As cold as it was, he flexed aching fingers to urge the blood back into them, but they wouldn't obey.

Before he could spare the matter any further thought, three hooded men appeared before him in what passed as a doorway.

"Here he stands…" said the first.

"A poor man", added the second.

The third said nothing, merely lifting his head a little to better regard the stranger.

Edgar produced a coin, quickly dropping it into the mud as his fingers failed him.

And as he stooped to collect it a hand clamped about his wrist.

"Coin won't do…It is nothing to us"

Edgar rose slowly and tried to see under the man's veil. It was a futile effort. The shroud seemed part of his skin, not just his mystique, overhanging like ancient moss by water's edge.

Without a word the three men turned and retreated into the ruin. Edgar followed.

Inside, the place made him feel unclean. Yet, for all its lack of grace, there was a certain sense of peace permeating its walls.

"We seldom entertain guests," said one of the men, his voice dripping with sadness. "But we can offer you something to drink, if you would but wish it".

Edgar shook his head. He had no idea as to what they classed as wine, but had no doubts that it wasn't derived from the grape.

"I was surprised to find this place so easily", blurted Edgar, awkward trying to make small talk.

Abruptly, all three men stopped.

The silence was like a vacuum.

Edgar could hear himself sweat and his heart skip a beat.

"Do you know where you are?" asked one of the men.

Edgar thought a moment on this. These were the kind of people who would likely speak in tongues and find answers bound up with more questions. He didn't want to get caught up in all that.

"No", he replied, settling on a terse answer.

The men said nothing, although one offered Edgar a length of rope.

Edgar stood incredulous, holding the rope at arm's length like he might a snake.

"What am I supposed to do with this?"

And as though he had woken up from a hard night drinking, the three figures seemed to blend into one. And at that moment a sense of clarity entered his mind.

Edgar wiped his forehead.

Delirium?

No.

Adrenalin.

The figures stepped aside to reveal a chasm in the ground. Cylindrical in design it was as though something had bored straight through the floor unerring in its pursuit of darkness. It was perfect.

Edgar had heard of such pits, doubtless bottomless. They were a myth, rumoured to be no more than a dozen in the world and perhaps all connected somewhere in-between to allow easy access for denizens of the Night to go about their business on a whim.

Edgar didn't believe in all that. He knew what pits like this were like. Sure enough, there was a bottom. And down there would be mud; mud and bones.

The monk's hood snapped around to face him.

And the next thing Edgar felt was a sharp prod in his back before a moment of free-fall. He never even noticed the rope around his waist.

Pain assaulted him as the rope went taught and slammed him against the edge of the pit. But now was not the time for concern over anything but mortal wounds. The adrenalin he had stockpiled soon resigned his current ailments to nothing but a near memory.

Spitting out a combination of moss and dust, after the second impact, he scrabbled around enough to look up to see a whole team of monks looking down from the rim of the pit, each with a length of rope in his hand. He didn't even want to think about what that meant. And he couldn't even tell which asshole had pushed him in.

For a moment, he began to climb back up. Only, the fact that he wasn't actually ascending at all made itself clear in the form of each monk happily feeding out more rope whenever he made a move to climb higher.

It was like a game. And not a very good game either. Not like "Hide the Onion", from his youth. He was good at that.

Shame.

As he hung there limp as a soiled rag, his eyes began to focus on the gloom below. And what at first had appeared to be endless, unbroken architecture now seemed to have imperfections along its wall; cracks…alcoves...

There were even iron gated doors set into the masonry as far as the eye could see, and further still, Edgar wagered.

They were scattered around at random and as he lowered himself he noticed the monks pass a rope from hand to hand between themselves, measuring its movements against his own, particularly when he made to navigate to one such alcove horizontally across from him. They were like a human mechanism, unfailing at first, but bound to slip at some point.

Edgar clung to this thought just as tightly as he did the iron bars of the first door he arrived at.

The rust instantly turned his hands dark and a foul musk came from within.

A small candle burned at the back of the vestibule. A sprawled figure lay at its base. And beside it, gear; armour, shield. It was all there. It reminded Edgar of Richter, but it was some other hero, long of arm and short on luck.

Understanding began to dawn upon Edgar then as his eyes adjusted to the darkness and the network of alcoves turned from a few into dozens and likely hundreds more unseen.

Once again he hung limp.

~

It felt like days had passed. And after Edgar peered through the bars of his fifty-sixth door, the novelty had begun to wear off. And not just the novelty; his hands were now raw and weeping from the relentless effects of the rope. Each new movement brought fresh pain and further exhaustion. Blood ran down from above as the monk's hands, similarly afflicted, sloughed skin wantonly from their pale, soft hands, used to no more than the quill and the question.

If only he had become a sailor...

The thought of door number fifty-seven filled his mind with a soup-like apathy, and he slid ever-so-slightly down the rope.

Somewhere during proceedings, he had soiled himself, and a faint stench made itself known. He descended faster, effectively moving into the faecal miasma as he went. And in his haste, he almost slipped by door number fifty-eight. It was not a door at all, really, but more of a window hewn into the stone. Perhaps the previous room was en-suite...

He peered in and could just make out a hunched figure at the back of the room.

But she...

The rope played out suddenly, and before he knew it, the darkness grew. He reached out and grabbed at another doorway, pulling away rusted ironwork as he went, but that didn't stop him.

Richter did.

The knight folded like a wet baguette under Edgar's weight and lay still as the grave upon the floor of the pit.

Edgar quickly took in his surroundings, and his initial fear from the fall evaporated and transmuted rapidly from smug to concerned, to panic.

It was dark; too dark, but not dark enough. And in the half-light of the moon far above, Edgar understood who lay before him. The dull glint of armour was unmistakable. It was new; untouched and untested, and would be ruined within days.

"Richter I..." he moved gingerly forward.

"Tell me you have the key", groaned the knight.

~

They sat in the gloom for longer than either cared to think about. Rain filtered down as an uncomfortable silence fell between the two.

A dozen pieces of rope dangled before them, though try as they might to climb, they moved nowhere as the endless coils just kept unravelling. That is, unless they jerked the rope quickly, then something seemed to stop it. The monks above had a sick sense of humour and more than once Richter tried to pull one over the edge to join them in their misery. But it was as though they were made of stone; works of granite, gargoyles perched upon the rim on solitude.

And now they were left with silence, albeit augmented by the occasional sobs from some random cell far above.

Edgar scoffed, "And to think for a minute there I actually believed in bottomless pits". He picked up some dirt and ran it through his fingers.

Richter raised his head. "What do you mean?"

Edgar poured the rest of the dirt onto the ground and clapped his hands together to dislodge any left.

"You know, the tales we were told as children. Can you imagine?" he grinned, though the expression was lost in the darkness.

There was a moment's pause before Richter chuckled. And then again, more enthusiastically until, before Edgar knew it, the olde knight was roaring with laughter, slapping at his mail-covered thighs and sounding like a bag of coins on the back of a plague cart.

Incredulous, Edgar waited until he had calmed down before speaking.

"What was that all in aid of?"

Richter wiped his eyes.

"Oh, nothing… It's just that… You came all the way down here without a key, but never expected to get to the bottom anyway. I just can't figure out what went through your mind…"

Edgar frowned. "I'm not sure that's all that funny, if I'm honest"

Richter sighed and his shoulders slumped. "I suppose not… But do you really think that you're at the bottom?"

Edgar looked around before tapping a foot on the soil.

"Well, I can't go any further can I?"

Richter chuckled again, but this time with less mirth, sobering shortly after.

"What?" demanded Edgar, irritated.

"Why do you think it's so dark down here?" asked Richter.

Edgar shrugged. "Most wells typically aren't lit"

Richter glared at him through the darkness. "And most voids typically aren't so inhabited"

Chapter XXII
Ire

"Do you know what this is?"

Edgar shook his head blankly. He was young and knew only the taste of porridge and the sting of leather, the weight of books, and the variety of chalk.

Every year he received a gift for his birthday, whenever that was (He assumed it was for his birthday anyway). But today wasn't his birthday and the travelling sage before him presented much more than just an ample sack. Indeed it seemed to contain everything and nothing. At least until he was shown how to use it.

"The Sack of Ire!" the wild man before him proclaimed enthusiastically. He gestured with the sack as if it were attached to his arm and too hot to handle. A beard jutted out at unspeakable angles and his hair mopped the floor.

Then he stooped and leaned in to fix Edgar with a piercing glare. Well, it would have been piercing but the man just looked too dishevelled and comedic to impress the right effect. In fact, he looked closer to an animated box of matches than a real sage, or wizard, Edgar thought to himself, but the man had come to town touting his wares, claiming precious charms and potions alike.

Patiently and indifferently Edgar just sat there and listened in quite a mature way for a ten year olde. But he was bored by now and the sun outside seemed obnoxiously bright for the time of year. He had come to think of it as "The Endless Summer", but every year he thought the same, regardless of duration.

He would stay indoors today then, as was his want.

"Tell me, young man", began the sage. "What is worst for you in life?"

It seemed like an important question, so Edgar took a full two seconds before responding.

"The Sun" he replied, petulantly biting his lip, squinting a little in the daylight.

"The Sun…" repeated the sage, letting the words drift off and seeming a little less sure of himself. He raised a brow. "Nothing else, then? Something…er, smaller, perhaps?"

Edgar frowned, thinking hard. He recalled a day when the kitchen chef had played a trick on him, amongst others, by coating an onion in toffee and giving it to him as a treat, insinuating that it was indeed a ripe apple. He still remembered how he salivated at the thought of the sweet shell cracking to reveal the juicy, sweeter still contents of the fruit within.

How his mirth had turned to antipathy as his teeth bit into a fresh, crisp onion.

And he had hated them ever since.

"Onions, then", he said at length.

The sage seemed amused.

"But of course"

And with a click of his fingers, a pair of large, golden-brown onions materialised in the man's palm. Edgar found himself laughing at the sleight of hand and poked one to check that they were real.

"Go ahead, take one" urged the sage, and Edgar complied, the dry outer casing sloughing away in his hand like a leper's last grasp.

The man then rolled the other down his arm and flicked it into the "Sack"

Edgar looked on in astonishment as the withered and flaky remnants of its twin slipped through his fingers, grey and empty.

The sage winked at him. "Oh no!"

Edgar looked as though he was about to burst with excitement. That or excrement. Either way, he was in a right state.

Unceremoniously grasping for the Sack, the sage pulled his arm away.

"This is no toy", he said. "What you put in here becomes nothing, and what you don't becomes everything. Do you know

what that means? I couldn't count them all if I tried. Each another rendition of Here..."

Once Edgar looked as though he was prepared to give the Sack proper respect the sage relaxed his grip. He smirked and began testing it with anything he could lay his hands on.

If only he hadn't laughed...

"You know, if you want, you can always reclaim something", the sage advised, revealing the onion much to Edgar's dismay.

He paid the odd man with as much gold as he could find in his Father's coffers and said no more about it.

And the very next morning, when the sun rose he looked out of the window to find the olde sage bowed and shuffling down the street to some other place or time. He also noted a furless rabbit and a wingless bird, limp and ragged upon the vast background of the valley. He vowed to remove those particulars from the sack.

But he never did.

~

Edgar has always been under the impression that the Sack was newly made, something for him only, given, or rather sold to, before anyone else. That it might be an heirloom or widely traded item had never crossed his mind. And so he would never forget the day he pulled something out of the Sack that he never knew was in there.

A small vial of liquid, tinged with amber, containing a single limp leaf stuck against the bottom. A wax seal covered a cork in the top and lasted about as long as a jockstrap in a brothel by the time Edgar had got his hands all over it. And seconds later he had necked the lot. It could have been poison, it could have been antidote. It was neither, but he didn't care.

And that night when it rained and rained it was all he could do to not lie out beneath the sky as the leaves turned brown and the air turn cold and damp about him.

Crops failed, men starved, Doom Sayers arose and heresy fell readily upon the lips of those who listened; and everybody listened.

But since he couldn't hear their prayers, Edgar learnt to follow his own heart, full of discord and harmony.

Chapter XXIII
Small Wonder

Richter was sick of hearing such reminiscent tales, and lay slumped against an apparently well-made grill at the bottom of the oubliette. The bars were as thick as his arm and the lock impeding their passage to the tunnels beyond was made of such stern stuff as Richter had never known the like.

The pommel of his sword now resembled a half-eaten apple, having made no forceful progress against the thing, and it wasn't long before his eyes drifted back to the bones on the ground and the dark shape of Edgar, similarly slumped on the other side of the pit.

Edgar uncovered his ears.

"Done?" he called across.

No answer...

At length, Edgar got up and ambled over to where Richter sat, his sweat-soaked hair slicked against his face and an upturned look upon his brow.

The knight ignored him when he approached, his head hanging lower until he looked as though asleep. Perhaps he was.

Edgar stooped to examine the lock. It looked ordinary, but one glance at Richter confirmed that this couldn't be the case. The man's sword was part of him, and now fragments of it lay about the ground amidst the assortment of bones.

No. That is not the way...

He took a step back and eyed up the bars. They looked ancient. And they would remain ancient.

Idly, he scratched at his head before the movement naturally found its way towards his groin.

Not now...

147

He looked back down at the bones, trying to distract his mind, but the macabre sight seemed even to worsen the problem.

He grabbed at his skull cod-piece. Things were becoming uncomfortable.

Another glance over at Richter showed that, blessedly, the knight still slept. At least there was that. And before long the cod-piece lay on the floor as Edgar sat on a small pile of coins that had issued forth from his gusset. He held his head in his hands and stared unblinking at the low-shimmering gold.

~

Richter awoke to a strange sound and sight.

Above him, Edgar stood, trousers around his ankles, shovelling what sounded like a fortune in coin using his fabled skull codpiece as a scoop.

It was an odd sight, but not wholly unexpected. Nothing surprised Richter anymore and, as a result, he merely climbed up the small, elaborate mound without comment and crouched by Edgar's feet before using his helmet to aid in the venture.

To the monks above the scene looked somewhat different, and it wasn't long before they departed, appalled by the display, but equally not surprised.

~

Edgar grasped the lip of the pit with trembling fingers, a second hand mirroring the first a moment later. Between his teeth, the crude visage of a familiar skull loomed over the rim and then he was up.

Seconds later, a battered sword and helmet emerged to clatter upon the upper floor before Richter hoved into view.

And it was there, stood like newborn foals, that they turned hollow eyes upon a hoard of the ages, the oubliette thoroughly obscured from view and a mountain of coin rising up like an ancient latrine of the Gods.

The Grey Monks were nowhere to be seen, apparently put off by Edgar and Richter's enterprising display of glittering fornication, and before long other hands appeared above the threshold.

Those below with enough strength left to aid in the towering construction emerged with blinking eyes and unending gratitude, only be stunned again by Edgar's flippant disregard for his fortune.

"Go, take a coin. Take a dozen. Take as many as would make your life worthwhile, and more to decorate your futures a new shade of gold…"

He motioned to take a step, but teetered then, on the brink.

Richter's strong arm caught him.

"Perhaps, pull up your breeches first?"

Chapter XXIV
Storm

A single tree stood upon an otherwise empty horizon. From a distance, it looked to be breathing in the storm clouds surrounding it like a pair of lungs. Beneath its errant branches, Edgar had never felt so at peace.

As he leafed through the pages of the Olde Book, his own tears added to the pulp that was emerging between the binding.

"We should move on", urged Richter. "This place feeds on misery and desolation. And to my mind, you are the perfect catalyst"

The open moors played host to more than just oppressive storms and occasional trees. The pair had been mindful not to draw too much attention from foragers seeking a certain plant, scarce anywhere else, but relatively abundant there.

Rumour had it that a tea brewed from the leaves could grant great strength to those who drank it. But the preparation was not without consequence; too much and the tea would drive a normal man into a frenzy until his heart gave out from exhaustion, too little, and the herb had the opposite effect, rendering healthy bodies into withered husks.

Richter regaled Edgar with the story of a lone knight who had ambitions beyond simple quests for glory and riches; a knight who wanted to be cast into the annals of history and be immortalised in song and prayer. A knight whose juvenile folly would have him sip of the tea long before properly brewed, in impatience and in ignorance. The knight survived, but only the knight. His mind was addled and his body turned infirm. Apparently, he could still be found wandering the moors, convinced that a fresh brew would bring about his vigour once again. But he could no longer see, nor smell, nor feel.

Edgar shook his head at the tale.

But despite Richter's concerns, he could not shift Edgar from his torpor. He was gone now and it would take some time to get him back.

Resigned to this fact, the knight decided to seize the opportunity and partake in a little foraging for himself. He had time to kill, so why not?

But, after an hour's ceaseless searching, he had found little to confirm the rumours of olde, succeeding in finding only the forgotten, bleached bones of some previous adventurer. Perhaps they belonged to the fabled knight from his tale after all?

He shrugged started back towards the tree.

By now the sky was a thick black soup coalescing above the branches of the large tree, as though stealing the thunder from all around it.

A concentration of malice loomed above; with tenebrosity before them and the void in their wake. It was definitely time to go.

The knight even managed a brisk jog to expedite the departure, but it was as he drew closer that he realised that Edgar was no longer alone.

Breaking into a run his muscles screamed as the weight of his armour fought gravity to hold him back.

And the nearer he got, the slower he moved, for the ground underfoot softened exponentially as if in violation of the will of the tree.

Or was it something else?

Gasping for breath, Richter cursed as he stumbled forward, rumpled and crawling on his hands and knees.

He looked up, brushing aside a ragged length of hair matted to his forehead by fresh and olde sweat alike. The tree seemed no nearer, and yet he felt like he had been running for hours. If he ever did reach its lofty branches he would be as weak as a kitten by then.

He straightened and took deep breaths to steady himself.

"Fuck", he uttered, hands on hips.

By now he was all but a beacon for a prompt lightning strike and would end up a cooked body in a tin shell; a prospect he could do without.

Meanwhile, the maelstrom raged, gathering in ferocity by the minute, by the second; by the thought.

In the distance, Edgar still seemed to be reading, but, in truth, he was fighting; if not for his life, then at the very least, his sanity.

Fervently he read the words on the pages as though enraptured by their very existence. Some strange sorcery worked its way through the tome and he could not look away. His eyes held the words like the intimate gaze of new lovers left alone for too long. His hands sought the pages like garments the in the way.

Before long, the tree was teeming with creatures half the size of a man, but as nimble as a monkey. They seemed neither here nor there and brooked no room for argument.

They descended down the barren limbs in a swarm-like fashion and fanned out as they met the ground before streaming towards Richter like quicksilver, hate in their eyes and magic in their wake.

In grim, resigned fashion the knight drew his sword, the motioning seeming to take an age. Battered as it was it would still tear flesh or, at the very least, bludgeon and rend.

But when the things fell about him it wasn't flesh that his steel met. Instead, each beast carved faded away as if no more than a memory, a cloud of ash or dust choking the air around him.

The creatures bore claws to bear but could do nothing about Richter's metal skin and so shrieked in dismay at a foe they could not harm.

But they were clever. And one by one they set about unmaking the buckles and straps that held up the knight's armour.

Richter span about, ducking and slamming foes to the ground. He whipped his own cloak around him like a shield, tangling several limbs before hewing the owners in half.

"Edgar!" he cried, slowly becoming overwhelmed.

But he did not look up.

And the sky grew darker, as though of night.

And soon after, Richter succumbed and went down in a heap, doing all he could but eventually vanquished by sheer numbers and exhaustion.

"Edgar!"

There was a crack like thunder and the dark skies flashed.

At first, Richter assumed it was thanks to the storm. But something ringing off his left pauldron, still clinging to his shoulder like a babe, told him he was wrong.

The creatures about him screamed in anguish at either the noise or the light and lessened their insistence upon Richter's form. The knight took the opportunity to clamber back to his feet and lay about him once again, taking down the apparitions in swathes.

Flash.

Crack.

Richter spun with the impact and landed face up in the mud.

The creatures scattered.

~

The olde knight found himself blinking rain from his eyes as though he had been wearing spectacles with rims fashioned from onions.

Good grief...

And then a figure loomed above him, the twin barrels of a pair of stout duelling pistols steadily aimed; one at his face, the other his groin.

"Off my land or so help me I'll make sure you end up wearing your manhood as a false nose for the hole I'm about to put there. And that's not meant as a compliment"

Richter wasted no time, rolling to the side and sweeping the man's legs out beneath him. He fell and landed heavily. There was another *flash* and *crack* and then Richter found himself scrambling backward as the man violently shuddered from the bullet of one of the pistols lodged into the side of his head, having discharged during the impact.

There was a good minute of juddering before finally the man came to rest, his skull stoved in like a dropped melon.

"Holy shit…" Richter whispered under his breath.

"What's going on over there?" called Edgar from the tree. "Did you find what you were looking for?"

Richter was in no good mood.

And as he pushed aside the slumped remains of the dead figure he vowed to exchange harsh words.

But when he rose from the mud he could tell that something had changed; something tangible, something odd strange.

Something wrong.

It was daylight. And Edgar was smiling.

Richter trudged through the slop to meet him, carrying an assortment of armour parts and a pair of ruined duelling pistols.

He sat back against the tree and almost fell asleep right there and then. But he caught himself, saving enough energy to ask the eternal question.

"So why are you in such a good mood?"

~

Edgar slammed the book shut, the damp pages clumping together to seal for all time.

He rubbed idly at his arm, a burning sensation hidden beneath the cloth, and was just about to examine it when Richter ambled over, tossing an apple into the air as the drizzle faded into nothing. At his side hung a pouch of some suspicious herb.

"What have you got there?" he said, nodding to the book.

Edgar furrowed his brow. "Just some words, they are nothing for your eyes…" he said, stuffing the tome into his satchel. He paused in the action. "In fact, no…" he then filed the book into the Sack of Ire and that was the end of it.

Richter looked put out. "Anything interesting?"

"Very", replied Edgar, annoyingly. He got to his feet. "Come on, which way?"

"You really want to go back to that place?" replied Richter.

Edgar shrugged. "I can't leave him"

"They're just… bones, Edgar, I…"
"I can't leave him"

~

Edgar made off across the moor. He'd been indolent too long.

He had outpaced Richter two to one as he loped along and now the olde knight lagged behind far in the distance. As the mists rolled in he was torn whether to wait or to press on. His mood was more sour than usual and all of a sudden he didn't know what to make of his companion.

I should never have read those pages.

Glancing over his shoulder he could just make out Richter's form in the distance, obscured by vapours, marred by fast-dwindling light.

At least, he was sure it was Richter…

A chill blew over the plains and his cloak responded in kind. Edgar pulled it tighter, but couldn't take his eyes off of the figure in the mist.

The knight survived, but only the knight.

But he could no longer see, nor smell, nor feel…

Chapter XXII
Lead

A leaden feeling fell about Edgar.

Where once he saw a friend and companion, he now saw an apparition. He witnessed no dream, no trick of the mind or false vision from some conjured miasma. The man before him was real, operating under the influence of a long and painful curse.

They had both been so blind.

He turned and ran ahead into the gloom until he located a stand of dead trees and a scattering of rocks. It was an obvious place to hide, but it was all there was.

"Edgar!" cried the knight as he shambled past in the failing light. "Where are you!?"

Edgar edged around the side of a splintered trunk and watched the broken man, his mind telling him, crying out for him, to answer.

But he stood silent; Grim, and silent.

"Help…me…." Stammered the olde knight as he fumbled through the remnants of a thousand morrows just the same.

Edgar slipped away and faded into the impending dusk.

~

Hours later, Edgar found himself eating some unnamed slop by the cracked window of a second-rate inne.

The Swagger Inne was known for its rambunctious nature but tonight the place was nearly empty and only a smattering of broken furniture littered the floor, half of which was now being used as impromptu firewood to ward off the damp without.

A minstrel sat in the corner and performed out of key and out of time.

Idly, Edgar stared out of the window, barely registering the grey sludge running down his chin and back into the chipped bowl from which he ate.

He drained the last drops from his tankard, of what he hoped was ale, and made a beeline for the privies. If there was one thing he needed right now it was to excrete some urine.

As it happened, the privy was, in fact, no more than a mere hole in the ground out back, but the proprietor of the inne had at least gone to the effort of nailing up a board outside to state its use.

As he relaxed, Edgar smirked at the thought of some of the lazy summer days gone by, before that sign had gone up, and the many innocent youths that had once used the hole as a sandpit to play in.

By the time he returned to his table he found it occupied.

Fucking hell. Richter.

"I couldn't find you amidst the brume", said the olde knight. "And when it started to rain I thought it likely you would seek shelter. I was out there some time…"

Edgar rubbed his forehead. "Richter, I'm sorry I…"

"Is the ale any good?" interrupted Richter.

Edgar shrugged. "Look…I'm going to bed".

He reached into the gusset of his trousers and pulled out a coin, laying it firmly on the table. "Get yourself a room, or a keg, or anything. Just…" He couldn't even be bothered to finish the sentence before turning away and trudging up the stairs to the modest suite he had hired for no reason other than casual opulence.

To be fair the "Suite" at the Swagger Inne meant that it had a bed with four equal legs, a stool bucket without holes, direct access to a pump for water and, to sweeten the deal, a hatch in the floor overlooking *the hole* in case one found oneself caught short in the night and didn't fancy fogging up the chamber with one's own excremental vapours.

A polished tray sat on the window sill to serve as a mirror and a comically stuffed deer's head adorned the wall opposite the bed, complete with broken antlers and a slack-jawed, dead-eyed stare.

Edgar doubted the quality of the forthcoming night's sleep, but still, at least he had some time alone.

As he lay in bed he picked at the scabbed form on his arm, the dark words of the tattoo crisp against his pale skin.

Introspection leaves no room for the living.

~

Edgar awoke to the sound of knocking at the door.

Mole-eyed and pissed off he sat up.

What time was it?

A glance at the low-burned embers in the fireplace told him it was likely the middle of the night or small hours. Surprisingly, he didn't even remember falling asleep but had welcomed the rest.

Apart from the subtle glow of the fireplace the room was pitch dark and he took a moment in making his way across the distance to the door.

"Who is it?" he asked through the keyhole.

"Richter…"

He sounded drunk.

Edgar sighed inwardly and drew back the bolt.

The knight stumbled in before slumping down heavily on a leather wing-backed chair by the remnants of the fire.

"Come in", said Edgar in withered tones, bolting the door behind him once again.

Richter began drinking from a half-empty mug of ale on the table.

Edgar shuffled back to bed and closed his eyes, hoping that Richter would simply sit, drink, and pass out.

~

A long time passed with nothing but the sound of the crackling embers and the occasional slurp to break the silence, and Edgar was hanging on the edge of sleep when he was started awake by Richter's voice cutting through the Night like a garrotte.

"I was there the day their world was taken from them. I was there that day..."

Slurp and silence.

"There was nothing I could do. For all my years and skill with a blade..."

The leather of the chair creaked as the olde knight shifted before continuing.

"I...I never meant to kill the man. I never mean to kill any of them. Well...*hiccup*...the Three, perhaps but...well, of course..."

Edgar rubbed his eyes.

Fuck sake.

"Before I knew it I had created the makings of a stray, a monster...I...I had escaped the Three, or so I thought. I quested on for the trophy I sought for all those years...The one I told you about... I knew nothing else...That damned cup, with its impossibly dark jewel, modestly set upon a graven aperture wrought from elaborate, skilled conception..."

Slurp.

"There...was no one else, just an olde cabin on the edge of the moors away from...from everyone; away from people like me. I didn't know what to say, but some part of me that was left decided I would leave them there. There was nowhere else..."

Sigh.

Hiccup.

"And when I returned to the moor the man's bones were picked clean and the guilt weighed upon my shoulders like a slab yoke"

"There was rumour of a charmed blade... a misericorde...some knights would use it as a coup de grace against a fallen foe or even a friend", he chuckled. "They were half right, I suppose"

He sighed.

Edgar lay prostrate, wishing Richter would stop, but in lieu of trying to drag the man out into the hallway, he continued to listen.

"I was told such a blade could undo all the wrongdoings of a man with one swift stroke. The simple price being that the wielder must also be the victim"

Slurp.

There was then a long silence then, an unspoken tension between the welcome release of sleep and a thought hanging upon the periphery of existence. To say it would be a finality, to ask would be a crime.

Richter slumped in the chair that little bit more.

"To me, it seemed like a bargain"

And whilst the fire played out its last few notes and Edgar began to drift, he was left to wonder what Richter was even on about. It sounded like a fairy-tale but, given what he had seen of late, he would pretty much believe anything, other than, of course, that the ale in the Swagger Inne was anything but three day olde urine.

It was some time before Edgar realised that the knight was asleep, tipped off by the beginnings of ragged snores and the fact that he had finally ceased in his moaning.

Reluctantly, the fire winked out and Edgar closed his eyes.

Chapter XXVI
Blade

The following morning, Richter was gone. Only the crease of his arse in the leather marked that he had even been there at all; that and the empty flagon.

And on the table beside the chair, a long knife lay unsheathed, glinting occasionally as shards of light fed through worn curtains before the pane.

Edgar slid into a bath of cold water and lay there unmoving for what seemed like ages.

Richter's words had disturbed his dreams all night and the modest light now creeping through into the room made his discomfort no better.

Idly he scrubbed himself with a rough brush before deciding enough was enough and clambering out to face the day.

A glance outside the window offered him a wet, overcast visage. At least there was that.

He donned the necropants, which were beginning to smell worse by the day, and then threw on his battered cloak before belting on his sword. Finally, he complemented the look by taking up the sack of bones.

Over breakfast, he considered recent events and decided upon sticking to one task at a time.

Richter was a man grown and it would do no good to run after him like some juvenile. Besides, it was because of him that he was where he was now, in more ways than one. That weight alone would guide his feet.

Breakfast consisted of more grey slop and Edgar found himself hard-pressed to tell the difference between the contents of his bowl and that of the nearby latrine. Perhaps they were one and the same. Even so, after one spoonful he left it, grimaced, paid up, and shipped out.

At first, he headed back towards the moors, re-living the desolation of the previous day's jaunt. He knew now where he would deposit the bones, but if he would find that place only time would tell. On the horizon, he saw the Mneme Tree, dark and foreboding as once before. Only this time, he would embrace it armed with knowledge and determination.

As he approached he could already feel the call of the earth around him, disturbed by the roots beneath, and flashes of insight forced their way into his mind.

Manipulation led to elsewhere entirely. And in that moment he saw, or rather felt, The *Link*...

Where?

He asked.

When?

Then before he knew it he tripped on a root beneath the soil, gnarled and broken as his own sense of humour.

Bending down and drawing back his hood, he dug deep to pull up no root, but the weathered bones of a forgotten man, now remembered.

All afternoon he toiled there in the rain, a grave robber in broad daylight. With occasional starts he would look up, expecting a mad forager or the Lost Knight, but he was met with only the wind and the rain.

Tired and covered in dirt, Edgar reflected that he was glad he bothered to take the time bathing that morning.

With a soiled hand, he mopped his brow, made use of the recently acquired facilities, and sat down for a snack.

The mound of freshly dug earth provided ample comfort for his posterior, arranging itself around every nook and cranny.

And as he bit down into a mouldy apple he turned to regard the fruits of his labours.

A cold, hard pile of bones lay arrayed up the ground, gradually being washed clean by the ceaseless elements and made free upon the plain.

~

The night had come and gone and dawn was but moments away.

What a way to pass the time.

Edgar was exhausted, and it was there, slumped by a pile of bones and a mound of earth clutching a half-eaten apple, that Richter found him.

Taking pity on the olde soul he gathered up the remains and slung Edgar over his shoulder before beginning the long walk back to civilization.

But civilization never came.

When Edgar removed the hood from his eyes he peered around in wonder at the remnants of an olde log cabin, replete with every variety of arachnid under the hidden sun. The Wilde had made its home here but there were faded signs of much love and attention, buried beneath the ages.

He sat up, half breaking through the pallet he was resting upon.

Richter stirred and came to greet him.

"What is this place?" Edgar asked, picking up a brittle figurine carved from wood.

"It was once a Home... Until a monster came one day..." replied the knight, offering Edgar a mug of stagnant water.

Edgar put down the figurine, becoming interested in a weathered dream-catcher that he had noticed in the corner of the room. Stretching for it, the effort made him cry out in pain.

"I feel like I've been on the rack..."

"You had a long day" Richter cut in, sternly. He reached for the object and passed it down.

"Thanks", said Edgar, examining the dream-catcher with interest. Within its weave vague hints of human shape presented themselves, and dust lay upon the fabric like birds upon the wire. Edgar pocketed it.

Richter raised a brow.

"I'm up to my guff in nightmares, Richter. The last thing I need are any more"

The knight sighed, laying a mailed hand upon a skull on the table, a shattered hole through the temple.

"I told you not to rake up olde graves"

Edgar regarded the collection of bones.

What a mess.

"I missed some", he said, noticing some errant pieces once they had all been laid out.

The knight shook his head. "No".

Richter took a seat on a chair that looked set to buckle at any moment, though for the time being it held.

"The pieces are all here, Edgar. But the image they construct is not a happy one. Can you…"

There was a rap at the door.

Edgar looked up sharply at Richter before drawing his rapier and one of the olde, cold duelling pistols, unsteady hands protesting against their weight. Richter merely loosened his sword in the scabbard but held an arming knife concealed along his wrist.

Moving warily towards the door he thrust it open without preamble and stood facing nothing.

For ten long seconds, the rain and wind were invited in before the door was summarily closed once again.

Richter looked back towards Edgar. "It's cold", he admitted.

"Then let us light a fire", replied the knight.

It took a good while before any flame would catch there in that damp place. And the blocked chimney served only to fill the room with smoke and ash. The effort of starting the damn thing warmed the pair more than the flames ever did. Still, they persevered, and eventually they had created something that passed as a fire.

With so many broken windows, the cabin naturally let out a sufficient amount of smoke for the pair not to smother, but it would be many days until the smell vacated their hair and beards.

~

"You never did tell me where we are" Commented Edgar over a cup of beans. The smacking of his lips was beginning to drive Richter to distraction.

"Who do you think lived in a place like this? So isolated from everything, from *everyone?*"

Edgar scooped some more beans into his mouth, silently praying they didn't emerge as a potent and noxious gas shortly after. The confines of the cabin were not ideally suited for that situation to take place.

Richter leaned in.

"There were never had any dreams, only nightmares. For their part, they knew nothing else, but those around them were doomed. They grew up away from others on the edge of a miserable village rife with incest and plague. Then one day, after one tragedy too many, those around them began to suspect became wary. But it wasn't until one night, when the moon was both full and unseen, on the longest day of the year that delirium turned to madness"

"I was away on an errand, but something happened that night, something dark and something grim. Upon sunrise, every red-blooded male was found withered and spent, like withered flowers and broken at a touch"

"I returned that very morning to find my home alight, a congregation before the door, spitting on the flames and watching as the place burnt from eave to eave"

"For two years my sword had remained un-bloodied, a rare thing for a sworn knight, but then the polished steel became thick with the paint of others; people I knew, people who betrayed me"

"People I betrayed"

"As the last press of women tried in vain to block my passage I cut them down like wheat; a farmer in his field after a glut had been gifted."

"I never stopped to think of my actions that day. And as I pulled them out of the flames I found my wife, burnt to a crisp, a blade in her grasp and a smile on her face"

Richter paused, taking a moment to wipe a cold approximation of a tear from the bottom of his eye.

"I've won battles against armies, witnessed duels between married men, slept in the mud, and watched the dying light go out in my horses' eyes. But to this day, Edgar, I have never seen anything so terrible, so...memorable".

His head hung low.

"Every night I see them in my dreams", he absentmindedly said into nothing, his head somehow hanging lower, impossibly low.

"It took me a lifetime to discover the true nature of darkness. Yet all I needed to do was invert my eyes..."

There was a long silence as the rain dripped through the weathered boards without a care.

Edgar swallowed his beans, not quite sure what to say.

"Richter, I...I found this"

Edgar fumbled for a moment in the lining of his cloak before producing a slender blade.

Richter's eyes widened at the sight of the blade.

There was a moment's rest before an unseen tension built between them.

"Hand me the blade".

Edgar hesitated before recoiling slightly. "I don't think that..."

"GIVE ME THE KNIFE!" bellowed Richter, so abruptly that Edgar fumbled the weapon and toppled backward off his stool.

Terrified by the man in front of him Edgar edged back towards the corner of the room to huddle in a damp corner next to a collection of dead plants and a broken bookcase, rank with woodworm.

Before him was a monster.

But it wasn't until the knight held aloft the blade in his trembling hands that Edgar realised his true intentions.

Here was a man bent on self-destruction, wracked with a forbidden guilt and trapped in a dark labyrinth of loathing and disgust. Here was a man who now had the tool he needed. Here was a man on the edge of Paradise.

And as the door to the draughty cabin forced open once again, the fire flared to shed light on a mortal scene; the flickering face of anguish, and the long grim shadow of remorse.

At some point, Edgar had found the courage to regain his feet and found himself within close proximity to Richter.

But it was too late.

And there by the fire he lay, his life's blood seeping out through an unforgiving wound, the hilt of a knife protruding from his flesh.

Richter knelt beside him.

"I am sorry, my friend. I have failed you. I will go now, to walk forever in your debt…"

And with that he turned, the sound of his armour stark amongst the rush of blood between Edgar's ears, and walked out into the rain.

Edgar stretched out a hand as he watched him leave. And with the last of his strength, he managed to speak.

"It's not your fault"

~

Through lidded eyes the blurred image of a dark woman came into focus; her raven-black hair, her fleeting aura, her pale skin like moonlight through sapphire.

On the periphery of his hearing, Edgar could hear the steady beat of rain upon earth. It was a familiar sound, a comforting sound.

The fire had gone cold; some indication of how long he had lain there.

The woman knelt beside him and ran deep eyes over his broken body, then fixed him with a stare.

The pain!

Seconds later the blade was out, blood pooling once more upon the rotten timbers of a long forgotten home.

His eyes closed.

And still the rain came down.

Chapter XXVII
Grey

It was morning when Edgar was greeted by a fine rainbow through the cracked glass of the cabin, robust in girth and length and piercing in its vitality.

He felt like he had a hangover and groaned at the mere sight of so many colours forcing themselves upon his retinas beneath thrice heavy lids.

Without thought he crawled on his knees, gathering up the Sack of Ire whereupon he stood uneasily and started towards the rainbow's end.

He continued to blunder his way through barren, scarred rock and irregular bluffs until he happened upon a still pool, pale in the dawn light and playing host to a whole firmament of colours.

Casting the Sack into the waters he wasn't satisfied until a bleak crescent of grey shot out over the horizon, soft upon the eyes and unremarkable for all to see.

He almost smiled then, but his eyes found something else.

Edgar watched as a woman slowly emerged from the silent waters of the pool. He did nothing to hide the fact that he was staring, though he could not pinpoint the apex of his attention.

But it took only a moment to register that she appeared completely bone dry, if not warm.

She spun with a flourish, hair trailing in her wake to form a dark cloak that revealed nothing.

Sparkling eyes regarded Edgar across the waters.

"Why do you come here?" she inquired, softly.

"I've been here before", he replied.

She narrowed her eyes. "This place?"

Edgar nodded.

The woman looked around her as if taking in her surroundings for the first time.

She turned back to regard Edgar before moving out of the water.

He took her hand as she approached the edge of the pool. She felt like the dead.

"They tell me you are quite the magician," she said to him.

"Do they, now?"

Silence.

"Are you not cold?" he asked, trying to change the subject.

"Quite", she replied. "But let me ask you this; if I was to lay down and stripped myself bare, how would you proceed, how would you dare?"

Feeling awkward, Edgar said nothing.

Tanera stared at him.

"The vision holds some truth, Edgar. After all, why do you think you are still here?"

Edgar looked down at his own hands, but when he looked up her eyes were sad.

"A dying wish can be a powerful thing, secondly only to the love of the lost..."

"But I..."

Tanera took his hands in her own, cold grasp.

"Do not dwell on these things, Edgar..."

From out of nowhere she produced a sack of bones, cleaned and cherished as a king's crown. And then she handed him the dagger.

With one soft kiss on his lips, she took his breath and uttered four short words.

"It's not your fault"

His breathing was shallow then, and he was acutely aware of his own fragility at that moment. Cold, naked, unarmed, and lost, he could be no further from comfort.

Yet he did not feel frightened.

The witch walked around him. No...*flowed* around him like silk in a stiff breeze, and the surface of the water flickered hypnotically.

Eventually, she moved near and he looked into eyes so intense he felt as though they were his own.

It seemed to him then that he viewed the room for outside of his body; a wraith within the room.

Her voice sounded hollow to his ears, and it wasn't just the strange acoustics.

His eyes were his own again, and as he looked up at iridescent pupils he shivered as he became aware of his now prone body.

The words were simple, the words were soft.

"You have a sadness in you", said the witch. And there was no malice there.

Edgar squirmed uncomfortably. "Can I get up now?"

She nodded.

Abruptly he sat up and grabbed his trousers. But before he could move any further she grasped his head with both of her hands and fixed his gaze once again.

"Wha..."

"You have a Sadness inside of you"

The intonation and emphasis, as well as her choice of words, gave Edgar pause for thought.

"I don't feel particularly sad...at least right now", he offered.

The witch turned away.

"I know".

"What's wrong?", he asked.

"Edgar, I can't help you ".

She looked uncomfortable.

"It's OK…"

She smiled then a little, offering him a goblet of wine, which he took briskly and supped abruptly…perhaps too abruptly.

He lowered the cup.

"Tastes like wilderness and afterthought"

Chapter XXVIII
The Gateway

When Edgar set foot upon wet ground between the two stone pillars before the catacombs he stood for a moment.

Nothing had changed.

A pair of crows watched, impassive from their monotone perches.

His eyes scanned the horizon. No, something *had* changed. There was peace here now.

He breathed deeply and caught the fragrant scent of rose upon the air.

Regarding the offending item, he turned to find something missing. There was no sarcophagus now, cold to touch or otherwise, and in its place, a pit of scarlet and thorns choked the earth where stone once stood.

And something else.

Had it been so long?

A gnarled yew bent over the entrance to the depths below, blessedly shielding the first steps from the worst of the rain. Its olde roots sprawled over a vast area, stopping abruptly at the portal.

Edgar took a step forward and peered in wonder, gently caressing the leaves with the tips of his fingers.

"Is it so hard to believe?"

Edgar clutched his chest and breathed in sharply.

"For fuck's sake..." he spat, turning to regard Herbynlocke. "Will you stop hanging around in graveyards?"

Herb remained stoic, but his eyes gleamed. "Touché".

Edgar relaxed and exhaled. "What do you want?" he asked the sage in curt tones.

"I'm coming with you".

"Really?" said Edgar, quirking an eyebrow. He had never known Herbylocke to lift a finger all his life.

"What are you after?" he added.

The sage sighed. "I'm sorry to be such a burden. But it is time to close this book"

"What's down there?" asked Edgar.

"You know what's down there" And with that last comment, he regarded Edgar's belongings, in particular, the sack of bones slung over his shoulder.

"And you won't need all those", he added.

Edgar stood mute for a moment before objecting. "So why did I spend a day and a night exhuming bodies? Was it just for fun?"

Herbynlocke shrugged, nonchalantly admiring the yew tree, fondling its leaves like a lover's hair. "Looks that way".

He then moved forward towards the catacomb steps, leading down once again into fathomable darkness.

Reluctantly, Edgar put down the sack of bones and rolled his shoulders. It *did* feel good to lighten the load, but he was reluctant to leave it unattended by the wayside and faffed for a while, trying to find a place to stash it.

"*Will* you stop messing around with skeletons?" reprimanded Herbynlocke, impatiently.

Edgar looked around before an idea struck him.

With effort, he heaved the bones into the rose bush. Maybe the thorns would dissuade any pillagers. But with ill luck the bag tore and the bones scattered throughout the blooms, half in and half out of the sackcloth.

What a mess.

"Great", said Edgar. "Exactly what I wanted to happen".

He looked back toward Herbylocke, who now wore a look of impatience. "At least they now look authentic", he said without empathy.

Edgar hurried over and together they turned towards the stone portal.

A low hanging branch of the yew presented itself to them and Herb reached up to snap off a twig, wreathed in miniature leaves, and glistening berries.

He held it up before them.

"A simple taste and we discover how shallow-a grave this truly is".

He nodded solemnly to Edgar who, weirdly without question, took the sprig and inserted it through pursed lips.

He never saw Herbynlocke cast *his* aside.

"It is time", he said. And Edgar heard the words as though through a fugue and a veil.

They moved onwards and down in delicate waltz, a soft torch held before them that Herbylocke had provided.

Deeper and deeper they travelled, way beyond Edgar's expectations. He had trodden these steps before, but now time soon slipped away beyond reach as they continued into the gloom.

Before long there was nothing left to see. The opening at the top of the stairs was lost to sight; a pinprick, winking out step by step.

And now there was a strange pressure. No cold, this time, just pressure. This couldn't be the same place. It seemed all wrong.

Edgar felt a pang in his stomach and reached into his pack for a sliver of dried meat to curb his appetite, but the morsel did little to aid his discomfort or pad out the hunger.

Rummaging around in the dark he laid hands upon another snack, but Herbylocke took hold of his wrist.

"That won't help. Come on, time is short now"

The sage's pace seemed then to quicken then and Edgar loped along to keep up, taking the steps two, sometimes even three at a time as his long shanks afforded.

By the bottom, he was exhausted and the cramps in his stomach had worsened. And, if he was being honest about it, he didn't feel right at all.

And the pressure…

"Herb…this Pressu…"

"It is nothing", snapped the sage. "Concentrate", he added.

"On what? There is nothing down here"

"Concentrate"

Edgar kicked some rubble in disgust, forgetting himself until his eyes fell upon what Herbynlocke's torch now illuminated.

Before him sat a great machine.

What?

Edgar's breath hung in the air for a length of time that became unusual, before it continued to bloom.

His eyes widened to regard a contraption that his mind could not comprehend. It was bending his grasp on reality, despite all he had seen so far. The mundane and the magic he could dismiss as fantasy. But this was tangible. This was elemental. This was real.

The thing shimmered in the darkness and was covered in all manner of copper and brass piping, along with various cogs and golden inlays.

Edgar had never seen the like, had never dreamed the like…

Dark pupils widened yet further still as he took in the scope and aspect of the machine. It was vast. The crypt had to have been sat on some kind of sinkhole.

Small wonder…

Edgar paced about the thing, letting his torch reveal the tiniest details; the inscriptions, the filaments, the diodes. It looked like a cross-section of some…mechanical brain, only so much more…

As he leaned in to examine one of the dials it appeared as if the machine itself protested and something in the room changed. The sudden pressure caused Edgar to feel as though he'd gone too deep too quick, or vice versa.

He licked dry lips and took a step back.

Herbynlocke watched with interest as Edgar paced about the curiosity with lingering afterthought.

But another wave of pain ripped through Edgar's body, his stomach folding in half, and he chose to sit upon the dusty floor like an olde tome, and he felt his heart rate drop.

"Herb, I…I don't feel right"

The sage knelt beside him.

"I am sorry, Edgar. You will feel some pain now, I'm afraid…"

Edgar looked at his distant friend, who laid a hand upon his forehead, and, leaning back, he closed his eyes.

In that dark place, Edgar curled foetal where he lay, his mind shrouded by wonder, his body a battlefield of agony.

And then he was still.

Immediately, Herbynlocke threw his cloak over the curled form of Edgar's rapidly cooling body.

"Come on!" he spat into the darkness. And three figures emerged.

Grim and noble, Richter stepped into the torchlight, followed by Tanera and then, an olde man.

"My Halidom…" breathed Richter under his breath, registering the olde man in the flickering flames. "You must be older than I am…" He stated, gaping at the withered, yet smartly dressed figure before him.

The bent man inclined his head.

"Please", said Herbynlocke, extending a hand to gesture at Edgar's still form.

Richter took hold of his feet, Herb his arms. And together they moved the body closer to the ominous, looming machine. Just then it seemed almost sentient.

"Tanera", spoke Herb.

The witch strode forward, producing a phial from the folds of a capacious sleeve. A green, iridescent liquid filled the small vessel and ran freely into Edgar's mouth as she upended the last of it, sealing the final drop with a gentle kiss.

Richter had begun stripping his armour and was nearly naked by the time the pleasantries had finished, save for a linen cloth around his waist and what appeared to be the form of a clenched fist, wrought of good steel, serving as a codpiece.

"Too much time hanging around in Graveyards…", added the knight, grimly, seeing Herbynlocke's dark expression.

The sage said nothing.

He turned to the olde man.

"Now it's up to you"

The man moved forward gingerly, clearly trying to hold back his torment at seeing Edgar lifeless upon the floor. But he persevered.

Bypassing Edgar's body he moved towards the machine until he stood before a kind of plate. There was less dust there.

Shakily he held out a skeletal hand until it met with the cool metal, a half glance thrown to Hebylocke betrayed some fear and a hint of prayer.

And then the pressure dropped.

Chapter XXIX
Skin

As Edgar's eyes adjusted to the light as he ran unsteady hands over the smooth pipe-work of the formidable machine before him and, in doing so, found himself feeling an unprecedented sense of wellbeing. He even hurt less.

He must have spent the best part of an hour looking for a way out of the crypt, but the stairwell was blocked and it was all a riddle to him.

And so damn cold...

Yet the machine...

Edgar shook his head and muttered to himself. It all seemed so vague. And now, left with a pile of dysfunctional brass piping and a layer of thick dust for company, he was not so sure what was real anymore.

He considered his options; He could dig himself out using his bare hands, but who knew how long that would take. Or he could call for help, but that plan was scuppered by the fact that the ruins were populated only by the dead. His only other option appeared to become a skeleton and join them, though that particular choice, whilst amusing, lacked appeal.

In frustration, he threw a small piece of rubble at the machine. The rock struck the piping and rang out clearly through the hall.

"Fuck!" exclaimed Edgar, as the reverberation went on never quite seeming to finish.

And then the tone *did* stop, punctuated only by occasional knocks of loose stones finding their way into the dust. And in that moment he found peace.

Until a voice called out.

Seconds later there was further commotion as masonry began to shift and groan from above.

Edgar covered his head and prayed for a quick death if it was coming.

But hadn't he already been here?

At length, when he looked back up he was stood in a shaft of light like some deity depicted in a hallowed book.

Edgar rubbed his eyes and mopped his brow respectively.

Why was he sweating?

"He's here!" Came the cry from far above and the shaft widened, preceded by a few more errant chunks of masonry making their way south.

Edgar squinted. He supposed he could pick out a figure at the top of the long, forgotten stairs, half-buried in remains.

Stumbling forward into the rubble and dust Edgar blinked particles from his eyes and called out.

The wind that sped down the shaft was strong and most of his words were sent back towards him. Something wasn't right. Even as he called out again and struggled up the shaft over the broken stones, he knew that.

As he walked farther from the machine he felt colder, heavier, older. And his vision was less keen than he remembered, yet he missed nothing. He blinked again and rubbed his face. He didn't remember shaving so recently. Then again, he didn't remember much.

My name...

Eventually, a strong hand reached out and took hold of his own. The unmistakable crunch of gauntlet upon gauntlet founds its way to his ears and as he emerged from the gloom he held a hand up to shield his eyes from the bright white light all about him.

Casting around he was surprised at how familiar everything felt, yet so strange at the same time, like the scent of a rose in the bedchamber or graveyard (Sometimes one and the same). And even then, who is to say which is the familiar and which the strange?

But here winter had hold of everything and the cluster of half-starved knights staring back at him did nothing to set his fragile heart at ease.

He could hardly tell one grave from another and it was with grim realisation that many of the humps were not mere sepulchres, but the bodies of fallen men turned rigid in the cold. There by bloodshed or by starvation, he could not tell, but every breath he took was another bought and paid for with life's precious heat. He motioned to draw his cloak about him.

My cloak?

"My Lord" Came a voice beside him, thrusting a worn helmet into his trembling hands.

No.

Catching his reflection in the visor his blood turned to ice.

He'd never known such a winter. And as he looked ahead upon the ruins of his family estate he idly wandered forward. That it had come to this; everything he had ever known, gone, and what was left could barely pass for an elaborate central heating system with which to warm a particularly draughty castle.

Edgar managed a grin. The irony amused him. So thee olde man had finally gotten round to spending some coin after all, managing then to waste it on the excremental experiment below.

And as he reached the frozen moat he thanked the knight who had given him the helm. His fingers were now raw, but he cared not. Right now he just wanted to find a decent cloak.

"My Lord, did you find what you were looking for? We thought we'd lost you"

My lord.

What was I looking for?

"Richter?"

Edgar tilted his head as he caught something on the edge of the man's voice. It was then he swept up his sword to take his head. He knew he was a good man and on a subconscious level, the act pained him. But it was no use crying over spilled innards, especially when there were more to come.

A few further strides and the next man was done, run through with the tip of his sword, the blood of both men mingling to pool in the snow, creating a fine, scarlet, slush. He was convinced he had ordered his men to wear strong plate instead of leathers or chain, but some people just couldn't be told or were too damn cheap, choosing first to spend their coin in brothels or innes.

But now the element of surprise was gone.

With four men left Edgar didn't fancy his chances, but it was not his body. This one was trained and honed. He lived for this.

One man, bolder than the rest tore off his own helmet and spat in disgust before moving forward to cross swords. But a casual sidestep had the man standing on well-iced timbers and he overextended to be easily nudged into the frozen moat below. The man fell ten feet to hit the thick ice with an awkward crack. It was hard to tell if the sound was from ice or bone, but the moat-water did not break. Edgar spared him no further thought.

The three remaining knights fanned out around him, looking unsure of themselves but determined and enraged, although one, in particular, looked sad more than anything and momentarily lowered his sword in hope of parlay.

Edgar wasted no time and took the man's sword hand at the wrist, giving it to the piled snow beneath before following with a backward slash that ripped through the knight's coif and arming hood respectively to leave him sprawling on the ground like a blind man seeking his cane or the last few coppers of his once former fortune.

The other two lay in without thought and were met with steel, elbow, and boot before retreating a safe distance to standoff.

"I'm going in there!" screamed Edgar, gesturing with his sword to the castle but not taking his eyes off the men. "To get what's mine"

As he said the last, his eyes began to well up and his shoulders relaxed for but a moment.

But that's all his assailants needed.

Seconds later he was backpedalling and fending off multiple attacks. Soon he would be gone and never did a worse knight live.

But fortune favoured him once more as one of the men briefly lost his footing, offering a clear opening.

A lunge left Edgar exposed but also left the other man impaled. And as the last knight slashed down to remove Edgar's arm at the elbow he let go of his sword and drew his dagger.

Protruding from the man's face the dagger frosted in the chill wind as his breath faded around grasping hands.

Edgar stepped in and withdrew the knife before slitting the man's throat without style or grace, though with some short mercy.

There he knelt in the snow for several long minutes, cleaning the blade beneath his hung head.

I was never meant for this.

~

When Edgar approached the threshold of the ruined castle he was unsure of what to expect.

Was this home?

To him, *home* had come to mean a whole firmament of things, including; dark skies, a threadbare gusset, and an empty chalice. That, and the plague of restless dreams, endless nights, and memories too far beyond the veil to be real.

He stood before the large oaken door, or what remained of it. Time had not been kind to the structure and the wood hung haphazardly from hinges long given up to rust.

He loped through the weathered wood, not daring to touch any such part of the portal.

On the other side gaped nothing, save the tired remnants of a well-used latrine, the frozen contents staring back like an opaque sculpture of horror.

The castle had been sacked long ago.

"I'm glad I bothered" uttered Edgar to no one, with thinly veiled sarcasm.

But he knew why he was there.

Picking his way over forgotten relics of time and through a veritable labyrinth of yet more crumbled masonry, he would occasionally happen upon something of interest; an olde piano, still out of tune, a torn painting, bleached from the elements. It could have depicted anything; a broken shield, ornamental, and a half-buried bottle of wine.

He stooped and collected the last, dismaying as the brittle cork crumbled into the vintage, but downed half the bottle nonetheless. He had forgotten a lot of things of late and wanted to add these moments to the list.

Skirting the fallen foundations, he edged around the perimeter of what remained of the rooms in the front half of the castle. But towards the rear, he found a familiar sight, though even that had changed too.

The empty cloister now harboured a frozen pool where once a fine willow stood. Edgar moved towards it and laid a hand upon the ice. It didn't feel right. Again, he caught his reflection and sighed.

Feeling the presence of eyes upon his neck he slowly turned to face an empty corridor at which end began a broken stairwell.

But those olde stones held well and though the moss between the cracks had died and flaked off with every step, Edgar trod tenderly upwards towards a room he never dared look upon again.

He tore off the first door he saw and threw it into the void before stepping into the chamber. Without thought, he made a tight fist around fragments of a curtain, decayed and brittle, yet with some small virtue, and wrapped the drapes about himself.

Casting his eyes around the room was not quite what he had expected. The bed was empty, the cabinet bare, and a hole lay open in the centre.

He sighed.

Poking around for a few moments before retiring back to the main foyer, or what remained of it, Edgar dragged his gore-encrusted sword along the stones and olde timbers, scoring lines haphazardly like some sort of, particularly heavy snail.

He returned to the cloister and sat by the pool, contemplating his next move. He should probably eat, he thought, feeling a slight pang. But the thought of food brought only a phantom pain in the pit of his stomach, and a bitter aftertaste…

After a while, he left the cloister alone. The absence of the willow had taken away some of the charm of the place for him, and there was precious little of that around as it was.

It was then he heard crying; the gentle sobs of a woman far from the throes of happiness. He followed the sound through a rear gate and out into a small walled garden beyond which a stone arch led to another room. The tears came from in there.

He rubbed his forehead.

Wasn't this a vestibule?

Looking around, grey walls stood around a grey floor beneath a cracked ceiling where flakes of snow drifted like apparitions through wild shafts of light.

In the centre lay a block, also grey, but of a stone that appeared far fresher than that of the floor and walls about it. Snow had piled around the edges but most of the top was clear. There was no engraving, no imagery or relief. But it was a sarcophagus without a doubt.

Just a plain olde sarcophagus.

Crouched before it was the woman he had heard, but he could not see her face and as he reached out to her she blew away in the breeze like softly spoken words. Edgar's hand met with the sarcophagus instead.

Removing a gauntlet, Edgar ran fingers over the stone. It was cold to touch and he found himself grinning for no good reason.

Then, after replacing his glove, he stood reversing the grip on his sword, heaving it above his head, bringing the weight of the pommel down upon the top of the slab. The stone chipped, but was far from broken.

Again and again, he struck, until his gloves wore through and his breathing became ragged.

How long he tried only the walls could tell, but by the time the stone was cracked, the hilt of Edgar's sword was a ruined mess and sweat poured from his face and hair to freeze upon his boots like cheap rhinestones cast about by the wind.

Wild-eyed and shaking with hunger, Edgar set to the gape in the slab, tearing apart the fragments with his hands like some feral beast upon a fresh kill.

Splintered and broken, the sarcophagus lay open like baked pie whose chef couldn't wait to sample the delights within.

And there before his very eyes lay the source of his nightmares, the sum of his worth and his mark on this place.

In the ruins of an afternoon's work, his sad olde bones lay grey and silent.

When the clothes had rotten off it was impossible to tell, but some sense of dignity remained in the form of a well-used skull codpiece still in place.

Edgar hung his head low.

Chapter XXX
Memories of Mhourningsyde

Edgar stood back, watching the flames as they devoured all. Timber by timber, the structure soon became a husk; one without complaint.

It was the warmest Edgar had felt since he could remember, yet inside remained a tundra.

Who even was he now? He had no body, no memory, and no legacy. He looked down at himself.

What a mess.

Even pride had escaped him.

For long hours he stood there by the frozen moat, alternating his gaze between ice and flame. He even considered cracking a hole in the moat and throwing himself in. His armour would weigh him down and within moments it would all be over.

But it was no good, he knew. He might drown today and awake tomorrow, only colder and wetter than before.

He turned away from the flickering sight before him. Only one road lay open then, the dark path back towards the crypt.

In a fury he pulled off the stubborn pieces of Richter's armour, exposing himself to the elements before walking naked back down into the frigid stone surrounds.

And it was there he sat until he was too weak to move, until late one hour when unexpected footsteps opened his eyes.

The silhouette against the light of the shaft offered little information, but as flakes of snow made their way down and found the figure's form they did not move, nor did they melt.

Edgar licked dry lips, trying to speak, but found himself unable.

The figure crouched before him in the half-light.

"Edgar, how do you fare?"

The familiar words echoed around the tomb for so long that he thought madness would take him at any moment. But as the crackle of the flames from above punctuated the pale stillness of the confines around him he knew he would be spared that destiny.

In his grey fragment of a heart, he was sure that he was a good man. And good men did not deserve to be robbed of their sanity.

"Look at me Edgar"

This can't be happening.

"Things have not gone as planned, I see"

No.

"Look at me..."

But before the conversation could continue any further, and with the last of his energy, he rolled to the side and made for the door. And with just enough adrenalin pumping through his veins the surroundings gradually dissolved around him. Where he found the strength he would never know, but the door was open now and the cell no longer his home.

With a torch in one hand and a leather-bound book in the other, Edgar found himself navigating the rabbit warrens that were the castle dungeons. But he was no stranger there. These were his halls, his home.

He had been played, but now was no time for introspection.

His mind conjured visions of the past, ethereal way-markers to guide his way.

He heard the shouts, felt the eyes, and fanned the flames, but soon he was where he needed to be.

The door opened and he lurched down the corridor past guards too busy tending the maids to bother standing watch. Money well spent, then.

And after an exhausting climb up the endless stairs, he found himself passing by servants and knights alike, all now alerted to his presence. It mattered not. Just a few more feet and...

...Running straight into a butler sent silverware skyward, and edibles south. The less said about the liquor the better, save the fact that most of it ended up in Edgar's face.

He screamed as the alcohol burned his eyes. But when he removed his hands from their aperture his breath was stolen away, for he straddled the parapet ledge that he had been looking for.

He looked behind to see two knights slowly edging towards him, and the familiar face of a man holding stained silverware, aghast and pale against a tapestry background of burgundy and gold. No, not burgundy and gold, but of grey.

For a brief moment, he caught his reflection.

Time stood still then, as he stood upon the edge of the stone. He took one last look behind him, at the face he had met, whose name he had never even known. At the Chylde he had failed, now a man grown.

The world faded and the blur of the walls became a comforting blanket of ash before the shock of moat-water engulfed him.

His fortune now was out of his hands.

~

Edgar lay shivering in the dark, naked as the day he came into his cold, miserable existence.

And it was there he remained until a shadow, a deeper black against the dark, loomed above him.

He felt his eyes strain to take in detail, widening to gather light. And then the darkness spoke.

"If I lay down and stripped myself bare, how would you proceed, how would you dare?"

"Tanera", he rasped, with some sense of relief.

A pouring sound accompanied her footsteps as she moved nearer. Sitting up, a goblet was pressed into his hands.

"Where have you been?" she asked in soft, probing tones.

Empty of stomach, Edgar sipped from the vessel and the vintage went to his head at once.

"I'm… I'm not sure…" he responded. "Though…"

"Go on"

"Parts of me seem missing, but which I couldn't tell you…"

He felt her hand brush over his hair as she moved closer to sit by him on the floor.

"Nightmares linger. They stay by you when all other thoughts disappear." She paused. "I'm sorry there was no easier way".

Edgar supped once more.

"I don't know how I can go on after all that has happened. What is to come? And what then?"

When no answer was forthcoming he began to suspect that Tanera had departed, vanishing, as was her wont, upon the winter breeze.

But instead, his suspicions were met with soft words.

"Welcome back" she whispered into his ear.

After that, his goblet fell to land upon the cool stone, its crimson contents gently pooled as the sound faded away to make room for others.

~

A single candle lit the room, the dark amber shimmer of the machine conspicuous in the background.

Tanera wore a thick cloak with her cowl up. Edgar could not see her face.

"We must leave this place," she said.

"Must we?" complained Edgar.

The hood nodded gently. "To dwell here too long would be an idle frivolity. And that is not what you need right now"

"Where are we going?" asked Edgar, lacing up his boots.

"To a place called Olde Acre"

"Olde Acre?", mused Edgar, out loud, his breath frosting in the deep recess of the crypt. "Sounds like…Well, it doesn't matter what it sounds like". He cleared his throat.

Tanera turned to him in the shadows. "Edgar. Do you remember what it's like, out there? Are you ready?"

He heaved the Sack of Ire over his shoulder with a shrug. "I remember".

At the top of the olde stair, they were met by a deeply still night. Drops of rain worked themselves down the branches of the olde yew and pooled before depositing themselves upon

Edgar's brow as he peered out onto the bleak vista beyond with untrusting eyes.

Spectres of the night drifted shyly in the background and moved away further still as Tanera lit a torch to guide their way.

She laughed, drawing an inquisitive expression from Edgar.

"As a child, one of my greatest achievements was being able to navigate the Endless Meadow after nightfall without the aid of such implements", she gestured to the torch.

"A useful skill", replied Edgar.

"Mmmm…Until you slide into an unmarked grave", she smirked, but the expression was lost in the gloom.

Edgar cast around.

"Speaking of which", he said, stooping to the side to where he had scattered the collection of bones prior to his visit to the Underworld.

But where once were bones, now grew thorns.

A brilliant rose bush, shaped into the crude fashion of a throne by some… rudimentary topiary, grew from a shallow pit.

Edgar turned to Tanera with a look of silent awe.

"What did you expect to find? Blood and bone make quite the conditions for growth, given enough time…"

"Time…" Edgar uttered under his breath.

How long had he been gone?

Absentmindedly he ran a hand across his face as if trying to feel for signs of age or distress.

But then the torch winked out and Edgar felt Tanera's hand grab his arm.

"We are watched" he heard her voice directly in his ear.

"Tread softly. Tread carefully". And she dragged him along.

And as they sped through the darkness he could feel the tug of lonely spirits upon his cloak, calling for some kind of strange companionship that he neither desired nor would entertain.

But Tanera knew the way, her misspent youth now shown to be a blessing.

And as they hurdled tombstones and earth mounds alike they soon approached the edge of the Meadow and left the denizens of the night to their nocturnal foray.

Soon the pair were traversing a wooded path that, despite the darkness, struck Edgar as well-trodden.

The rains then began in earnest and Tanera slowed her place, relighting the damp torch with no small effort and guiding them onward to this "Olde Acre" that Edgar had only just learned of.

"I know you must be hungry", she said. "But this will have to do for now".

She shoved a half-bottle of mead into his hands and he drank from it deeply.

Instantly his head swam and the surrounds of the forest took on embodiments of their own.

Night noises, the shadowed sky, and the dark earth beneath his feet grew closer and closer.

Idly, he threw the bottle into the bushes and continued on.

For hours then, they followed the trail, sometimes led by moonlight, sometimes firelight, as the clouds rolled over and under. But still, Olde Acre remained a mystery.

Edgar was beginning to flag and stumbled several times before Tanera turned back to offer a gentle hand.

"We are almost there," she said, gently.

Edgar wanted to be sick, but there was nothing within him to facilitate the action.

Had he been well-rested and well-nourished it would have undoubtedly been a pleasant walk, but he soon found himself wishing for the carefree release of unconsciousness once again. And in that regard, at least the mead was helping.

And then, without warning, Tanera stopped.

Edgar's heavy breathing seemed to irk her and she covered his mouth with the palm of her hand.

For a brief moment, he considered licking it, but she wore a look of caution and so he fought against the childish urge.

"Listen," she said.

Amidst the sound of rain on the leaves and earth it was fairly hard to hear anything untoward. But slowly, eventually, something broke through the monotony.

"It sounds like someone crying", stated Edgar, furrowing his brow.

Tanera nodded. "And they are not alone"

A kind of eerie music, if it could be called that, seemed to fill the air then; one dismal wailing after another. Soft sobs followed by inconsolable peals of anguish drifted upon the night air and blended with the unbroken wash of the rain.

And as they turned the corner a small village spread out before them like a lake growing steadily from the stream. Hundreds of flickering lights punctuated the vista. It was almost beautiful.

"Mhourningsyde", stated Tanera. But she did not miss Edgar's confounded glance.

"A forgotten place; a magic place... a sad place", she added. And with that, she strode forward.

Edgar pulled his cloak up further and followed her down about the twinkling lights of the strange village.

In many ways, it seemed enchanting. But something had happened here - something ill.

As they trod cobbled paths and passed by modest homes, the sights of dozens of men, women, and children, wracked with misery played out before their eyes like an elaborate painting gone wrong.

Paint flaked freely from the building exteriors and the hung remnants of martyrs lined the walls of others.

In the distance, one building, taller than the others, stood a little straighter, a little prouder.

More than once, unknown hands pawed at the hem of Edgar's cloak and the leather of his coin purse as they passed unannounced through shining streets of darkened stone. Every owner of those hands had the wet, bloodshot eyes and sunken cheeks of folk that had not known peace in years.

It was as though Tanera had read his thoughts.

"Peace does not come here. Not to this place. These people wear misery as a courtesan might wear an expensive perfume; liberally and without question".

They made their way through myriad paths of slick cobbles for another quarter of an hour. The moon had vanished but the rain continued and they welcomed the sight of the first inne they came across.

The promise of warmth.

The promise of food.

A rotten sign hung limply from the post outside and Edgar could not even decipher the scrawl upon it.

Just another nameless inne…

Again, Tanera seemed to pick up on his thoughts.

She didn't miss a thing…

"These people have no use for names… Not anymore"

She pushed open the door, which made a stereotypical creaking noise and entered the building.

Inside, the inne was much like any other Edgar had frequented in his time. But the clientele were exclusively fed-up. It was bizarre.

He'd seen plenty of men drowning their sorrows, moping over a lost bet, or errant lover. But he had never before seen a man actively topping up his own pint with fresh tears.

"What happens when they run out?" Edgar vaguely mocked, not bothering to clarify if he was talking about ale or not.

"They never run out", Tanera replied with a blank expression.

Edgar chose then to hold his tongue. This was clearly not the time or place for larks or indeed japes.

After a few minutes of searching around the various tables, alcoves, and nooks of the inne, Tanera started to show signs of frustration.

"Who are you looking for?" asked Edgar becoming bored at just hanging around, listening to nothing but whimpering, not to mention how hungry he was.

"Just make yourself at home", she replied before heading to the bar and engaging a somewhat miserable-looking barkeep in what appeared to be conversation. But it could as easily have been consolation.

Edgar took a moment to look around for a good spot to sit. He had been walking for longer than he cared for and his head span from hunger. But most of the empty seats were on tables already occupied by miserable patrons and he didn't fancy trying his patience with any of them.

And so he pulled up his hood and went back out into the rain. There was an olde cask outside that would do for now. And at least there was solitude.

Or so he thought...

A few minutes after feeling the sensation of his legs disappear, after having them draped over the rim of the cask, Edgar shut his eyes, as tired as he was, and held tight to keep from falling.

He took deep, slow breaths and tried not to think about food, letting the cleansing rain lash upon his face with abandon.

But when he opened them once again he was astonished to find a creature of odd description perched above him on the ruined sign of the Inne.

He pulled back his hood to get a better view, letting some of the rain into his eyes.

The creature was avian in nature, and about the size of a cat with a thick, black bill and ruffled feathers that resembled dead roses. Sharp talons scored moss from the sign and an intelligent glint made itself known within black, soulless eyes.

"Hello", Edgar heard himself say, numbly.

Hello, hello, hello... He could almost hear it say back. But he knew that all he really heard was the rain on the cobbles and kegs.

The bird flew down to him then and groused about the stones.

Edgar watched it curiously for a couple of minutes before instinctively slipping off the cask and bending down to try and pet the creature. As his hand moved closer he could feel some unexplained notion encroaching upon him, some disquieting anxiety and dread.

It was then the door to the inne burst open and Tanera strode out into the rain.

She didn't say a word as she passed Edgar and the bird on the road but continued to walk off into the distance toward the tower they had seen on the horizon earlier, although now, admittedly, it looked less unfitting and more...unwelcoming.

Edgar left the bird alone and hurried after Tanera, whose cloak whipped and flapped about her like a sentient being. He knew that beneath its folds, unlike him, she would somehow be bone dry. That was a skill he yearned to acquire.

As he staggered at her heels she shoved a hessian sack into his arms. Within, a paltry selection of meats and sour grapes offered temporary sustenance of which Edgar basically inhaled, swallowing any his body regurgitated with satisfaction, only to be regurgitated and swallowed again.

Bliss.

Tanera paid him no heed. She had her eyes fixed upon the hill. And as Edgar glanced behind him he fancied he caught a glimpse of that bird again…

Smoke on the wind told him parts of the village burned, but he saw no flames and heard no alarm. The persistent wails were now just background noise once more and, if anything, his own silence seemed louder to his ears than any commotion could be.

Eventually, Tanera slowed.

"To touch the Merrow Bird is to guarantee misery and invite disaster". She said.

"But I didn't…"

"It is not from *Here*", she added, didn't elaborate.

"Right…" began Edgar with a grimace, not quite sure he could take the credit for that, having almost just stroked the thing.

"Out of interest, what did it look like to you?" Tanera asked.

"What?"

"The plumage…"

Edgar forced down another morsel before responding. "Roses…Deep red roses, some withered to a darkened brown," he replied, somewhat baffled by the question.

Tanera looked away.

Was that a smile on her face?

"To me, they are orchids black…"

She drifted off.

Edgar stared at her unsure what to say, before glancing back to see if the Merrow Bird was still following.

"Anyway" snapped Tanera, returning from her reverie. "If you see it again, leave it. Lest you want to spend the rest of your poor life sobbing into your own cup or accidentally adding salt to your porridge"

She was about to march off again when Edgar spoke up.

"What happened in there?" he asked, gesturing behind him. "Who were you looking for?"

"It doesn't matter" she replied, Seeming annoyed by the question. "Our answers lie there", she pointed forward into the dark, to the keep on the hill. Shuttered windows and black fascias lent a grim sight indeed. And as the rain continued to pour it wasn't exactly what Edgar had in mind as a stop-over.

"What answers?" demanded Edgar, moving closer. "Ever since the crypt, or even before the crypt, I've been following you under some…delusion or pretence that maybe there will be some understanding to follow. The only thing that has made any sense all day has been a bird compiled of roses. And that's not a thing I thought I'd have to admit"

She stopped then. And for a few moments, they were alone with the rain.

The bricks of the many buildings soaked up moisture like ancient moss, and olde flagstones stretched either way, ignored and broken through neglect.

Edgar saw something of himself in these austere surroundings and could find no words to continue.

Tanera stared into Edgar's eyes and took his head in her hands. "Up on the hill lives a man in a tower made of memories. He asks no questions, yet gives only answers. You may not speak to him. But rest assured, he will show you the way to Olde Acre"

She walked off then, leaving Edgar standing by himself to soak up the rain like a man made of litmus. And, around him, the sky deepened as the strange bird made itself known on the horizon.

Chapter XXXI
Olde Acre

The door opened with profound silence. Whatever his vocation, the man responsible for maintaining the estate knew his business, lubrication-wise.

But as Edgar and Tanera stepped through the lofty portal a sense of loss overcame him.

Olde carpets, faded through the years, showed signs of wear but remained intact, a testament as to their quality. Dust motes played about like sycamore seeds in autumn twilight and sad paintings hung upon the walls, noting their presence with eerie eyes.

To Edgar, the place looked abandoned.

"It is not," Tanera said.

Again...

Edgar coughed. The dust really was thick and there was a hint of mould on the air too, though he was familiar with that olde tang.

"So who is this man?" Edgar asked, clearing his throat and idly looking around at the various paintings whilst pawing at oddities and artefacts that lined the entrance hall. In particular, a silver quill with a black plume piqued his interest.

As he approached the item he was met with a strange feeling. And, upon picking it up, he was elsewhere entirely. In that moment he saw, or rather felt the quill's last writ. A missive to a lover, no longer in favour and the poisonous seeds acquired to deal with such a malady. Edgar felt both the pain and the misery imbued within the pen. And then it fell from his fingertips to the stone floor, leaving a feather-like impression in the dust below.

He looked up nervously at Tanera, expecting some small reprimand. But she had moved on.

To that end, he saw this fact as free reign to examine other items including a glass cabinet that housed what appeared to be a clean human skull resting upon a bed of snow. How the snow had survived he could not fathom, but upon pressing his hand against the glass he discovered it to be cold all the same, his breath fogging up the pane as he viewed the charmed spectacle within.

A plant, withered and brown-ed sprang to life at his slightest admiration, stealing the moisture from his palm and taking on various shades of green as it started to recover vibrancy and lustre.

And a gem, cut from a ring; an heirloom, shone dully from shafts of light filtering through the modest window of the keep's outer walls. As the street lamps burned brightly, little did they know that their colours might touch the jewel of a woman long since forgotten, yet once an austere source of wealth, forced to pawn her finest possession for want of a single night of ecstasy.

But as strange an item, even for this place, that Edgar did not expect to find, was a length of rope, cut and frayed beyond a certain point. It seemed vaguely familiar and was coiled neatly on a plain table in the corner. No cabinet, no façade.

Edgar only had to go near it before he felt its imprint force into his mind.

Tanera turned to see the still image of Edgar, racked in pain, tears emerging from hollow eyes as his breath failed him. To her, the moment was but mere seconds. To Edgar, it was much too long.

She moved quickly over to him and tore the rope from his hands, shockwaves flowed through her own mind, but they were fleeting.

Edgar stood mute.

"Ah, my favourite heirloom…", spoke a smooth voice from behind them.

There was no need for the man to be looming by the window, but he did so, all the same, arms clasped behind his back, clutching onto something.

Still stunned, Edgar looked over to take in the figure.

He was basically a gaunt shell of a man without an inch of hair upon his person. A dark shawl or scarf was draped across his body to preserve his modesty and as he drew his hands forward it was revealed that in one hand he held a thick book between impossibly long fingers.

Tanera turned. "We seek passage to Olde Acre", she stated simply.

The man bit back a grin. "And have you the coin?" he replied.

"You have it", she said, gesturing to the rope.

The man moved forward to pick up the artefact before closing his eyes and breathing deeply.

A few seconds later his eyes reopened and briefly regarded Edgar before turning back to Tanera.

"*He* has paid. But I still require something from you"

She looked at him then, the Curator, and her eyes narrowed and darkened, slowly twisting into something else. At least, so it seemed to Edgar.

"What would you have?" she replied.

The Curator now openly grinned.

~

As Tanera helped Edgar pack for his journey to Olde Acre she considered the error of her ways.

The Curator had duped and cursed her all in one stroke, bargaining her happiness so that she might join Edgar on the next part of his journey, yet simultaneously robbing her of that option by the simple fact that doing so would cause her more mirth than she now otherwise felt. And even then, she could not now hope for his return, for once again death loomed as the penalty; a geas upon her heart to beat no more should it beat too quick.

Indeed, it was now with quiet dignity she kept these thoughts to herself.

Edgar had no real idea of where he was going, but Tanera assured him that there was something for him to find and that

To this man both are one and the same; an avalanche of entrails and a forbidden pool, the dying and the dead.

There is no regret.

Show me a vision far from this. I cannot stand the malice, and the colour is too much to bear.

When next we meet I shall recall only fragments, sharp edges of a nightmare, broken between the fist and the forge.

There is no regret.

Now only clouded thoughts remain. Amidst forgotten stone and frequent shadows...

Edgar closed the book. He needed a drink.

~

Having followed the darkening clouds for half a day he was comforted when it started raining, for his wineskin was dry and his bladder thrice-empty.

He'd taken to sucking on a ruby for a while to try and lessen how parched he felt but eventually abandoned the idea, having nearly swallowed one wholesale. And, much as the thought of eventually shitting out rare gems appealed to him, he wanted to leave that for another, less demanding time and really *savour* the experience.

He lay on the edge of a mirage, his mouth wide open until enough rain had fallen to create the basics of a genuine oasis around him.

He got to his knees. The mountains were not so far. Another half-day and he would be beneath their lofty reach, the soft, welcoming beginnings of green surrounding their feet and harbouring all manner of beasts and derelict structures.

He staggered several times as night drew in, but thought only of the witch. The path seemed darker here, more superb.

And when the plains wore out he grabbed at the first berries and fruits he could find on the fringes of the forest, regardless of the risk, until he looked like a clown that hadn't washed in weeks.

His mind reeled through a thousand thoughts over and over, but he was unable to settle on a single one of them. And eventually, he focused on the rain; its unbroken banter upon the leaves above him and the broken earth beneath his feet. He felt it run off his nose, and fall free of his hair. And even his cloak could do little to ward off such a prolonged torrent.

In the end, he wandered shirtless, breathless, and soulless.

He couldn't tell at what point he sank to his knees, but from there it was only a short way until his hands pressed against the dirt, his nails becoming dark with soil, and his vision becoming blurred.

The night was blessedly still, and so he did not shiver, but how long he had stayed there he did not know.

He was deep in the wilds now, and with no sense of emerging any time soon. The last road diminished into faded memory, the last person, barely a name upon the wind.

But as the hours crept by and he wondered if he would ever again have the strength to find his feet, the briefest nuance of the forest aura seemed changed. There was music now.

He checked again. No, not music… that was too kind a term. But it broke through the night nonetheless.

He hadn't noticed it at first, but there was also another smell amidst the others. Of a darker wood, of bitter leaves musk within the pine…

There was the smell of damp fire and the aroma of death. His mind recalled the Corpse Flower and that somewhere it still bloomed. Like a crown upon a velvet cushion...

Edgar looked up. Nothing had changed, but his eyes had adjusted to the night. And now he could see in the glimlight, the familiar glow of embers or bright candle. Some… faint structure loomed beyond, masked by low boughs and deep dark.

His feet moved now, with a will of their own, his mind a failing source of sensible thought.

He emerged from the forest by the olde manor. His face was grey and rain fell upon his brow from the drip line of the trees above.

He stared long at the ancient structure, his eyes taking in the missing paint, the broken glass…. The whole thing looked like a discarded toy, but it was beautiful in its neglect.

Edgar wiped his brow and composed himself as waves of music assaulted his mind once again. It was strong there and he knew that finally…at last, he had found the source of that relentless dirge. But that now too, was beautiful.

A striking fox with a coat of embers silently made its way past the front porch and entranceway of the magnificent building. Edgar hardly noticed it. His eyes lingered on the mausoleum, with its stone walls slick with rain and standing stoically in the gloom, the winking light of candles within.

Night made everything so perfect.

He strode over and fox departed, followed quickly by another that he had not initially noticed.

A tiny graveyard of plain slabs of ash adorned the damp earth, crumpled or overgrown, and not a withered bunch of flowers in sight.

The mausoleum was a squat rectangle of solid stone, with a wrought iron fencing about its waist, and ironwork grating about its feet.

He moved inside and out of the rain, following his instincts. He found a dry torch within and a box of fashioned bone with matches and several more candles.

He grubbed around on his knees, fumbling at different areas of the floor grating until eventually, he found what he was looking for.

The metal pulled loose, and a stone drawer emerged.

Inside he found a small music box, a vial of belladonna, and a finely cut ruby the size of a fist. He pocketed the music box and the vial, replacing the secret drawer. The ruby he absently tossed in his hand like an apple, the cold finally starting to creep into his bones.

He spent the night in that place, laid out on the central sarcophagus like a slab of meat. And when sunrise broached the forest once again, he could see his own breath upon the air.

He was still between worlds and, though the music had stopped the night before, he considered that perhaps he now possessed the tool of his own absurdity.

He turned the music box and slowly consumed the nightshade one berry at a time.

Eventually, his fingers failed and the music box dropped to the ground, along with the gem, a dull echo in that haunted place.

He remembered hearing the lowest note on a piano, presumably from somewhere in the manor, and seeing the flash of firelight as someone lit a torch. His eyes were wide. The ruby was gone.

A hand brushed the hair from his face, intangible words finding his ears…

"Amidst forgotten stone and frequent shadows, in search of a new shade of gold,

The persistent joy of inevitable horror and, for a brief moment… a dreamer's moment,

Until enough rain has fallen…"

~

A turquoise river stretched out before Edgar like some serpent, twisting this way and that until its end was lost to view.

Rivulets of cold water ran down his back and a mist hung above the surface, obscuring the trees to either side.

He shivered as a Raven took flight to his left, but he didn't feel terrible. In fact, as the remnants of the elixir turned in his stomach he could recall no other time when he felt so bad, and yet so good.

It was then he retched into the gently flowing waters and dunked his head once more.

As the murk faded from his eyes he heard the crunch of unknown feet on pebbles and turned to regard the sound.

A dark figure moved away from him and further on into the mist. Edgar thought about calling out but decided against it, the moment lost between the passing of time.

There was peace now and plenty of it.

Emerging from the clouds a cool sun sought to burn away the shroud about him and soon his skin was dry as he stood upon the bank, wringing the last of the stream from his clothes.

As he sat on the shore a bottle of wine floated past and he collected it up, forced in the cork, and took a swig.

Not the best vintage, but fair for the price.

After about ten minutes he decided to move on, the wine taking the edge from the sting of the elixir.

Again, he pondered the futility of this expedition.

So he just walked.

With no other logic than that the mysterious figure had walked that way, Edgar headed in the same direction.

For a time he met no one, but not no *thing*.

The Raven dogged his progress and annoyed him from time to time with its various vocal interludes and eventually, the thing flew near enough to him to consider it a sign of friendship. But only when it inhaled the biggest slug he had ever seen did Edgar realise it only wanted him for meat. It had probably seen him getting undressed in the river.

After a while, a cut-through into the trees offered him some relief from the sun, but the price was a fresh attack from the various insects residing beneath the canopies. It was as if they were waiting in ambush, and he lost much blood then.

Before long he was clad once again in his full over-clothes and cloak, sweating in the forests by the river, keeping an eye out for anyone else.

But whether he really saw them Edgar would never know; a figure once again on the horizon, soft hair with the wind and cold surf about the ankles.

He blinked and the mirage was gone.

"What am I even doing here?"

And only the Raven heard his words.

Eventually, he succumbed to tiredness and hunger and flattened down a small clearing in which to spend the night.

Not being an adept woodsman nor having easy access to a box of matches, he let the darkness take hold gradually and was pleasantly surprised to find a family of fireflies providing the evening entertainment, as well as the evening meal.

As he crunched on not one, but two of the phosphorescent creatures, and juices flowed gently down his chin, he idly watched the spectacle before him.

As the flies danced and wove he found himself using the Sack of Ire as a make-shift pillow and gradually drifted into a gentle sleep, the sound of unknown wildlife filling his ears like a foreign song drifting above amber highlights.

Dreams came to him then, rare of late, but present nonetheless.

His mind turned to the forgotten abode of a by-gone magician; a great house, dark and brooding upon an open cliff, with only the world before it. As he traversed the rooms he found he already knew which way to go. A living door, touched by the Art; such secrets lay within. If only he knew the words...

Dozens had tried over the years. All had failed. And now the inhabitants of the house were among that number, whose minds had been wantonly addled by the charm upon the door.

And as he dreamt, several hooded eyes watched from a discreet distance; glittering gems beside the fire. And when his lips moved they noted what was said with patient precision. But by morning they were gone.

A pale form reached out, blurred to his mind's eye, holding a scarlet rose. He sat up, blinking in the half-light of dawn, clutching nothing more than the rapidly fading memories of his astral foray.

Stretching, he strained to hear the sound of a waterfall not too far away and decided to make towards it. He never noticed the marking upon the floor.

~

The sound of water grew louder and it was then that Edgar laid eyes upon an absolutely textbook waterfall, its silvery mane descending from on high to create a heady mist of spray below and feed the river of which he had followed up until now.

He edged forward until, caution aside, he stood beneath the curtain.

He thought his heart might stop then, such was the shock, but he instead found himself laughing.

He never saw the Three.

Behind every magic door lies a risk, an unknown, an Unknown unknown.
Behind every magic door, there is a chance for everything or nothing.

Or worse.

Chapter XXXII
Relief

Edgar wiped the spittle from his face. Or he would have were he not tied to an antique chair, rough, homespun cord chaffing his wrists like a champion wrestler.

Hot words landed upon his ears fashioned from ill-tempered tongues.

He was still laughing.

Three crones circled him like vultures would an abandoned carcass and it wasn't long before they tired of Edgar's good humour.

The eldest and most gnarled of the three thrust a wizened hand in the direction of a nearby window. It imploded, filling the room with shards of glass like razor-sharp confetti. Rainbows of light shot forth from moving prisms in a dazzling array of enmity.

The youngest and most beautiful crone held aloft her arm until the ruffled feathers of the Merrow Bird alit upon her wrist. If it weighed anything, Edgar couldn't tell. But the woman's face held a permanent solemnity that could have been painted with oils, framed with gold, and hung on the wall.

She turned then to Edgar, gesturing the bird closer.

"Laugh all you like now…"

Edgar calmed a bit then and shook his head.

"You have the wrong man"

The Three looked at each other then.

"He lies", they spoke together in a trio of discordance.

Awful.

Edgar eyed all three of them in turn.

"I speak the truth…"

"He wears the armour!" the three interrupted, crowing amongst themselves.

It was no use. This was not going to end well.

Edgar let his mind wander and the chatter of the Three drift away like a paper boat.

Oh, you don't dream. You just...fade away...

His mind turned then to flames; their luminescence against the stark nothingness of the void.

He felt their warmth, their brilliance, their pain.

And through those unforgettable visions, he channelled their fury, their ire, their aid.

As his surroundings came into focus once again the ropes about his wrists fell away in charred mockery of their former selves; remnants of forgotten restraint and a sign of things to come.

The first of the Three had only half-inhaled to speak as Edgar's mailed fist clamped around her throat. The second tried to interfere and bit off her own tongue as a second fist connected with her jaw, blood bubbling out like a backed-up sink.

The Third, and the most cowardly by far, struggled frantically against the door, her wits beside her and her dignity on the floor.

Edgar dropped the first, rapidly cooling body without ceremony or sadness.

The second lay choking on her own blood and turned glazed eyes towards a horror.

~

Richter loomed like some malfunctioning dreadnaught of which tales were once told by children around a failing fire, faces half-stuffed with mallow and bags under their young, haunted eyes.

Then, without a care, the Merrow Bird appeared and gently landed upon the tip of his sword, ruined as it was, without weight nor apology.

And in the glint of those eyes, those uncannily human eyes...
For a brief moment, a dreamer's moment ...

Numbly, Edgar dropped to one knee, the hollow sound of the door rattling beside him. A peculiar rage of guttural aspirations beyond blended into the sound of the blood pulsing through his ears.

He looked at his own hands then and saw one stained deep red with the blood of men, the other black from the quill. One retained calluses of some other life, the other, the burn from a match burnt too low. These weren't his hands.

His eyes began to fill.

These weren't his eyes.

He dropped his sword with a clatter and the Merrow Bird vanished beyond sight, a withered rose trailing in its wake.

And as he breathed deeply he wasn't even sure whose lungs he used; which mouth he opened, what air he breathed.

Turning to the door he glanced down at the last crone, shivering in a heap beside it. She had tried and failed.

He opened the door and saw the world before him.

Edgar took a step forward and Richter followed. They closed their eyes, the last of a rare precipitation forcing its way from concealment.

And quietly, but carefully, lips moved; the last breath caressing a dry tongue to form a singular, rough-hewn word…

Relief.

Chapter XXXIII
The Edge of Paradise

Autumn rays fell low upon the fallow fields.

How long must he spend there, a wraith amidst the brume, a careless thought within the cluster? Olde leaves adrift, heavy foot fall, in that place where daylight fades away...

Tanera was waiting.

And when he crossed the Bridge of Grith, with its lichen-encrusted long-hallowed boards nothing could touch him again.

It took some time for the smoke to clear and the timbers to become visible and corporeal, but in the end, he stood at its apex.

Herbylocke reclined against a tree on the other side, idly flipping a coin for no good reason.

"Slugabedde. I was wondering when you would bother to show up. After a hard day doing nothing, it's finally time to wake up..." he called across.

Edgar didn't bother to humour him.

And as he approached the edge of the Bridge, Edgar stooped to the verge-side, plucking a flower from the ground – A Snakes-Head Fritillary.

Edgar stared at the running water for a while then, and eventually, his gaze shifted from its restless design.

Beyond stretched the wild, roving vista of a dark Winter Gloaming; Olde stones, tall trees, and vast lakes. The moon perched gently now, whilst the sun went patiently, hiding from view.

Somewhere out there formed a new refrain, the signature as if Quinne drew new breath, the notes drifting on the wind like an alluring spell.

And beyond... the cavern.

Richter approached, breathing deeply, his eyes glistening like late-summer rain.

"Where will you go?" he asked Edgar.

"I will return to the Blacke", he replied. "I don't think I'm quite ready to let it all go" He turned to the knight. "Perhaps… I'll take one last look at that olde castle we visited. I think there may be something for me there."

Richter stared at him for a moment, trying not to break into a grin.

"You mean you want another look at that *chest*"

Edgar shrugged, kicking a stone from the edge of the shore into the water where it disappeared without remark.

Richter sighed, looking ahead distractedly. Even his exhalation on the cold, moonlit air seemed to smooth the furrow from the knight's brow, and as he leant upon the rails of the olde bridge, he spoke softly.

"You know, there was a time when all I thought about was my final breath. And now ahead of me I can see so much more"

He turned to Edgar. "And you helped me, Edgar. You opened my eyes. I owe you everything". He paused, the crisp air blowing a lock of long-grown hair from his eyes.

"But tell me, truthfully. What do *you* see?"

Edgar turned to look, his eyes glazing as of pale morning frost.

"Honestly?"

The olde knight nodded slowly, the subtle dilation in his eyes succumbing to a form of hope.

Edgar sighed, his shoulders not even slumping.

"Nothing"

~

In the cavern, pale moonlight filtered in from without, and the sweet scent of cinnamon embers took form amidst the black, gently fed from an ill-tended fire by the edge of the pool.

Tanera floated upon the water like a forgotten garment, her eyes fixed on some unseen mark.

And this was how Edgar found her.

His heart leapt and failed with equal abandon and, casting his sword aside, he hurriedly picked his way down the small rocks and along the black sand before she stopped him in his tracks, her voice permeating the space like an over-ripe fruit.

"If I was to lay down and strip myself bare, how would you proceed, how would you dare?

"What if I was to tell you there's something here? Do you see it, something there? A terrible fascination; a darker mote against the grey; gone when you look, there when you stray"

"I have stood on both sides of the coin; the very edge and the metal in between. When it's beneath it's too late, and by then, it's on top. Melodies of affliction adrift upon ebon waters, discord beneath the surface and bones beneath the wake. And as I sink back into the Void I take with me the tenets of reality, the foundations of hope and the truth of solitude"

Edgar just looked on as she slipped beneath the oily deep, a pale stone thrown to grasping hands, an enigma of existence. And where she would go he did not know, only that he could not follow. At length, the fritillary fell from his hands to lay gently upon the surface of the water.

And soon before the last, a dark mirror lay undisturbed before him. No fracture or distortion, but perfection of night behind the glass; reverberations of a fading voice, a haunting lamentation.

He knew then that he was alone.

Part III

Chapter XXXIV
A Song by the Fire

It had been a month since the Bridge of Grith, and Edgar found himself going around in circles. He was haunted by his final conversation with Tanera, and try as they might, his feet never found their way back to the Blacke.

Instead, he had squandered his coin in every tavern from Sluice to Ire and it was there his feet began to slow.

Richter had joined him begrudgingly at first, but as his past began to creep up on him once more the thought of solitude within the keep stole the resolve from his heart.

There was work left to do and, now finding themselves back in the area, the pair sought to tie up loose ends. But it was an endeavour that would require an embellishment to their meagre company.

And so the pair shouldered their way into Thee Olde Leathern Glove tavern. A known location for adventurers, merchants, and thieves, and as the only establishment for miles around, it was standing-room only.

Edgar had heard of it but never imagined he would actually end up there. By contrast, Richter knew the barkeep well.

The pair could barely breathe so heavy was the smoke that hung about the common room, the fog and rain without that seemed so hostile before, now a pleasant memory.

"Just let me do the talking", said Richter through the corner of his mouth as they inched closer to the bar.

He had heard that before…

Upon spotting the proprietor amidst the throng of flailing arms and foaming beer, the knight called out.

"Forsythe! Stand an ale for an olde friend?"

The barkeep looked up instantly, his current mug of ale spilling over as the keg remained pouring. His face darkened and then he broke eye contact.

As the pair reached the taps, Richter pressed the matter. "Forsythe!?"

The man kept his head down and busied himself with half a dozen orders and wiping down the countertop. It was loud in the tavern and Richter's voice disappeared within the aural maelstrom.

Edgar looked around uncomfortably. There was clearly some unfinished business between the two, and he wasn't quite sure how much longer he wanted to linger amidst the hostile faces he saw around him.

However, eventually, his eyes fell upon a group of men in heavy leather armour and rusted chain.

Daggers and swords hung off them like dew. They seemed just the sort of people he was looking for. After all, that's why they were there.

He was about to suggest to Richter that they venture over to the table and make enquiries when he noticed that everything had gone quiet.

He snapped out of his reverie to find Richter pinned down behind the bar, the man known as Forsythe holding a knife to his neck.

"What going on!?" demanded Edgar.

Forsythe favoured him with a glance. "You in with his man, boy?" uttered the barkeep.

Edgar made eye contact with Richter.

"I am…"

Forsythe bared his teeth. "Don't trust him, lad. He still owes me more than just coin, and I'd be willing to wager he owes you, too. Claims to be a knight, and he's worse than any highwayman I ever knew, aren't ya!?" he slammed Richter's head down against the counter.

"There's no need for that!" cried Edgar, trying to placate the man.

"Here" He doled out several rubies and sapphires from a pouch onto the bar, the candlelight enhancing each facet to bestow wonder upon the viewer.

Forsythe dropped Richter like a sack of offal; his eyes never leaving the gems.

"And there's more where that came from, *if* you can help us out", added Edgar.

The barkeep hastily scooped up the jewels as though he was afraid they would disappear any moment, and slowly looked up.

"Who are you?"

~

Later on that evening Edgar and Richter each nursed a flagon of ale by the failing fire of the innes' common room.

Arrivals had dried up and the place was now nearly empty, not one traveller having taken them up on their offer of coin in exchange for unbridled brandishing of cold steel.

Either they were paying too little, which seemed unlikely, or the task was simply too daunting. Edgar wasn't sure. Not having been an adventurer for long, he had no real expectations of what lay ahead, only that he couldn't or rather didn't want to go alone. Richter on the other hand didn't really possess the mind of a sane man, having lost of his fear of death long ago and simply living bowel movement to bowel movement in search of redemption.

It could be entirely possible that the task was too great.

Just then, a thin wretch of a man edged his way in from the outside, rain dripping from the bells of his hair and warping the wood of the battered lute slung over his shoulder like a week olde pheasant. He loped over to the bar and mutely placed a large coin on the counter with finality; a silent exchange that saw him leave with a full bottle of brandy.

Edgar and Richter exchanged glances.

As the man took up residence in a dark corner of the tavern Richter shrugged and pushed out of his chair. When he was within about three paces of the newcomer and his shadow darkened the corner further, he was stopped in his tracks.

"Leave me alone"

It was a voice a breath above a whisper, draped in sadness, but with an undertone of threat.

The man was an enigma and Richter wasn't sure how to proceed. He was about to talk when the man threw his head back, the bells in his hair rattling with a flourish as the bottle pressed against his pursed lips. Several long swallows later and the man's head hung low once again.

Richter returned to the fire.

"Not interested?" asked Edgar.

Richter said nothing.

~

The next morning saw the inne playing host to only a few patrons, those starting their day with cheap meals or beginning their night early with cheaper ale.

Edgar and Richter partook in neither, having slept late, and forfeited what time they could spare refuelling their bodies for a few more precious hours of slumber. It was a fair bargain. Besides, Richter didn't really fancy another encounter with Forsythe, preferring to slip away with the debt still unpaid. Again, it was a fair bargain.

To add further to the deficit, the pair had purloined a couple of good horses from outside the inne to expedite their departure, having forgotten the price to be paid upon their unfamiliar arses.

For a change, the rain had ceased and the harsh morning sun was doing its best to work light out onto the world, succeeding only in a developing grey. Puddles glinted here and there and steam rose up from the ground like a cauldron.

"What now?" asked Edgar as the pair ambled down the road aimlessly, the monotonous clap of horse hooves upon the road becoming a mantra.

Richter was quiet for a long time, eventually releasing a sigh and sagging slightly in his saddle.

"I honestly don't know"…

He stared ahead, eyes unfocused, heading toward a dark place. Edgar knew the signs.

"We'll just have to go by ourselves", he said at length, trying to sound positive, though he couldn't believe the words came out of his own mouth. But then, he was in search of treasure.

Richter merely offered a deep shrug, the sound of his mail stark against the natural sounds around them.

They carried on down that endless road for what seemed like days, not seeing a soul to tell a tale or a wagon upon the dirt.

As late afternoon approached and the puddles were drying up, a sombre sunset began its slow descent over the realm. They would need to make camp soon or simply continue under the modest shroud of darkness until the next inne.

It was then that the pair noticed a singular form trudging along the side of the road in front of them, head bowed and what appeared to be a lute slung over his back. Richter urged his horse to a trot until he came level with the figure, who kept walking despite the interruption.

"I thought it was you", Richter stated, with a forced laugh, leaning down from his horse.

"Leave me alone. I have a headache", Came the curt reply.

Richter sat a little straighter in his saddle, breathing in the heady, early evening air, trying not to seem too put out.

"I say, I wondered if you wanted some company on the road. We were considering making camp soon and could use an extra lookout. We have provisions".

The man continued to trudge at the exact same pace, his eyes fixed on the ground, the gentle tinkling of the bells on his hair and boots making a mockery of his mood.

Edgar trotted up to join the solemn pair and, upon seeing Richter's expression, decided to try a different tack.

The stranger briefly looked up at Edgar's approach, his cracked mask barely hiding his disdain.

"Will you be following me all the way? Or do I have to cut out your tongues to get a minute's peace around here?" he asked.

Edgar backed away.

At this, Richter began to unsheathe his sword, but the very moment he had cleared the hilt the stranger stopped and withdrew a slender blade quicker than Edgar could follow.

Within a moment he had Richter's horse by the reigns and a knife against its throat.

Richter froze, his sword only half ready, and there was a moment where the two locked eyes.

It must have been something that Richter gave away in that glance, but the man cocked his head to the side, and it seemed to Edgar that beneath the mask an impish grin made itself known.

He then drew the full length of the blade across the horse's throat, causing the animal to go berserk and jet fountains of dark blood in all directions.

Richter was summarily thrown to the ground and Edgar's own horse carried him briskly away in a panic. As he turned to look back he caught a glimpse of the strange man standing over Richter, seeming to relish in the spray of blood washing over him. The noise was haunting, and by the time he had convinced his own horse to slow it was no longer interested in returning the slaughter.

Edgar dismounted and within seconds the horse bolted, taking everything with it apart from the sword on his belt and the map in his pocket.

He could hear thunder now and, in the distance, it had started raining again. It would reach them soon.

Meanwhile, Richter crawled around on the ground like a beast, the wind knocked out of him and spitting blood from the impact of the fall. The maniac above him had stopped revelling in the blood and now stood calmly fiddling with a stiletto.

The clouds reached them then and Richter looked up, blinking blood and rain from his eyes, a placating hand held up, grasping at the loose ends of reason.

"A warm meal, the companionship of others, and a song by the fire…" he rasped.

The stranger just looked at him.

Richter tried to straighten.

"Is this it then?"

Edgar skidded to a stop, seeing the exchange, feeling foolish for even having his sword drawn.

There was nothing he could do.

The stranger turned to regard him, trails of blood and water mixing like watercolours upon the mask fixed to his face; a macabre palette upon a portrait yet unveiled.

He began to laugh.

~

That night Edgar, Richter, and the stranger now known as 'Grey' sat huddled around a fire on the edge of the forest. Conversation was minimal, but the meal was passably good. Edgar had never tasted horse stew before, at least not to his knowledge, and he had come to the conclusion that he wouldn't mind tasting it again.

Once he calmed down, Grey had pragmatically suggested that they drag the beast into the forest and eat like kings until the sun came up. It wasn't until Richter somewhat sullenly informed him that the wine they had left over was in the bags stowed upon Edgar's horse, which coincidentally had run away, that the smirk finally disappeared from the jester's face. At least, that's what Richter figured. The man had continued to wear his mask until he found a suitably dark shadow in which to eat, the flickering of the fire offering teasing glimpses but nothing more. He was unreadable.

The rain maintained its heavy descent and, although the tree canopy was thick, fat droplets continued to work their way down to nestle amidst the travellers, and it wasn't long until conversation dried up entirely, each man pulling a cloak over his head, before leaning up against a tree to prepare for a shockingly bad night's sleep.

Grey had suggested a gentle song by firelight, but was promptly shut down by a close-up view of Richter's middle finger.

"No need to be rude," he said and closed his eyes.

Edgar focused his thoughts on the rain, the irregular patterns somewhat soothing in the bleak wilderness; a mantra from which he could slip away to serenity amidst the dark.

But, of course, his mind would not let him fully let depart, and before long he began to dwell on Richter's words, lamenting their quest and thoughtlessly spoken by a midnight fire.

I fear it is beyond us…

He looked over at Grey, and then at the knight. Both were asleep.

He stayed there then with his own thoughts; those about their task, the taste of horsemeat, and of the patterns of rain…

Chapter XXXV
In the Twilight Hours

In the twilight hours, Edgar climbed the hallowed steps of the cathedral and found himself met with an enormous, iron-banded, oaken door, framed with peaked stone. Tentatively he motioned towards the handle and made his way inside. A wave of peace and the flicking light of a thousand off-white candles assaulted his senses and his shoulders dropped somewhat as he took in the spectacle. Richter ascended the stairs behind him, leaving his sword sheathed, for now.

Together they took a moment to drink in the atmosphere. It was the best Edgar had felt in weeks.

However, it was all a charade; a trick of the light, some faint magic or charm, and the desecration was obvious. When viewed straight on they were faced with perfection. But from the corner of their eyes, all they could see was ruin.

Richter took a few steps forward, tossing some coins onto the ground in offering, and they rang out clearly into the silence of the night.

And gently, along the fabric of sound, soft singing insisted itself upon the visitors, though where it came from, none could say.

"There is a strong glamour here"

The voice was that of Herbylocke, who had come to join them beneath the high-vaulted ceilings.

Grey was there too.

Herbylocke had his eyes closed as if listening to the beauty of the music, only to be lost within the folds of its endless memories. And then, by inches, the harmonies drifted into discord, purity no more, to reveal a place of anguish and bleak lamentation.

When he opened his eyes Richter stood ready, his longsword resting unsheathed, lightly on one shoulder. Edgar looked over at Herbynlocke whose eyes now smouldered as he had never seen before; a latent power held back by conjured will.

Grey stood silent, his head bowed, a blade in each hand.

For a moment, Edgar felt foolish. He was no adventurer. He was no great conjurer or swordsman. He was nothing.

And yet, a blade somehow found its way into his hand, and he stood just like the others.

The meagre group approached the altar and Richter pulled aside the cloth.

It was a sarcophagus. It had always been a sarcophagus. And now, with chalice and candle, it became an inanimate charlatan of ill-practised art.

Without preamble, Richter passed his stiletto, the misericorde to Edgar.

"You must be the first", uttered the knight, his hard voice ringing clear about the walls and stone columns.

Edgar approached the mock altar and began to inscribe his own name onto the stone. But a pervasive ringing began insisting upon his consciousness and each stroke of the blade became a hard-won chore. And, before long, he had stopped altogether.

Richter exchanged a worried look with Herbynlocke, who took a step nearer to Edgar.

"Still your thoughts, embrace the distractions. They are but of a distant symphony. "They are just noise"

Edgar completed his name, though it looked written as though by a child, and looked up for approval. He was met by the stern face of Richter as he took the knife and braced himself against the chiming within his own mind; the wind against leaves of gilded iron, tumbling upon hills of gold.

Eventually, Richter's name had been added to the macabre roster and Grey took a sharp step forward, the strange man's bells tinkling in mockery against the misery he heard from the voices without; chains against stone, and empty cans passing along endless corridors.

He leant his head back before holding out the knife. His mind was already elsewhere with an aural assault of the faded echoes of drums and gentle voices.

Which left Herbynlocke, whose own battle was left unanswered, for one reason or another, and before long all four had their names inscribed upon the sacred stone.

It was a marker of their passing, a memory of their demise; a statement of their dreams.

And one by one the mage began to extinguish the candles upon the altar, each incrementally opening an aperture beneath the sarcophagus until only a single flame was left lit; a shining hope, the last remnant of normality.

A set of stairs yawned into view beneath their feet, vanishing beyond or normal sight. Herbynlocke caught Edgar's eye before peering into the gloom.

"Remember, Edgar, there are many things down there, none of which require light"

Edgar met his gaze.

"Then I'll be right at home"

~

Grey danced like a flame. The bells in his hair and on his boots gave the scene a chilling edge; a once joyful sound now entwined with the melody of death.

The tune came to him like a rehearsal, the violence a fitting performance for a timely conclusion.

Nobody knew what sweet sounds drifted through his head at that time, but when he emerged from the utter gloom and covered in gore, he wore a smile not only of contentment but of joy.

He wiped down bloodied steel and brushed back the braids in his hair. And, for but a moment, he removed his mask to dab at his brow, but it was too dark to see. Though, from what he saw, Edgar considered him to be a handsome man. But again, he reminded himself, it was too dark to see.

Herbynlocke brought to life a lamp, and with a dusky glow the party witnessed the slick floor beneath their feet, a half-dozen grotesque figures delicately sliced apart with faces against the dust.

Grey replaced his mask and furnished the company with a flourished bow. Herbynlocke merely raised an eyebrow as he led them on, through the labyrinth of darkness and debris.

Fallen idols were commonplace, and occasionally, gems and coins made themselves known, only to be quickly pocketed by Edgar before anyone else got their share. It mattered not; they were not here for trinkets or gold. They sought the Heirloom.

~

The four pressed forward through the shadows by meagre lamplight, the ancient map no more than a tattered rag by which they stacked their hopes. It would have served better as a dishcloth, or as something to buff a shine to their shoes. In that dark place, the markings meant nothing, mere scrawls upon the paper, indiscriminate and indecipherable.

And, despite Herbynlocke's best efforts, it wasn't long until they were lost.

"You were supposed to lead the way!" growled Grey through gritted teeth, a blade held up against Herbynlocke's throat as he pressed him against the wall.

"Grey", Richter said sternly.

The minstrel cocked his head sideways to regard him before finally yielding and releasing the mage.

He turned away in disgust, the bells in his hair a muted charade.

Richter leaned in.

"This map is useless" commented the knight, casting aside the parchment. Up until now, he was content to follow, sword at the ready should danger occur. But he soon realised the full weight of their folly.

They were at a crossroads within the dungeon labyrinth. And it was anyone's guess at which trail to follow.

"Worse yet" added Herbynlocke. "But my magic down here wains. The pressure is too great"

Even as he spoke the lamplight had dimmed between breaths, and he moved like smoke.

It was nearly pitch.

Edgar looked around, aghast. "What are we going to do!?" he asked, panic limning his voice, the words disappearing quickly down the dark corridors.

"Ah, fuck this", spat Grey, interrupting. He pulled out his twin blades, performed a fancy bow, and marched off down one of the many tunnels. They would never see him again.

Richter exhaled deeply, the tip of his sword coming to rest on the dusty ground. "I'm hungry"

There was a moment then, where the three remaining companions simply stood at stared as the lamplight ebbed away and they could no longer see the hands in front of their own faces.

This is all wrong.

And from the black came other noises. As their hearing became more acute, the sounds they heard before returned until they had bodies of their own; material behind the madness.

Edgar heard the slight shift of Richter's sword scraping against the ground, a sign that he had readied his blade, but against what he could not say. And from where he did not know.

Just then, a dim light made itself known on the peripheral of vision, a distant star in an otherwise empty night.

Edgar noticed Richter shuffle his feet, presumably to face this new terror, when he heard the tinkle of bells.

Three long heartbeats later and who he thought to be Grey was upon them, his wild hair and macabre outfit streaming out behind him like a torn banner.

He carried a lamp, though where he had acquired it none could say.

"Not that way!" the figure shrieked as he loped past, even shouldering Richter out of the way in his haste to outrun his pursuers.

It was only then that they realised their newfound light source was quickly making away from them.

"After him!" cried Richter, moving from a jog into a run, such as it was in all his armour.

What followed next was a blur in Edgar's mind.

At some point he stumbled, tripping over his own feet, perhaps, or even some coin. It didn't matter.

The sounds came upon him like a wave.

He became aware of Herbynlocke stood over him, eyes like coal, worse than coal. Richter was shouting.

There were sparks, perhaps of some blade against the wall, or maybe armour.

And then the hallway filled with a light so bright Edgar found himself screaming along with the rest.

He clawed at his own eyes and saw such dreaded afterimages as would disturb his sleep forever.

~

Somewhere else, a different part of him thought he witnessed a court jester cartwheel down a hallway, a blade in each hand and a smile from behind a cracked mask.

A knight picked up a dented shield, blood pouring from the tip of his sword in horrific rivulets of deepest claret.

And all the while some, there was a haunting melody, permeating everything. It became a rictus; a chaotic rime beyond explanation, to create a place so wrong as to become obsession, ravens tapping on the window… laughter on the wind.

~

Edgar awoke bathed in sunlight filtering from a shaft above.

He lay upon a sarcophagus that was not only cold to touch but had the lid mostly removed.

No…Not *on* a sarcophagus.

In a sarcophagus.

And whilst bright rays played down upon him, some, olde moisture crept down the walls as though the room held its own sadness.

Edgar sat up. There were birds down there and footsteps on the threshold of hearing.

Where was Richter?...

And Herbynlocke and that strange fellow, Grey!?...

Oh yes...

Edgar swallowed with a dry throat accompanied by dry lips and slowly pushed himself free of the tomb.

He began to recognise fragments of his surroundings. Not so much by sight, but by feel. The atmosphere was rich with memory and, whilst disquieting, was somewhat charming in its own, forgotten way.

He took a deep breath and found with it came a sound upon the peripheral of hearing.

It sounded like piano, a familiar note upon the wind.

He shared a brief laugh with himself and braced against a wall. A few tears fell then, and as he pulled his hand away the grime of ages showed upon his palm.

He turned and made towards the stairs leading up from the tomb.

He climbed each step as though it were a mountain and slowed before the top, frightened of what he might see.

And the further he climbed the clearer the melody became.

His mind reeled back to days of olde, of casual opulence and colourful words. The grey veneer peeled back to reveal a staircase fringed with gold, a painting on each wall, laughter through the halls, and wine upon the rack.

His breaths became deeper until he was dizzy with the effort and, by then, he found himself at the top.

The cloister was just how he remembered it, the bent willow brushing the flagstones free of snow, the several arches, and the minarets bathed in shadow.

A wind blew gentle eddies of snow about his feet, dancing as though celebrating a winter ball.

And when Edgar looked down he found a small note, written with familiar hand, fetched up against his boot, which he stopped to collect and then pocketed.

Brushing his hair aside he moved on and followed the sound of the music. It was comforting, inviting, warming in that desolate place; a place he once called home.

He moved through the cloister and made for the keep.

A single door lay open, strange considering the weather.

He peered through and only then realised he had drawn his sword.

Here he found Herbynlocke delicately playing the piano, Richter by his side, clad in a rich, red tabard and enjoying a large goblet of wine.

Both wore broad smiles and greeted him warmly.

Edgar listened to the music and tasted the wine, and as he sank back into a leathern armchair he closed his eyes for a moment in contentment.

It wasn't right.

It was all too wonderful, all too perfect; all too magic.

His eyes flicked briefly open again, as though drugged. But he managed a second glance.

No, Richter was not left-handed…

Come to think of it, could Herbynlocke even play the piano? *Perhaps…*

He took another swallow of wine to steady himself, and the liquid was like ice upon the pallet and hands about the throat.

The soft singing he had heard in the background now began to fade.

There was a flash, and the melody began to unravel.

No.

No…

~

"No!"

Edgar came round to witness what looked vaguely like a head being removed from its torso, bent double, mere inches from his face, and the metal-clad arse of a knight replacing it.

Seconds later, the arse and the body it belonged to crouched and another body flew overhead, heaved up by the knight.

Richter.

233

The man span as he finished the throw and cleaved into another horror emerging from the dark, until a fourth figure assaulted him from behind, driving him to his knees with wicked strikes.

He flailed wildly in front of Edgar's unfocused eyes, his sword rendered useless as he could not reach behind him to remove the assailant.

And then the thing undid itself, exploding like a balloon filled with offal and Edgar found himself inhaling some of the remnants, his mouth slack at the spectacle before him, his wits gone and clinging onto the edge of sanity.

Fire then followed in a blazing arc, bringing a curse from the knight, but ultimately giving him enough time to disengage from combat and bring up his guard. It was all he could do not to cast aside his armour as hot as it was from Herbylocke's attack, but he stood firm.

Herbylocke released another bolt and the walls cracked. Shrieks fell upon sensitive ears like crockery tossed into an empty well and droves of unseen denizens lost their grip on life.

Edgar continued to stare as the knight before him stood guard whilst his olde friend, who had never so much hurt a fly before him, tore lives apart like they were bread at a feast.

"My power wanes here…"

Edgar shuddered.

Just then, Richter noticed him for the first time.

"Come on!" he shouted, looking confused at Edgar's lack of reaction.

"Get up!" he offered, shouldering his shield and lending a hand.

Unsteadily Edgar gained his feet.

"We've got to get out of here, but it's a dead-end!" cried Richter.

Edgar merely looked around; at the carnage, at the blood, at the darkness…

"The map was a sham. There is nothing back there but an olde tomb. A place where I don't particularly want to spend the night! At least not *this* night…"

"Where is Grey?" asked Edgar, considering it a weird question to be so concerned about the strange man at this time.

"It's just us!..."

He took a moment to slay another creature that had avoided Herbylocke's assault and turned back to face Edgar.

"Can you hold this?" the knight gave him his shield.

Edgar took it without question and looked on as Richter carved through another body that seemed fashioned from many. The two-handed stroke saw the thing almost vertically halved.

He tried to blink the madness away, but the sounds remained and he found himself losing control, if indeed he had any in the first place.

But before he knew it, his feet had taken a step back; then another. And then another.

The sounds grew less. The shadows grew darker.

And then he was in the tomb.

Chapter XXXVI
The Cold Dark

In the cold dark, Edgar handed the cup to Richter.

"You first"

Reverently, the knight took the gift and brought it gently to his lips.

Edgar held his breath as he witnessed the warrior imbibe, his pupils dilating in that darkest of places, the furrow smoothing from his brow and, eventually, he gently closed his eyes.

Small drops clung stubbornly to Richter's upper lip, the haggard knight's ragged beard soaking up the eager remnants.

As he continued to watch it seemed as though his torch grew brighter, at which the man before him appeared somewhat younger, less beaten, further toward elusive peace…

No… It was just a trick of the light.

He saw what he wanted to see, an apparition brought forth by his own realisation that indeed all he saw was an olde man swallowing wine from an even older cup.

No… It was something else.

But before he could formulate another thought and push his mind in another direction, Richter had pressed the cup into his hands.

"Go on", he urged, a light shining in his leaden eyes.

Edgar looked briefly down at the dark liquid and the unseen shapes within, taking a moment before he brought the cup to his own, parched lips.

He caught Richter's eye as he tasted the initial tang of metal, and felt the cool, smooth rubies pressed against his fingertips. A subtle glint of gold was the coup de grace.

Only then, when the wine met his tongue did he relent and afford himself the luxury of closing his eyes.

And when he did it was as though he could still see, albeit through a blackened veil.

The world around him had changed.

He sat upon a mossy bank of chipped gravestones, somewhere beneath the night.

Rain soaked through his clothes just as sweet carmine worked between his lips and sought his wanting veins.

Edgar rested his head against the austere slab behind him.

So it had all been a lie.

For a brief moment, a dreamer's moment, he had thought he'd seen the same look in Richter's eyes that he'd seen beneath the surface of the pool.

Only now there was no reflection, and within his own mind, the pieces began to float away.

Stricken upon weathered boards that fell beneath undulating waves, his eyes grew darker, his breathing less keen, until he felt the need to lay down in that very place, the broken earth a gentle mattress, and fractured stone amidst the rains.

His body twitched and his breathing caught.

Smiling now, he remembered that dark place, where he was before, and the indefinable halls beneath his feet; of midnight foray's and staged laughter, the forest between worlds, and a touch of new-born sky.

Music wove throughout endless galleries, home to a dozen forgotten portraits and the smell of burning of parchment, beyond which the beautiful taste of onions and frequent tears would shed. There was treasure somewhere too. But that could have been anywhere, the glistening smirk of a coin half-hidden...

At last, he lay still.

And that was where they found him.

And so it was my curse;

I vowed to unearth, all the secrets of the underworld.

And dark are the paths, unhindered by light.

Grey skies and grey winds.

And a tide that stole the madness from a dreamless slumber…

Epilogue
Waxing Theta

There was only one standard left flying; a tattered rag upon a broken shaft, but still catching the wind enough to resemble a trapped crow.

About its base, a cluster of heavily armour knights lay piled upon each other and through the top of the mass, a lone fist remained to hold the flag, rivulets of blood running down knuckles free of skin.

Edgar and Richter cautiously approached, a few nearby crows taking their leave. The level of carnage was beyond anything Edgar had ever seen, even the most descriptive of paintings.

Richter merely looked on.

As they neared the standard-bearer the insignia became clear; A bejewelled cup, shining gold upon a field of ebony. It was a simple design, yet it held a reverence that still felt powerful even though the material was soiled and torn.

Richter leaned in and prised the banner shaft away from cold, still fingers. He turned to face Edgar.

Could it be?...

Edgar looked around at the mess.

Where to start?

He did not have to wait long, as Richter, having cast aside the standard, hauled cadaver after cadaver from the pile and into the mud.

Edgar set to the task as well, though with less success, and found that the deeper he dug, the more horror he saw. And by the time the pair had gotten to the bottom of the pile, there was nothing left but an assortment of limbs and a heady mush of thick mud and gore.

Richter wiped his hands on the banner, casting a despairing look along the line of bodies.

Edgar echoed his thoughts.

"None of them have it"

Richter thought for a moment before something caught his eye. He reached down and uncurled the fist of one of the dead. Within lay a ruby the size of a good acorn.

Richter straightened up, holding the gem to his eye, and then his gaze swept the horizon.

Edgar held his breath in anticipation.

The response came at last.

"No"

~

The fire had gone cold; some indication of how long he'd lain there. Peripheral visions came and went; the mist before sunrise, the fall of night. Tales around a failing fire, haunted eyes of shocking vesper, and the brilliance of twilight augury...

The cup lay half-buried in the mud, tarnished and clinging on to the dregs of a memory, submerged beneath an amber pool of inebriation.

Edgar's face mirrored the state of the cup, as did the rest of his body.

Beside him, Richter lay draped over a log, resembling a crushed tin can. His hair was matted against his face and his sword was slowly becoming one with the earth.

Edgar began to push himself up, but the world span and he fought the urge to vomit. And then he thought, why fight it? And he retched into his own bodily impression in the mud; a somewhat bleak mould to create a half-digested simulacrum.

He shook his head and picked up the cup. And it was then his blood ran cold.

It wasn't the one.

He wiped the hair from his face and looked more closely to be sure. No, it didn't feel the same. And wasn't it encrusted with rubies and not garnet?

It was too early for this...

He cast his eyes around the camp. A dozen more cups lay scattered about, each a pale reminder of what precious quarry Edgar had once held close.

"Richter", hissed Edgar, his voice sounding hollow in his own head.

"*Richter...*"

The knight didn't respond and, in his armour, Edgar couldn't quite be sure if he was even still breathing.

"Damn" Edgar muttered under his breath before staring down at his reflection in a shallow pool of his own vomit mixed with the now heavily increasing rain.

Eventually, he slumped back down into the mud and let his mind flow between moments of clarity and half-dreams that shifted between spirals of ebony and bleak aubade...

Some time passed then, as Edgar lay, blinking away a mix of rain and tears. He had come so far, gone so far...

And as he drifted on the edge of consciousness he turned his head to the side, and there his eyes fell upon Richter's hand and of the cup within his grasp.

A vessel of unbroken gold,

Red eyes by firelight,

And the elaborate scars of a handsome feast,

Brought down with blackened lustre and crows upon the plain.

~

As dawn rolled in that day Richter found himself wondering where the time had gone. One minute he was on his face in the dirt, the next he was stripping his armour and walking through fields of tall grass and streams of gilded burgundy.

He shook his head and prodded the remnants of the fire. Taking a quick swig from his flask, the knight could feel sweet warmth return to his limbs. But it was then Richter noticed a shiver creep across his bones.

His eyes fell upon Edgar and his unmoving gaze; an aura of nightmare and a lack of breath.

Past the point of decorum, he whipped the cloak off his still body like a magician performing an elaborate trick, and the motion caused a small parchment to fall out of some pocket and land upon fresh ashes.

Curling up, the parchment sought to burn, but damp as it was only smoke emerged before Richter had his hand in the fire and snatched it out.

Idly, he threw the cloak on the floor before moving nearer to the flames to examine the note, which simply read;

'Do not bury or burn'

When Words Are Not Enough...

Aural
www.lordtdrums.com

Visual
www.lordtimages.com

Literary
www.lordttomes.com

9 781800 310315